THREE *simple* RULES

NIKKI SLOANE

Dingbats Edition

ISBN 978-1-5009516-4-1

for my husband

chapter ONE

My best friend Payton and I were celebrating her best month yet at her job, where she'd pulled in forty thousand dollars, more than I'd make all year after taxes. Actually, she'd made it in a handful of nights, and she'd made it selling her body to men. Payton was a bonafide high-class whore.

"I'm providing a service," she joked. "The ugly and fat guys can fuck a girl who looks like me."

She was a hooker with a heart of gold, as in gold-digger, and had chosen this 'career' even though she held a degree in communications from Northwestern. She'd *chosen* it. There was no need or goal that had forced her into the position, although I often wondered if there was an emotional one she was desperate to satisfy.

We'd been randomly assigned roommates for the semester of college we studied abroad in Amsterdam. I'd selected it because attending school abroad looked great on a résumé, and she'd gone because, I suspect, she was bored. It was in the red-light district that spring when she discovered her exhibitionist streak. The entire dorm floor of Americans decided to go together to a sex show, mostly as a joke, and the host running the show had gawked at my gorgeous roommate.

My mouth fell open when the performers invited Payton to join them and I'd watched in fascinated horror as she made her way triumphant to the stage. She hadn't participated in the actual sex that night, but had no problem showing off the creamy skin of her breasts or touching both of the performers anywhere and everywhere.

It made me uncomfortable, but if I'm being honest, also envious. Not so much of the performance, but her total lack of inhibitions during, and absence of shame afterward. Confidence oozed out of every cell of her. She was attractive, but her unapologetic personality made her insanely hot. Even though I'm straight, I had a girl-crush on her.

We stood now in one of the quieter corners of her favorite spot, a trendy bar where no drink was less than twelve dollars and which was also overrun with assholes looking to get laid.

"These are from the gentlemen over there," the thin-as-a-soda-straw waitress said, passing us drinks and gesturing to the other end of the bar. Usually the assholes traveled in pairs, and the less attractive of the two would try to make conversation with me while the other did his best to land Payton. She was tall and slender with vibrant blue eyes, and I was the poor man's version. I had mousy brown hair to her glossy, black cherry locks. My curves were my thighs, whereas hers were located up top for maximum appeal. My face was plain and unremarkable, and hers was exotic.

"I think you should do it," Payton said.

"Do what?" I asked. The pair of suits had noticed we'd accepted their drinks and now were making their approach.

"Come with me next time. Give it a try." This was at least the third time she'd suggested it.

"No way. Have you not met me?"

She gave me a knowing smile.

"I'm Todd," the guy said before he'd even reached us. He couldn't have looked more cliché douche if he'd tried. "This is my friend John."

How fitting. The quiet one locked eyes with me for a

moment, and then seemed to struggle with the urge to look around for better options.

"Thanks for these," Payton said. "We were thirsty. I'm Payton and this is Evie, and I was just telling her to consider joining me next time I'm seeing clients."

"You two work together?" Todd asked. He smelled like he'd been standing too close to a cologne factory when it had exploded.

"No," she continued, "but I think she'd like it."

"What do you do?"

"I'm an escort."

Todd blinked, stunned. Then, a smile widened on his face and gave us a look at his too-white teeth.

"Oh, yeah? Me too. What kind of benefits do you get? Dental? Vision?"

"No need for the vision, I wear a blindfold during. Both my clients and I like our anonymity."

"Of course," he said, seeming to want to play along. "So, Evie, are you—"

"That's my bad," Payton interrupted. "You don't actually get to call her that, only friends and family do. Her name is Evelyn."

Her sweet, oddly possessive streak over my nickname had developed after we'd graduated and my first great love had dumped me. His loser friends knew me by the nickname, and after a disastrous run-in with them post-breakup at the Taste of Chicago, she decreed the name from now on had to be earned.

"Evelyn, got it," Todd said, pushing the cocktail straw to the side so he could take a sip of his drink. "Are you going to become an escort like your friend and I here?"

My face flooded with heat at the thought of it. "No, I

couldn't."

"Would you pay money to sleep with her?" Payton asked.

Todd gave me an evaluating look that made me feel more like a piece of meat than I ever had at this bar.

"I don't know, maybe," he said, indifferent, "I don't usually pay for sex." *Usually,* my brain noted, which implied he had.

"It's not just sex." Payton set a hand on Todd's arm and drew him closer to her. "It's an experience. You're buying the opportunity to be in complete control, to do whatever. Even the dark, twisted fantasy you've been secretly wanting to try."

"Yeah?" He tried miserably not to look too excited, but the thought of doing whatever sick idea he had to Payton was too much. "You're into the hardcore stuff?"

"Absolutely. But Evie's not a freak like me." Her blue eyes went to the other guy, who was focused on me. "What about you? Would you pay to do whatever you wanted to her?"

"Don't use me in your recruiting material," I said. I'm not sure why I cared, but a small part of me waited to hear the answer on whether or not this random stranger would pay for the privilege to have total command over my body.

"Well, she's hot and all, but I'm not into the weird stuff," he answered. My heart beat just a little faster with his flattery.

"He's vanilla, plus he's broke," Todd added.

"Wow," Payton said. "Sounds like our friends have a lot in common."

I was broke, thanks to huge student loans which, coupled with rent in downtown Chicago and utilities, left me with virtually nothing. I don't know if I'd say I was strictly into vanilla sex, though. I was by no means a prude, but by comparison to Payton, I was a nun.

"Wait, how does it work?" Todd asked. "If you're

blindfolded, how do you make arrangements?"

"The club handles that."

The smile faded from Todd's face a little, like he was worried she was actually serious. "What club?"

"The private club I work for." She finished her drink and pulled a business card and pen from her purse, and then handed her bag to me. "Turn around."

I did so and finished my drink, knowing we were about to make our exit. She set the business card on my shoulder and scribbled a word on it.

"If you're interested in learning more," Payton said, and handed the card to Todd, "go to this website. The password on the back is good until Sunday at midnight."

"What?"

"Thanks for the drinks," she replied, taking back her purse and dragging me away. Leaving them wanting more was her specialty, but the two men standing there looked more confused and disappointed than anything else.

⌘

The rest of the team waited for our boss to arrive and begin the Monday meeting, idle chitchat about the fading summer weather filling the silence. Logan Stone was now eleven minutes late to the meeting he had called.

"Should we give him five more minutes?" Kathleen, one of the senior designers, asked. I would have preferred to leave now. The order for my first major account had come back from the printers, and the finished sample was waiting for me in a FedEx box on my desk. Seeing your design work in a finished piece was deeply satisfying, and I had a bit of Christmas morning anticipation about it.

He came in with no excuse or apology, and gave us

barely a greeting. It made me wonder if this was a deliberate tactic to let us all know how little he thought of our time, or to make sure we knew where we stood.

Logan had been a senior designer when I started, and last year he beat out two other senior designers to take over as department manager. The power had gone straight to his head. He'd had difficulty accepting client feedback before the promotion, and now he was a nightmare. Negative feedback was met with what I like to call "education" lectures, where he'd spew all the design reasons for the decisions he'd made in the artwork. It was impossible to argue with him.

He always got his way, and the worst part was he was usually right.

Logan's tie was askew like it had been thrown on in a hurry. Maybe his lunchtime quickie had run over. He was attractive with short, perfectly styled brown hair and a trim, lean frame, so it stood to reason he had a girlfriend. Or maybe a fuck-buddy, since his strict personality would make him difficult to date.

He plugged in his laptop and navigated to the critique folder, where the entire department dumped their work-in-progress proofs. It was anonymous to everyone but him and the artist who'd built it, and occasionally it could be brutal. But today he seemed to be in a decent mood, elevating his "Start over" critiques to "Needs work."

If he was going to be like this from now on, I had no problem with Logan being late to every meeting. After we concluded, I packed up my things and overheard his discussion with another coworker about his weekend. He'd run a half-marathon on Saturday and finished at the top of the 30-34 year old division, but it had come at a price.

He'd been late to the meeting because his muscles were

tight and sore, and he'd gone to get a massage. Today, in the middle of the workday. If I was Payton, I would have told him how ridiculous that sounded, but because I was me, and because he couldn't see, I rolled my eyes and hurried to my desk.

I tore the box open and pulled the case card out, admiring the glossy sheen finish the new clients had splurged on. It seemed silly to be proud of a printed piece of cardboard that advertised a bottle of vodka, but I had worked so hard to marry together the concepts the client wanted. It was eye-catching and stunning. Even Logan had said so in critique, his gaze falling to mine that day in the conference room. I had decided I disliked him a little less then, until he laid into another designer's piece and had sent her home in tears.

A sensation of alarm trickled through me. Something was wrong. The printer had gotten the colors just right, perfect for the branding I was going for. Was the shadow off? A typo in the tagline? I had proofed it endlessly, surely that wasn't it. What was it that made my mouth go dry?

My gaze continued downward through the advertisement, down to the bottom, searching . . . That was where I found it, the horrible mistake that would put me out of a job. How the hell had this happened? In a panic I flew to my keyboard and searched through emails, terrified to confirm what I already knew was true.

I stared at the screen for an unknown amount of time in disbelief that I had been so stupid. And then an even longer time trying to figure out what the hell I was going to do. Not only did I need this job, but I *loved* it. I'd do anything to keep it.

Shaky legs carried me to the doorway of Logan's office.

"Do you have a second?" My nervous voice drew his eyes

up, and he nodded. I held the case card sample in one hand and used the other to shut his door, indicating how serious our conversation was about to be.

"I made a mistake," I breathed out, clutching the cardboard so hard it started to bend under my grip.

"What did you do?" It wasn't accusatory, more concerned.

"This is the sample for Player's." I set the board in front of him and sank down into the chair opposite his desk. Long fingers picked it up, and his chocolate-colored eyes scrutinized every inch of it. Like me, he couldn't spot it right away. He searched for a typo in the tag, and when he came up empty, he dropped down to the legal disclaimer at the bottom.

The cardboard dropped silently to the desktop, and his face filled with anger. "How the hell did that happen?"

"Player's is a new client, so I didn't have their brand guidelines when I started building. I grabbed a legal off someone else's artwork to use as a placeholder until I had it. I thought I had updated it, but . . . I didn't."

"Of course you grabbed their competitor's legal line."

It wasn't possible for him to be any angrier with me than I was with myself. It didn't matter that the customer had signed off on the proof I'd sent them. The customer was always right, and there was no way they were going to pay for twenty thousand pieces of advertisement they couldn't use.

"Call the printer and get estimates on stickers to cover that," he barked, and ran a hand through his hair.

"I already thought of that, but we can't."

He looked closer at the sample. "Shit."

The legal was positioned just so on the background that the stickers would have to be perfectly placed by hand to hide it. That kind of labor would be too expensive. It'd be cheaper to just print 20,000 new ones. And using the sticker would alert everyone to what a dumbass I'd been, including the brand new client, who'd probably bolt.

"I need to ask," I said, a tremble in my voice, "for a really big favor."

It was like I'd just told him I loved the font Comic Sans.

"What do you need?"

What I needed was to fix this mistake and keep my job. Agency jobs were hard to come by, and freelancers were making the design industry more competitive every year. I'd made tough choices before, and I could do it again.

"No one knows about this. I need you to have the printer destroy these before they go out tomorrow."

"That's a given, not a favor."

"I need you to place a rush order for 20,000 more, with the correct legal."

"I think the customer's going to notice an extra ten grand on their bill." His long, elegant face twisted with sarcasm.

"No," I said, my voice fading into almost nothing, "they won't, because I'm going to pay for it."

"What? You're not going to do that." Confusion made his eyes a shade darker.

"You and I are the only ones who'll know." I hated that he'd be able to hold it over me, but right now I had to focus. I needed his help. "If Player's finds out, they'll walk and my head will roll."

"Maybe that's what should happen."

"I'd like to point out that you signed off on the proof, too." I hadn't wanted to bring it up, but he'd left me no choice.

"I sign off on dozens of rounds of artwork a day. I don't proof legals because I expect my people to be able to execute simple things like this."

I tried not to let it sting, but his truth cut into me. "Your boss might see it otherwise." As my manager, his job could be in jeopardy for my mistake.

His eyes went narrow. "You've got that kind of money?"

"No," I said, "but . . . I think I can get it."

"That sounds ominous. How?"

"Don't worry about it." Because lord knows, I was plenty worried about it enough for both of us. "Please, Logan. I made a stupid mistake that I'm going to beat myself up over about for the next ten years. I love this job. I need this job. Please."

He leaned back in his chair, his gaze drifting away from mine and falling down onto the case card.

"If I do this, you better not breathe a word of it to anyone else."

I wasn't sure if it was relief or trepidation that filled my body. "Of course."

"Go back to your desk and get me the corrected file. Hurry before I change my mind." He passed the case card back to me with a pointed look. I scrambled for the door but froze.

"I'll have to know," I said, "how much I need to come up with."

His face was unreadable. "I'll let you know."

I couldn't look at the FedEx box when I returned to my desk. I jammed the sample in the garbage and updated the artwork, then emailed the file name and location to Logan. My phone rang a few minutes later with his extension flashing on screen.

"Ninety-six hundred." That was all he said before hanging up, and even with that few words I could hear the anger in his voice. Anger that I'd drawn him into this terrible situation.

Yeah, well, the joke's on you. I'd put myself in a much worse situation.

I was about to become a whore.

TWO

I followed Payton into the upscale salon, and I was sure I was going to throw up on the marble tile floor inside. We were meeting her manager, Joseph. Her pimp, who, assuming everything went okay with our meeting, would become my pimp.

"Just breathe," Payton said. She was beyond thrilled when I'd confessed what I needed. She felt bad how I'd come to the decision, but she had absolute certainty that this was the first step on my road to sexual awakening.

It wasn't a step, this was like being strapped to a rocket.

It seemed odd to meet here, but if Joseph agreed to let me see clients, he would have a say about the way I looked, specifically the downstairs area. Payton had filled me in on what to expect, but Joseph wasn't what I had expected. He was a thirty-something, elegant man with coat-hanger shoulders and a devilish smile.

"Nice to meet you, Evelyn. I've heard many good things." He shook my hand and then gestured for us to follow him past the wash sinks and into the back. He led us into a room I guessed was used for the waxing, and he sat on the table, assessing me with his gaze.

"I'm sure Payton has told you how this works, but things would be different with you. Your friend is a rare woman, which you probably already know."

"Yes," I said, the nerves making it difficult to speak.

"I understand you're looking for a one-night only sort

of thing?"

"Right." Payton had a contract. Not a legally binding one, since what she did was highly illegal, but she'd agreed to work a set number of nights at the club in exchange for a much larger percentage. "I don't really think this is for me, but I—"

"You need the money," he said. "I get it. I'll extend a one-night contract to you because I trust Payton. She thinks once you've had a taste you're going to want more."

I highly doubted that, but kept my mouth shut. It was totally dry anyway.

"You're very pretty. Can you take your hair down for me?"

My hands fumbled to release the ponytail, and then I let my straight, chestnut brown hair fall down in a wave.

"Have you ever gone darker?"

I shook my head. I liked being low maintenance, hence the hair thrown back in a ponytail.

"I'll need to see the other assets you've got now, to ensure you're the kind of woman our customers desire."

The air in the room went thin. I knew this was coming thanks to Payton. And since we'd been roommates, it's not like she hadn't seen me naked before, but it offered me little comfort now. This was the moment it started to feel real.

My hands lifted the shirt up over my heaving chest and then over my head before I set it in Payton's waiting arms. Joseph was calm and collected, not leering at me, which I appreciated. I hurried to undo my jeans and shoved them down over my hips. I wanted it over as soon as possible, but my haste made me clumsy and awkward. If he had expected a sexy striptease, he wasn't getting one.

I passed my wadded jeans to Payton, who ignored my shaking hands.

"Very nice," he said, making me believe he was satisfied,

until he added, "Please continue."

I twisted my arms behind my back and undid the clasp of my bra, my nervous fingers fumbling with the hook. I wasn't overly shy about my body under normal circumstances, but standing in the cramped room with the harsh lighting and two pairs of eyes on me made everything upside-down. The straps slid off my shoulders and down my arms, falling to the floor.

I didn't give myself time to check with him for feedback. I hooked my thumbs under the waistband of my panties and yanked them down my legs, leaving them beside my bra, on the floor. Then, I rose and set my hands on my hips and lifted my eyes to Joseph's. I was naked and vulnerable, but struggled not to reveal any of the insecurity threatening to paralyze me.

"Can you turn?"

My feet were cinder blocks, but I complied. I finished the turn, looking at him for some sort of confirmation or disapproval. A lifetime passed and all he did was stare and evaluate. I ached for a response.

"Excellent," he finally said, and gave me a crooked smile. "I have to gauge your level of comfort now."

He stood and his hands undid his zipper. I hadn't noticed that he was already semi-hard and bulging through his pants.

"What?" Instinctively I took a half-step backward.

He had his dick out in an instant, stroking himself until he was completely hard. "I want you to suck me off. Right now."

"What?" I said again, my eyes darting to Payton. "Here?"

Was he serious? Payton had her lips pressed together, and then . . . she gave me the slightest nod. Oh, yes, he was serious.

"I need to know you're not going to get cold feet with a client. If you can do this, I'll feel comfortable putting you on the list." While he talked, he continued to stroke himself slowly, and I couldn't help but watch, hypnotized and disoriented.

"Evie—" Payton whispered.

Was she going to tell me not to? Because I'd already come too far to back down. The prints had been ordered, and I couldn't get a loan or borrow from my parents, and Payton had blown all of her money on a new car.

"I can do this," I said, more for myself than for anyone else. It's not like this was the first blowjob I'd ever given, but it would undoubtedly be the least sexy. I took a tentative step forward and sank down before him, my knees resting on the cold, unforgiving tile.

I used a hand to tuck a lock of my wayward hair behind an ear. His dick was fat and hard, and right in front of my face. So I reached a hesitant hand out and wrapped my fingers around the firm flesh. My brain disconnected, I parted my lips, and slid him inside my mouth.

"Fuck, that's good," he whispered.

I was sure I would feel immediate revulsion, but instead I felt nothing. I wanted to focus and get my task done. I didn't like failing. I pulled him out and then slid him back in until the head of his dick touched the back of my throat. *You can do this,* I repeated over and over, and when I began to bob my head on him, I started to believe.

"Use your tongue." His breathing was ragged.

I obeyed his command, drawing a moan from him. I'd never had a guy tell me what to do before. I think usually they were just thrilled I was down there.

"Suck on it."

I did, and he let loose another deep moan. Honestly, his commands made this easier, but after a while my knees began to hurt, so I picked up the pace.

"That's so fucking hot," I heard Payton say. I'd been concentrating so hard I'd forgotten she was right there, and if I didn't have her pimp's dick in my mouth, I might have told her to shut up. But that was the anger I felt toward myself, misdirected at her. She may have encouraged this, but she certainly hadn't forced me.

"You like watching me fuck her mouth?" he asked her. "Yeah, me too. She's going to make me come."

A hand wound into my hair, and his other hand seized my head under my chin, using his grip to guide me to pick up the tempo. His hips thrust faster and deeper, just barely avoiding my gag reflex. It was an unfamiliar feeling, not having control, but a part of me didn't mind. I kind of liked it, and admitting that to myself made a small wave of pleasure and desire wash over me.

"Swallow," he ordered. Then he was coming violently, filling my mouth with hot, thick liquid.

I did as asked. As the pulsing inside my mouth began to ebb, I withdrew from him, and rose up from my tender knees, stunned that this hadn't been that bad. If I was truthful with myself, his commands had turned me on a little. I'd felt eager to please him.

The room was warm, and both pairs of eyes were on me as if waiting for me to do or say something. I crossed my arms over my bare chest, feeling awkward and hot.

Joseph recovered and zipped up, looking rather smug.

"I told you she'd be good," Payton said quietly.

"You can get dressed now," my new pimp said. "We've got a lot to talk about."

⌘

I sat in the stylist chair. My long, neglected hair had been trimmed into a swing cut, so it hung longest in the front and brushed just over my shoulders. Joseph chose a deep coffee color, and while I was seated, my hair drenched in hair dye, he presented me with a four-paged contract.

"Read it and let me know if you have questions," he said. "I don't want you to sign it today. Consider everything and make sure it's what you want. If it is, I'll need it back by Thursday."

"If I do this, when does it happen?" I asked.

"Saturday."

Oh, god. So soon. But maybe that was good. It gave me less time to talk myself out of it, and I'd need the money quickly if Logan were going to keep it off the books. "Do I get paid right away?"

"Normally no, but Payton told me you're in a spot, so I'll be understanding."

"Thank you." I figured it couldn't hurt to be gracious.

He gave me a startled smile. "No, honey, thank you." Then he left me alone to study the contract.

It wasn't written in legalese. I would offer my body for sex or to fulfill whatever other desire the customer had, and in return I would receive money, minus a percentage going to the club. How many clients I chose to service was my decision. The first page included what was required of me, which wasn't much – arrive on time to the specified location, recently bathed, clean of any drugs, and not intoxicated. The percentage I received would be calculated when I returned my "willing list."

The "willing list" was a menu of what I would allow

clients to do to me. I didn't think I was naïve until I scanned the two columns on the second page, and one-third of the things I'd never heard of. I'd have to ask Payton to explain them to me later.

The last two pages were more about security. Since the 'employee' would be restrained and blindfolded, there would be someone from the club with them until a deal had been reached, and there were security cameras. Which meant they'd be watching during the sex. It also outlined what would happen if a client became aggressive, or if at any point the employee wanted to stop. It was both reassuring and disturbing.

I hadn't really thought about how dangerous it was, what Payton had been doing. She said she felt safe, and honestly, I didn't ask a whole lot about it because it made me squeamish. Plus, she enjoyed it and I believed she knew what she was doing.

"Questions?" he asked when it was clear I'd finished.

"No, not right now."

"Okay, I'd like to stick around and see the new you, but I should get going." He handed me a card that was similar to the ones Payton passed out when trying to attract new clients. This one had a phone number printed on it instead of a web address. "Don't hesitate to call if you need anything."

I will admit the hair color and new cut looked great. But I barely got to enjoy it because as soon as I was done the stylist whisked me into the back, into the same room I'd knelt on the floor ninety minutes ago. My first Brazilian wax was excruciating, and I viewed it as excellent warm-up punishment for the stupid mistake I'd made. I'd never get a legal disclaimer wrong again.

Payton drove me home in her new black Jaguar,

explaining the most unsavory items from the list like she was explaining something simple and not how a guy would want to urinate on me.

"I don't think I can do this," I said, feeling sick to my stomach.

"Just check the stuff you can handle. Half the stuff on my list no one's even tried. Most guys just want to have sex. They come in the door with all these elaborate plans, but when they see you all tied up, waiting for them . . . it goes right out the window." A wicked smile bloomed on her face. "I had one guy finish in less than two minutes. I probably should have given him his money back."

"But you didn't."

"Rules are rules. It's not my fault I'm that good."

My eyes fell back to the list. "What's Greek?"

"Anal." Even though she was driving, she saw my pen move past that, leaving it blank. "Evie, you've got to check that box."

"No way, no." I capped the pen and put it in my purse. "It's gross." The irony was not lost on me. Most people would say having sex with a total stranger for money was gross.

"Get past your hang-ups. You might like it," Payton said. "And seriously, you'll never make enough in one night without it. Unless you want to do more than one guy."

My shoulders slumped. The idea of one stranger was bad enough, but multiple? "Oh, god, no."

"You've got, like, three things checked on that list. How are you going to know if you like stuff if you don't try?"

"I think I'll be trying enough new things that night, don't you?"

She nodded, knowing when to stop pushing.

⌘

On Wednesday my nerves were wound tight as a spring. I feared the slightest push would snap the coil and I'd break apart. I used my lunch break to get tested and prove I was free of any STDs. Otherwise I stayed hidden at my desk, desperate to focus on anything other than Saturday.

The unsigned contract was tucked in my purse, whispering to me. I felt like I couldn't escape, and yet the dirtiest part of me was excited. The ship would be leaving soon, and I was going to have to decide once and for all whether or not to get on board. I'd already made the decision, though, hadn't I, in the back room of that salon? The memory made my stomach clench. As if on cue, my personal email chimed on my workstation. I thought it would be another daily pep talk from Payton. It was from Joseph, checking in. The email had the logo of the club in the corner, the same from the card, a classy black and white diamond shape with a modern font. Elegant. If it had been from anywhere else I would have added it to my inspiration folder.

"Planning on doing any work today?" Logan snapped. My cursor clicked the email closed as fast as possible. Of course he'd catch me in the one minute I'd taken a break. I spun in my chair, my face hot with embarrassment.

"I was working. Did you need something?" I said, desperate to sound normal and not guilty.

He towered over my chair, his face hard and cold. "The printer overnighted the sample to me. It's on my desk." He turned and went without a word, expecting me to follow.

He could have picked up the phone and called me into his office, but that wasn't Logan's style. He liked to float around the department and keep people on target. Jamie, three cubes to my right, liked to surf Pinterest all day, rather than work.

I'd only been in Logan's office a handful of times, so each visit made me uncomfortable. He'd taken the management position a year ago, but hadn't done much to decorate. Maybe he didn't like the distraction of artwork on his walls.

He held out the proof for us both to examine.

"It was good work," he said, "other than the sloppy mistake." Well, if that wasn't a backhanded compliment I don't know what was. "If it had been anyone else, I would have let them go. You have to know you're the best one out there."

It was by far the nicest thing he'd ever said, and the power of his statement left me stunned. Yet he seemed completely unaware.

"When will you have the money?"

That brought reality crashing back down on me. "Saturday night."

"Saturday night?" he asked, skeptical.

"I meant Monday," I said quickly.

He gave me an odd look, but pressed forward. "Good. I'll get the prints released to Player's this afternoon." He rounded his desk and dropped down into his chair, and when his attention went to his computer screen, it was like I ceased to exist to him.

I carried the new proof back to my desk and looked at it with bittersweet eyes. This was my art, paid for with my own money . . . well, with the money I'd make. There was no turning back, I told myself, when I hit "send" on a response to Joseph's email, letting him know I'd signed the contract and would drop it off tonight. He emailed me back almost immediately and said to bring it with me on Saturday night.

It was done, and I was done worrying about this. I liked

sex, so maybe I wouldn't hate this. Hopefully.

⌘

Payton was on time, as usual, but I was running behind. As usual. She sat on the couch in the living area and watched me put makeup on through the open doorway of my cramped bathroom.

"I don't know why you do this to yourself."

She was talking about Blake, the man I'd been hopelessly in love with for the last year. I ignored her, swiping my lashes with mascara. Blake and I had met our freshman year in Art & Design 101. He was a programmer trying to keep his options open in case he wanted to shift into web design, but thank god he didn't. He was all left-brain.

I had a boyfriend back then and mistook Blake's friendliness for just that and not flirting. When my high school long-distance relationship collapsed, I wanted more than a shoulder to cry on from Blake, but he'd started dating someone the week before. Our horrible timing continued through college, through my semester abroad, until we both fell in love our senior year . . . with other people.

We drifted apart for a while, but reconnected when he moved to the city, and it was like no time had passed in our friendship. The longing for him flared back up, stronger than before. But Blake wasn't single. In fact, I suspected a marriage proposal wasn't far off in his girlfriend's future. In spite of everything, I liked her. Amy was geek-chic, a perfect match for him.

"It was nice of Amy to arrange to have her birthday on a Friday." Payton picked at her nails. "Did you fill out any more boxes on your willing list?"

I paused at her sudden topic change, and then recapped

my lipstick. "No."

"Evie." She directed a serious look at me through the mirror. "Please, check something else. Anything. I know how it works with the club. They're already doing you a favor, they're not going to do any more when it comes to the percentage."

"Okay." I wanted her off my back. I didn't want to think about it, like a patient with an upcoming surgery.

They were already seated at the restaurant, surrounded by a few of Amy's co-workers I didn't know, when Payton and I arrived. Blake's gaze connected with mine from across the room, and my heart beat faster. He was tall and lanky, just a few pounds of muscle short from being ripped. That was Amy's doing; she'd gotten him hooked on going to the gym. He'd never looked better than he did now. His light brown hair curled over his ears in an effortless look that made me want to put my hands in it. He'd been an adorably cute boy in college, but now he was a flat-out beautiful man.

Fate had been so completely unfair to me. That was what I thought every time I saw him. His amber-colored eyes lit up when I came toward the table.

"Wow, your hair," he said. "Looks nice."

"Thanks." I tried not to blush.

Conversation flowed easily between the group at first, but soon after it split down the center – Amy and her co-workers on one side, and Blake, Payton, and I on the other, although Payton never had much to say. I was surprised she'd agreed to come along. Payton and Blake were always friendly, but they were *my* friends and not friends with each other.

"What made you decide to go dark?" he asked, gesturing to my hair.

A huge grin spread across Payton's face. "She's going to

be joining me at work."

That was why she'd wanted to come. She wanted to see the moment when Blake learned what I was going to do.

"What?" I think he stopped breathing.

"Oh, yeah? What do you do again?" Amy asked. I hadn't realized they'd rejoined the group conversation.

"Customer service," Payton answered.

"Right." She gave a polite nod and went back to discussing something with her coworker. She didn't know the truth about how Payton made her living, but Blake did. This past New Year's Eve, when Amy had gone home to Minnesota for the holidays, Blake and I had gotten sloppy drunk and spilled our guts to each other about everything.

I'd told him that Payton was a prostitute, and he'd agreed, not understanding until I explained it all in detail. He'd had a lot of questions but promised not to judge her, for me. Then, I'd told him about my repeating crush through college, and he revealed he'd felt the same.

Then the margaritas in me told him I loved him.

He didn't say anything. Instead he kissed me ferociously, and the alcohol allowed it. We'd made out on my couch for a good twenty minutes until I stopped him. We were drunk and he had a girlfriend.

We never spoke about that night. I'm not sure if he remembered it or if he wanted to pretend it never happened, because Amy returned from her folks' place, and a month later she moved in with him. They got serious, fast.

"Tell me she's kidding," Blake said, horror splashed on his face. His eyes pleaded with mine.

I swallowed hard and nodded. "It's true."

He stood abruptly and stormed away from the table.

"Is he all right?" Amy asked.

"He's mad at me." I pushed back from the table. "I'll get him to come back."

Blake was waiting for me in the parking lot. I hadn't made it through the outer door, and he stalked toward me, getting in my face.

"What the fuck, Evie? Why would you do this?"

I told him about the stupid mistake and how I was doing it to save my job. I left out the part where I'd gone down on Joseph minutes after meeting him.

"It's just a job," Blake said. "You can get another."

"No, I can't, not in Chicago. Agencies talk to each other. I know where my coworkers came from and whether they left by choice or not." I despised how shaky my voice was.

Other than a rude boss, it was my dream job, and I loved living in the city. I loved walking in a herd with other business professionals on blustery Chicago winter mornings, and escaping into an air-conditioned cab after bar hopping with Payton on steamy summer nights.

"I'll be a senior designer by the end of the year, if not sooner," I continued. "Even if I could go somewhere else, I'd be starting from the bottom."

"There's got to be another way."

"Sure, you've got ten grand I can borrow?" I asked, bitterly. "It'll only take me a decade to pay it back."

His face changed to shock. "Jesus, it's that much?"

I nodded, grim. "Look, I'll be fine. It's just sex. It's not any worse than going home with some random guy. It's actually safer."

"Except you don't do that."

No, I didn't. I'd never had a one-night stand. I hadn't seen the appeal of doing something so intimate and then never speaking to them again. "Well, I guess I do now."

He glanced over my shoulder to the window of the restaurant. Then he closed the space between us, pulling me in his arms. I shut my eyes, set my cheek against his chest, and allowed it to happen without feeling guilty. I listened to the steady, quick thud of his heartbeat.

"Please don't do this," he begged.

"I'm sorry," was all I could say.

"When?"

"Tomorrow."

He pulled back, his golden eyes cloudy and dark. "Where?"

The rational part of my brain screamed not to tell him. Nothing good could come from him knowing, but I would do almost anything for him.

I told him the address. He squeezed me into a hug and brushed his lips over my forehead, the closest he could get to kissing me where I felt like he wasn't cheating on her. I pretended my heart wasn't hurting the rest of the night. When it was time to head home, he pulled me aside.

"I'll see you tomorrow," he said.

THREE

Payton pulled away from the curb and didn't speak until we hit the traffic on Lake Shore Drive.

"Tomorrow, are you still—?" she asked.

"Yes." It came out tight.

"You would have told him eventually," she said. "You tell him everything. At least he got his chance to talk you out of it."

"Oh, so that's why you did it?"

"No." She slammed on the brakes to keep from rear-ending the cab that cut her off. "I told him because he only wants you when he can't have you. I thought you two were just friends."

I'd downed my beer quickly and had loose lips. "You're kind of being a bitch right now."

She took her eyes off the road for a split second so she could lock them on me. "True, but you deserve so much better than that douchebag. You should be someone's first choice, not an option they keep open on the side."

She had a point, but it was hard to accept. I couldn't just turn off my feelings for him, no matter how much I wanted to.

Payton dropped me off at home, promising to be back for me in the morning. She had the whole day planned out before the main event. We went to a spa. Spray tans, mani-pedis . . . anything we could do to make sure we looked as good as possible while naked, her treat. Then we went shopping.

It didn't matter what we wore to the club. We could have shown up in sweats, but there was an unwritten rule among the ladies that you make an effort. Something you'd wear if you were going out on a hot date or to a club opening. Payton pushed me to try a shimmering, low-cut silver dress that clung to my curves, and then pulled out her credit card.

"No, Payton –"

"Shut up. I'd pay ten grand to sleep with you in that dress."

An eerie calm washed over me at dinner, and as I geared up to leave all my inhibitions behind, I started with my words.

"I need to know why you care so much about this," I asked Payton. "Why it's important to you."

Her blue eyes searched my face. "I like it. I want you to like what I like."

I'd never known her to lie to me. "I need to know your real reason."

"I'll tell you, I swear." She gave me a sad smile. "But I can't tell you until after."

That only increased my curiosity and skepticism. "Why? Are you getting some sort of commission off of me?"

"There is a bonus, but trust me, it has nothing to do with it."

We each had one drink. I would have liked some more liquid courage, but respected the rules of my contract. I couldn't afford not to. Time went too fast and too slow, and as it got closer to ten o'clock, I became restless and giddy. The dirty girl buried inside me was excited.

Payton drove her sleek car to the club, parking two blocks down. One of the advantages of arriving with her meant I was on time. Early, which was helpful because just across the street from the deceptively vacant-looking building that housed the club, a lanky man waited for me. I felt like I'd just done a somersault.

"What the fuck is he doing here?" Payton hissed. Her eyes narrowed. "Why did you tell him where?"

"I couldn't help it," I confessed. "He asked me."

She stared at me expectantly. "Well? Go listen to him tell you why you shouldn't do this. How you should continue to wait for him to get bored with his girlfriend. I'll be here," she said, pointing to her feet, "when you're ready to finally move on."

I swallowed hard and shuffled across the deserted street. Concern was painted across Blake's face. God, I'd been so stupid telling him. Seeing him now destroyed the shred of excitement I'd been clinging to and replaced it with paralyzing dread.

"Hey." His voice was grave. "I'm asking you not to go in there."

"Please don't make this harder than it already is."

I'd never seen him look like he did now. He was an even mixture of desperation and fear, and I ached for him.

"Don't do this to us," he whispered.

I froze. "Us?"

"It'll destroy any chance for us to be together, Evie. Please," he begged.

"Wait, what?"

"I love you." He reached out for me, tried to pull me close, but all I could hear were Payton's words echoing. I wanted to believe him, but it had rolled off his lips strained and forced.

"What about Amy?" I asked when his arms circled my waist.

"I know, it's complicated."

A spark of anger ignited a fire deep inside me. "It's really not that complicated. You can't love two people at once."

"Believe me, you can. I do."

I twisted out of his arms. "Let me clarify. You can't be in love with me and be in love with another woman, too."

"Evie, stop." He took a step toward me. "Let's talk about this. Just don't go in there."

We'd had time to talk. Months and months. If he wanted to leave her, he would have done it. "Does she even know you're here?"

He tore his gaze away from mine, guilty.

I took in an enormous breath, letting it make me feel strong. "You shouldn't have come."

He nodded toward Payton, a sneer on his face. "She's a whore, and she'll drag you down."

I didn't understand her reasons, but she'd never betrayed me, and she'd certainly never hurt me the way he had right now.

"Get out of here," I said, turning away.

Payton didn't judge. She loved me unconditionally, the way a true friend did. So I left him standing there and returned to my friend.

"You okay?" she asked.

"I'm fine," I lied. "Let's go have some fun."

Immediately inside the door, a large black man was perched on a stool with a clipboard and an earpiece. The room was small and dark, and the focus was the white door across from us with the black club logo on it.

"Hey, girl," he said to Payton, a genuine smile on his lips. He buzzed us through the white door, and as it swung shut behind us, I heard him say into his earpiece that we had arrived.

This room was wide and short. An oversized couch rested on one side and a bar on the other. The friendly-looking bartender also gave Payton a genuine smile when he saw her. He was also wearing an earpiece.

"This is the holding room," Payton said, directing me to the bar. "Sometimes the client needs a few minutes before parting with that much money.

"Or for the Viagra to kick in," the bartender said. He'd said it like a joke, but I was sure he was serious.

"Two shots of tequila," Payton announced. The bartender didn't hesitate.

"Is that okay?" I asked. I wanted the help the alcohol could provide, but what about the contract?

Payton knocked the shot back. "Joseph just doesn't want us plastered. A little lubrication isn't a bad thing." Her fingers nudged the glass toward me. I snatched it up and downed it, ignoring the burn.

"Thanks," she said to the bartender, and pulled me away as soon as I'd set my glass on the bar top. This door spat us out into the center of a long hallway, facing a seemingly endless bank of doors. She didn't have to say what kind of room was behind those doors. I'd find out soon enough.

We didn't go into the rooms. I followed her to the end of the hall and up a set of stairs. I could hear female voices coming from the room on the right, but she went left.

Into Joseph's office. He was seated behind a desk in a black suit and black shirt without a tie, a row of darkened video monitors behind him. The contract had detailed that the sessions were videotaped strictly for security purposes. Payton had reassured me it wouldn't wind up on the Internet.

I wasn't that concerned about it. A grainy black-and-white video of a woman with a blindfold on would be tough to identify. Plus this club made serious money, why would they jeopardize their operation for a few extra dollars selling amateur porn?

"Evening, ladies," Joseph said, rising from his seat. "You both look lovely."

"Thanks," Payton said. I struggled to find words and just

nodded. I was more nervous now fully clothed than I'd been when I was naked before him.

"Do you have the contract, Evelyn?" he asked.

My trembling hand dug it out of my purse. The paper crinkled when I handed it over, but then I couldn't release it.

"I need a pen," I blurted out.

Payton looked at me, startled. "I thought you signed it already."

"I did." I didn't want to explain, and thankfully Joseph produced a pen so I didn't have to. I turned to the willing list and checked not one, but *three* more boxes. This wasn't the tequila talking. This was my response to the man who had said he loved me not five minutes ago.

She gasped when she saw what I had done and then gave a wicked smile. "Aw, we're going to be sorority sisters."

I held my breath as Joseph evaluated the contract and waited to find out what the magic number was after the house took their cut.

"The best I can do is twenty percent to the club, and I'm sorry, that's not negotiable." Joseph pulled open a drawer in the desk and filed the contract. "And ten percent on top of it to Payton."

"Forget it, I don't need it," she said immediately.

My heart sank. Even with Payton dropping her bonus, I'd need to get someone to agree to sleep with me for $12,000. It was so much money. Who would pay that?

She threaded her hand in mine and gave it a squeeze. "You can do this."

⌘

There were four other women offering their services for the evening, and they'd all arrived by the time Payton and I entered the lounge. She introduced me to them, but I couldn't focus and forgot their names immediately. They were stunningly beautiful and exotic like Payton. Was I there as some sort of twisted affirmative action? The token average girl in case a customer wanted a helping of that?

And while these women were friendly and pleasant, they were also my competition. I was so screwed in every sense of the word.

"It's okay," Payton said. She must have sensed I was mentally freaking out and eased me down onto a chair. "Let's go over some of the code talk."

"Code talk?" There was a red drink in my hand suddenly, delivered by a blonde woman who looked like she'd just stepped out of a magazine ad. I thought I'd already met all the other women, but she was new.

"That's cranberry and vodka," the woman said. "I'm Tara. I'll be your sales assistant."

"You?" I took a sip of the drink blindly. "They're going to want to sleep with you rather than me."

Payton gave me a tight look. "Tara's the best at sales. I already told her where you need to get to."

"I'm sorry," I said to the mesmerizing blonde, trying to calm myself. "I'm really nervous."

Tara sat beside me. "I've been there. You just have to let yourself enjoy it. There are plenty of women who would pay to have this happen to them. It's a fantasy."

I set the drink down on a nearby side table. I suddenly didn't want any more alcohol in my system. I wanted to keep my wits about me. "Tell me about the code."

"If I talk about the weather when a client first comes in, he's average looking. If I talk about sports, he's hot," Tara said.

"And if he's fugly," Payton added, "she'll talk about

traffic." Tara shot her a knowing look as if they shared an inside joke.

"But if I'm wearing a blindfold, why does it matter?"

Payton's eyes fell on me like I was a dummy. "Ugly guys pay more for pussy. A lot more."

"I'll negotiate the price," Tara said, "but it's always your call on accepting the offer. You won't be able to see his body language, and he'll think that's to his advantage. When he makes a bid, where I touch you indicates what I think I'm seeing. The closer to your head I get, the closer I think we are to reaching his limit."

I didn't understand. She was going to touch me?

"For example," she continued, "if he offered ten thousand for Payton and I touched her on her ankle, I think we can get him up quite a bit. If I touch her on the shoulder—"

"I'm going to take it," Payton said.

Okay, I guessed it made sense. I hadn't thought much about the pricing or negotiations, and I was relieved not to have to.

Time was rushing along, and when I glanced at my phone it was ten minutes to eleven. There were noises downstairs, stirrings as if clients had begun to arrive. Joseph appeared in the lounge, chatting with a few of the women near the door. I wondered dimly if he'd had his dick in everyone's mouth at one point or another.

"Number four, Tara," he said when he passed by.

That was the number of the room I'd sell myself in. Tara handed me a silk robe and showed me where I could put my clothes and purse, and then looked at me as if waiting for me to do something. I couldn't fathom what, until the five other women in the lounge started to undress.

They weren't bashful. Two of them laughed and told

jokes with all their business hanging out. Some of them were watching as if judging me. I hurried to catch up, pulling the silver dress over my head. I couldn't wear a bra since the dress was backless, so that one move told them I came to play.

I stepped out of my underwear and heels so I was as naked as a jaybird, and shrugged into the soft robe. Payton slid an arm into her own robe and cinched it shut as she gave me a wink. In spite of everything, I cracked a smile.

My bare feet were cold on the stairs as I descended in a single-file line, and then marched determinedly down the long hall to my room.

"Enjoy yourself, Evie," Payton whispered as she passed by. "If you like it, he'll fucking love it."

I stared at the brass number four attached there, wondering what the hell was going to happen to me behind that door.

I turned the knob and pushed the door open.

FOUR

There wasn't a bed in the room softly lit by a crystal chandelier. Taking the center of the space was a long table with a leather cushion top, similar to a doctor's office, but . . . decidedly less clinical. It was, for lack of a better word, sexy. Every inch of the walls and ceiling were covered in alternating textures of black fabric in an intriguing sequence. A clever disguise for soundproofing. In the corner sat a white wingback chair I knew wasn't for me. There was an easel with a dry-erase board on it. My willing list in big, easy to read print.

The door latched behind Tara, and I was gripped with full-body terror.

"Can I take your robe for you?"

Her voice was like honey. My clumsy hands undid the knot at my waist and let it slide off my shoulders, catching it in my hands. It felt like real silk. I handed it over and watched her hang it on a hook behind the door.

"Is it warm enough in here?" she asked. "I can adjust the thermostat."

She must have asked because I was trembling. "I'm fine."

Tara's hand was warm when she set it on my arm in a friendly way. "You've got a beautiful body, and I'm not going to have a hard time finding a buyer for you. But it's your first time here, so don't worry. I'll find the right buyer. One who deserves you."

It was a simple gesture, but it calmed me.

"Do you mind?" Tara gestured to the table. I took a deep

breath and sat down, and was surprised to discover the table was soft. "Scoot back and lie down, please."

As I did so, I steadied my breathing. This was happening, deal with it. Tara bent down and opened a cabinet beneath the table, and when she stood, she had two pieces of black fabric in her hands. The first I recognized – a blindfold. The second was a long swath of black ribbon that disappeared over the side of the table.

"I'll show you how this works." She dropped the blindfold beside me and held up the ribbon. "Can I have your wrist?"

I held up my hand, and she wrapped the end of the ribbon around it, pressing it closed.

"Velcro?" I asked.

"It's strong. You won't be able to undo it with one hand, but if your client wants to, it's easy." She undid it and handed me the blindfold. "It's time."

Oh, god. I slipped the elastic over the back of my head and then lowered it over my eyes so everything was black.

"Make sure it's where you want it. You won't be able to adjust it in a minute."

I did as she suggested, putting the elastic behind my ears. My breathing increased when her hand closed around my right wrist and strapped it down to the table.

"Can you test that for me?"

I tried to lift my arm but could only move it a few inches. Her high heels clicked softly on the floor as she rounded the table to stand on the other side. It took no time for her to do this one.

The modest part of me cringed inside. Yet there was a darker part that was turned on. It's better to have regret of what you've done, than what you failed to do, it whispered.

"How are you?" she asked. "Does your nose itch? My

nose always itched as soon as I was bound."

"Well, now it does," I replied. She laughed and ran her fingers over my nose, and then they were gone.

"Room four is ready," she said in a hushed voice, obviously not to me. She must have an earpiece as well. Her heels tapped out a slow rhythm away, and I heard her sink into the chair.

There were a million thoughts running through my mind while we waited in silence. The straps weren't uncomfortable, but they weren't great, either. I wanted to get on with it even as I was petrified. What if he wanted to start with one of the three boxes I'd checked at the last minute? Disaster, that's what would happen.

I heard the door swing open and I stopped breathing. Heavy footsteps entered, and I could make out his raspy breathing.

"Good evening, sir," she said. "Can I show you what I'm featuring tonight?"

"Yeah," he said. The heavy footsteps plodded closer. "Good lord, I think they get better with each room." He had a southern accent.

"I don't know, I think you'll find she's the peak. And she's an exclusive."

"What's that mean?"

"She's here for one night only. She can be yours alone."

"Yeah?"

They lapsed into silence for a moment before Tara spoke again. "You don't sound like you're originally from here."

"Nashville."

"Oh? Bet the traffic took some getting used to." So, he was fugly, as Payton had put it. Maybe he could put up top dollar and be done in five minutes . . .

He sighed. "She's real pretty and all, but I'd kind of like to see them all before making a decision."

"Of course," she said in her honey-sweet voice. I heard the door open and close. "Thanks for telling me he's show-rooming," she grumbled, again I assumed into the earpiece. "Okay, got it."

It sounded like she returned to the chair.

Without my vision, it felt like hours had passed.

I waited.

And waited.

But the door never creaked open. I tried counting in my head to distract myself. What if no one else came? Whoring myself out was bad enough; what if no one wanted me?

"Tara?" I asked, panic rising in me. It had to have been at least thirty minutes, and I worried she'd left and I hadn't heard her, or she'd fallen asleep.

"Yes?"

"Does it usually take this long?"

"No, but we've . . . run into a situation."

What? "What kind of situation?"

"Someone's requested a hold be put on you. He's not a member of the club, and only members have that privilege."

My heart leaped into my throat, making it difficult to breathe. Blake. Was he going to screw this up for me? Was he going to come in here and have me? The door swung open abruptly, and there was a sharp intake of breath that made me tremble.

"Good evening, sir," Tara said. "I believe this is what you've been waiting for."

"Yes." It was almost inaudible, making it impossible to recognize.

"She's an exclusive, one-night only experience. Please,

take a closer look."

His footsteps were quiet as he came near. I had to remind myself to breathe, to relax.

"Are you a sports fan, sir?" Tara asked.

"I'm sorry?" he said, sounding caught off guard. And not at all like Blake. Maybe familiar, but my nerves made it difficult to concentrate.

"I usually try to work it into the conversation subtly, to let her know when I think a potential client is attractive. I wanted to make sure she understood the level of attractive we're talking about here."

"I'm flattered." I could hear the smile in his words.

"Would you like a taste?" she asked him. What did that mean? Then her breath was warm on my neck. "I'm going to touch you now."

I jumped when her fingers dragged across the skin of my stomach. Lower, and lower. Was she going to–? Soft, delicate fingers stroked me. I tried to jerk away, but the straps kept me in place. I'd never fooled around with another woman. I could appreciate the beauty of the female body, but I never had any desire to explore anything outside of my own. I liked good, ole-fashioned sex, and knew I still had a lot to learn there. Adding women into the mix seemed overwhelming

It didn't matter. Her fingers were stirring my folds where I was shamefully wet, and the slightest of moans slipped out before I could choke it back.

She drew her hand away from in between my legs, and there was a noise I couldn't place, like a kiss. No, I figured it out. He was sucking on her fingers.

"Does she taste good?" Tara asked. Heat poured through my body.

"I'd like to drink straight from the tap," he said. *Oh god.*

Oh my god.

"There's a fee for that, but I'll waive it if we reach a deal." I assumed that was acceptable to him because Tara again leaned over me and whispered in my ear. "Slide down near the edge of the table, and enjoy." She sounded envious.

I did as asked, my trembling body gliding over the leather. When I was down far enough and my feet dangled awkwardly over the side, Tara's warm hand closed around an ankle and lifted it, setting my foot on the flat surface of the tabletop so my toes curled over the edge. She guided the other ankle so I was laid out before him, my knees bent up in the air. Sliding down had also forced my arms to be bent up by my head.

The pads of his fingers were cold when they touched the inside of my knee and gently urged it to the side, opening me to him. My bottom lip quivered. No, my whole body quivered. The fingers dragged across the inside of my thigh until they reached the hollow where my legs joined my body. I wanted him to say something. I wanted him to—

"Fuck," he said in a low, deep voice when his finger brushed over me where only a few men, and now Tara, had touched me, making me shudder. "You're so wet."

His touch was gone and replaced by warm air as his mouth hovered over my sensitive flesh. He kissed the hollow there, then just above my slit, then the inside of my thigh on the other side. Teasing me. Delicious anticipation grew and strangled my breath.

I bucked hard on the table when his tongue grazed me. One of his large, cold hands clamped down on a hip to hold me in place. The sensation wasn't like anything I'd felt before. The blindfold focused everything on the pleasure that was spreading outward through my body from his indecent kiss.

He licked me again, starting at the bottom of my entrance and all the way up to my clit.

"Oh my god," I said out loud, and then went wooden. I wasn't supposed to speak until spoken to, according to the contract.

"You like that?" He didn't wait for me to answer, he just did it again. And again. The beginning of an orgasm developed off in the distance and then was right upon me when he eased a finger where I was soaking wet.

"She's yours for twenty thousand," Tara said. The logical side of my brain tried to function, but the physical part of my body was in control. That wasn't true. This man, this total stranger, was in control of my body when he was fucking me with his mouth and finger.

"I was thinking more like nine," he responded. Then his mouth was back on me. How could he negotiate like this? His head was buried between my legs, and she was just standing there, watching. The orgasm threatened closer still, and I moaned.

Nine was close. It was already more than I thought I could get, seeing as how Tara had said he was good looking. But Tara's hand brushed over my ankle, demanding I focus. She could get him higher. I shook my head quickly at his offer, and then moaned when his tongue slipped inside me.

"She seems to like you." Tara's voice was sultry. "How about sixteen?"

"Ten." He murmured it against the side of my thigh, his finger working in and out of me. Desire built, pinpricks creeping over my skin, begging for release.

"We both know she's worth way more than that. Fifteen."

His hand withdrew and it was cold as if he'd stepped back. *No*, the dirty voice in my head cried. He was going to leave me when I was so close. So close to not just what I needed, but so close to tumbling over the cliff into a sea of pleasure.

"Twelve." His deep voice filled the room. My heart lurched and relief overwhelmed me. I barely noticed when Tara's hand skimmed my knee. His hands and mouth had already shown me he knew what he was doing and promised I would enjoy it.

"Yes," I whispered.

Tara's hair fell on my arm when she drew close to whisper, "Are you sure? I think you're leaving money on the—"

"Yes." The need in me was too much already. How had he been able to bring me right to the brink so quickly? I was ready to pay him to get the tongue back.

"Congratulations, sir," Tara announced. "She's yours." Her footsteps said she was moving to the door to leave us.

"Do you want to stick around?" he asked.

The footsteps stopped, hesitating.

"If you'd like me to watch, I wouldn't mind." Another wave of heat burned in my core with the thought of it. She'd almost sounded eager. She wanted to watch what he was going to do to me. Soft footsteps announced her return to the wingback chair.

The deal had been made and, honestly, I wanted it. I longed for his mouth to be where it had been before my orgasm had stalled. The excruciating ache between my legs took my breath away.

Fingertips traced over my right breast and made me flinch, and I gasped when his hot mouth closed around the nipple of my left. The ache in my center intensified when he sucked at me. Holy shit, I wanted him. Usually I loved foreplay, but I was out of control and desperate. My hand tried to push him down and show him what I wanted, but the dull thud of the restraint going taut answered back.

"Did I hurt you?" He'd bitten me gently a split second before I'd tried to move. It hadn't hurt, not where he used his teeth.

"No, sir," I replied, frantic.

He might have laughed; my brain was foggy with thoughts of lust.

"Then, what is it?" He didn't sound concerned, he sounded smug. "What do you want?"

I was allowed to answer because he'd asked, so I tried to be sure not to waste my words. "I want your mouth between my legs again."

"Where?" The sin in his voice was addicting.

I wasn't huge into dirty talk, but since everything was getting thrown out, I let this go too. "My pussy."

"Yeah? I believe this is mine tonight." He buried a finger deep inside me, causing my back to arch off of the leather. He revived the stalled orgasm in two slow, wicked thrusts, and just as I reached the precipice, the hand was gone.

A frustrated whine tore from my lips.

There was the sound of clothes rustling and a zipper being undone.

"Condoms are in the top drawer beneath her," Tara said. I'd already forgotten she was there, watching, and her voice was uneven and rushed. Was she turned on watching us?

The table barely moved when he opened the drawer and then shut it a moment later, a noise of foil tearing. I had mixed emotions about it. I craved what he was going to do, but I desired his mouth even more.

Wet, velvety bliss licked at me. His mouth was aggressive, sucking at the bundle of nerves, making me gasp. I climbed again, inching closer and closer, and he forced my body to writhe with need. While his mouth was busy, it sounded like he was fiddling with the condom, rolling it on.

His tongue ran over me again. As he pulled back, the faint stubble along his jawline brushed over the skin on the inside of my thigh.

"I'm going to fuck you now." From his words I could tell he was standing again.

I moaned, a desperate cry of eagerness.

Hands slid under my legs and yanked my body down so my ass was just at the edge of the table and my bound wrists were above my head. Every muscle in my body went tense when the head of his dick touched my entrance. The length of him slid once through my folds, either teasing me or making me aware that he was long. He lined up where he needed to be and pressed inside, just a tiny bit. I let loose a whimper. He was thick.

"You're so goddamn beautiful," he said, inching in. The words made my walls clamp down on him, an involuntary reaction that only made it harder for him to get inside. "And you're so tight." He withdrew and then pressed in again, further this time. I sighed. It was uncomfortable with his size, but the pleasure of the fullness overruled it.

"Do you want more?"

"Yes," I said, breathless.

He pushed deeper, forcing his way. Even though I was wet, he was so hard and big, and it had been a long time for me. But the orgasm he'd held at bay reared its head and I was about to explode. He continued his descent into me, filling my mind with nothing but the sensation of his presence.

He buried himself as far as he could go, until he was completely inside, and ground his hips against me. "Now come for me."

He'd known all along how close I was. And when he demanded it, holy shit, I gave it to him. I came hard in one of the most intense orgasms I'd ever had, bucking on the table, crying out a sob of pleasure. My body seized and convulsed, fighting against the straps. I'd wanted to reach out and grab something but there was nothing within range.

He didn't move as I came on him and milked him with my body. I heard his rapid breathing followed by a deliberate long, slow breath as if he had to even himself out.

"I could watch that again," he said. His smooth skin was on mine, warm, our bare chests pressed together. I could feel the crisp fabric of his button-up shirt on my sides, like he'd undone his shirt but not removed it. Lips skimmed my pulse on my neck. "Would you like me to make you come again?"

"Yes," I said, still shuddering with aftershocks of my orgasm. He started to move deep inside. With me, sometimes a second, smaller orgasm piggybacks on the first, and I could feel the tendrils of this second one tugging me along, pulling me back up.

"I have rules," he said. "You don't get to ask questions, no matter what." His deliberately slow, indecent rhythm made me crazy with need. "Do you understand?"

It was already a house rule, so I didn't struggle to answer. "Yes."

"Yes, what?" He thrust into me once, harder, getting my attention.

"Yes, sir."

He resumed his disciplined pace, sliding his flesh inside mine and building the desire to an alarming level. "Good. Rule two is you answer my questions, and you have to answer them honestly."

I could do that, so I nodded quickly.

"The last rule is your body belongs to me, so that means your orgasms are mine. You don't come without my permission." His wet tongue dragged from one breast, down the valley between them, and on to the other one, circling the taut nipple. "There will be consequences if you break any rule."

I gasped. Did he know I was already close?

"Understood?"

I swallowed a breath. Three rules, simple enough. "Yes, sir."

He whispered it against my flesh, "Good."

It was out of my mouth a second later. "I want permission to come."

He laughed. His body was gone from mine so he was only touching me where we were joined. "Already? No."

No? Why? My legs shook and wrapped around his back, trying to pull him in deeper. To pull him back to me.

"Do you like having my big cock in your pussy?"

I didn't have to think about it. "Yes."

"Then I think it's time to lose the blindfold," he said. "We're both visual creatures."

The room fell away and everything shifted horribly. His fingers slipped under the mask and eased it up, and even though it took my eyes a few blinks to adjust to the light, it didn't matter, I already knew. I'd heard him use that phrase before.

"No," I cried. *No, no, no.*

"Hello, Evelyn," Logan said.

FIVE

Logan didn't slow his pace. His large hands clamped down on my hips and braced me to the table when I tried to slide backward away from him.

"I don't think so," he said.

"Why?" My voice was as shattered as I felt. "How did you—"

"I believe that's rule number one."

In the low light and with my vision restored, I could see the thin sheen of sweat on his chest and defined abs. His mocha-colored brown hair was perfectly tousled. Tara was right. I had always thought he was attractive, but when I pushed his personality to the side, I could see he was undeniably hot. I squirmed under his hands, but all it did was create a seductive smile on his lips.

I could stop him. I had a signal. If I opened and closed my hands quickly and repeatedly, I could have him thrown out in less than a minute. I'm sure he knew this, just as I'm sure he knew I couldn't use it. The damage had been done. He'd seen me naked, he'd gone down on me, and currently he was fucking me. My boss. Wasn't it enough that I had to struggle to please him at the office?

"What are you thinking about?" he asked. "Honestly."

"That you're my boss."

He continued to pump his dick into me, and although the pending orgasm had faded significantly when he revealed himself, it lingered.

"Trust me, I'm aware. I'm not supposed to do what we're

doing right now with an employee, no matter how much I've thought about it."

What the hell was he talking about? "You don't even like me."

He leaned over me, burying his face in my neck and sucking on it. "You sure about that? I just dropped twelve thousand dollars to be with you."

The reminder of how much money he'd spent whispered to the orgasm to come closer. The idea that he wanted me and wanted me that badly was powerful. It left me breathless.

"Maybe I overcompensate at the office," he admitted. "And your thoughts on me?"

I shut my eyes. How in the world could I answer that? The steady rock of his body against mine was beginning to drown out all other thought. One of his hands left my hip. It traveled up my skin, leaving goosebumps in its wake and settled on my nipple.

"You're not going to answer me? That was rule two." He pinched hard enough that it was just short of pain.

"I don't like you," I said.

He laughed, like it was doubtful. "Maybe not before, but now you fucking do." He pulled out of me and ran his hand where he'd just been, causing me to gasp. "And this," he shoved his wet fingers into my mouth, "This is the proof of how much you do."

I could taste my arousal, and . . . I liked it. In the office, Logan was abrasive and strict, but he was also driven and fair. Logan outside of the office . . . holy shit. I did like him.

"Do you like my big cock in your pussy, Evelyn?"

I couldn't say no, he'd know I was lying. "Yes." It came out quiet and ashamed.

He entered me again, and I'd swear he was harder now.

My traitorous body shifted to take him deeper, and he gave a sharp breath as if enjoying it. His deep brown eyes were almost black and hypnotizing, and I stared into them, trying to understand why he'd done this. I had to focus on that. Not how good it felt. Oh my god, it felt too good.

"I wanted to ask you to get drinks right before the promotion," he said.

"Why didn't you?" I didn't realize I'd asked it out loud.

"Rule number one again." This time he used his teeth to nip at the underside of my breast, a sharp pain dulled immediately with the swipe of his tongue. His thrusts increased in intensity and I bit down on my bottom lip. *Oh, no.* I was getting close.

An odd expression crossed his face, perhaps regret. "I'd heard you had a boyfriend, the guy you've got a picture of on your desk." He was talking about the picture of Blake and me at an alumni Northwestern football game.

"He was never my boyfriend." His hand left my breast and slid down to curl under my knee, pushing it back. "Shit, don't do that," I said, panicked.

He ignored me, leaning in to my neck and tracing the edge of my ear with his tongue. "Why? You don't like it?"

"No, I like it. I like it too much."

"That's a terrible reason for me to stop." He was moving furiously now. My body fought for control, begging me to stop resisting. Desire flowed through my veins, thick and hot like liquid fire. I wanted the release. I needed the release. Or I might lose my fucking mind.

"You can do this," he whispered. "Hold it back. It'll be so much better if you wait."

My eyes fell shut, but in an instant my head was cradled in his hands, forcing it up.

"I want you to watch me fuck you."

We're visual creatures, after all. He knew it was torturous for me to see his massive dick disappear inside me. I'd never seen anything so erotic, and I gasped for breath, straining to push the orgasm back.

"Good, you're doing so good," he said. "Just a little longer."

I think he wanted me to fail. He trailed one hand down my body, over my breast, down my stomach, and moved between our bodies to circle my clit. It was too much, overwhelming me.

I sighed in frustration, or desperation. "Logan . . ." I was ready to beg for it.

His eyes were framed with long lashes, and I realized how beautiful his dark brown irises were. When I said his name, his eyes filled with heat. His expression was fascinating and my total undoing. I didn't have a prayer of surviving rule number three.

He realized it just before it started to happen. "No, not yet. You don't have permission."

It was way too late for that. This time my hands reached back and curled around the ribbons holding me, gripping them as I came.

"Oh, fuck," I cried, throwing my head back and closing my eyes. It wasn't as strong as the first, but it was still powerful and knocked me sideways. As I came down from where he'd taken me, I opened them again and looked at him timidly.

He was furious.

One hand latched onto my wrist, while his other ripped open the Velcro, freeing me. He didn't say anything. He went straight to the other wrist and undid it as well, then pulled out of me and yanked me up so I was sitting before him. I wanted to ask what he was going to do to me, but I'd already broken what I could tell was the biggest rule. I didn't need to do another right now.

"Stand up," he ordered, stepping back to allow me to do so.

My gaze never left his as I put a timid foot down on the cold floor. That was as far as I got before he pulled me down off the table and turned me in his arms so my back was against his sweat-dampened chest. Hands shoved me down so I was bent over the table.

"Put your arms out."

Because he wanted to bind me again. My hands slid slowly up the leather, shaking with both nerves and excitement.

"Any chance you could—?" He wasn't speaking to me.

"Of course," Tara answered. Crap, I'd forgotten she was there again. Her face was flushed as she came to the table and wrapped the restraint around my wrist.

"If I can help you in any way," she said to him, her words dripping with innuendo, "don't hesitate."

Wait a minute. What had she just offered? A sharp pang of possessiveness stabbed into my core. Logan had paid to have me, not her. My thoughts had me too distracted to notice she'd closed the other restraint before it was too late to do anything.

I watched her return to the chair, her hands pressed against her thighs.

His hand came down hard on my ass, and I cried out with shock. I hadn't really been spanked before. This was one of the three boxes I'd checked this evening, and apparently my consequence for disobeying him. It stung hot, and went cold as the hand left, only to strike me again, now on the other cheek. This time the hand remained where it had landed, and it pulled my cheek to the side . . .

So he could put his mouth *there*. Where no one had

been before.

I jolted and my knees slammed painfully into the cabinet beneath the table. His mouth moved down so he could dip his tongue inside me, but the hand remained where it was. He set his other hand on my other cheek and eased it away so my backside was totally exposed.

It was shocking and taboo when his tongue moved up again, and sent me into a frenzy. Soft, warm, wrong. My body liked it but my brain did not, and the war between the two left me dizzy. I thought I could catch my breath when he stood, but it got much, much worse.

I felt him nudging there, pressing into me.

"Wait." I turned over my shoulder in panic, every muscle in my body tense.

He hesitated. "What?"

"I'm not sure I can do that."

His gaze went to the list on the easel. "It's on the menu."

"I know, but—" How to explain that I'd only done it out of desperation? "I haven't done it before."

"You don't want to?"

I didn't like giving up. I didn't like failing. But I thought I'd fail at this.

"I don't." It came out defeated. What was going to happen now that I'd backed out–

"It's okay," he said, "I can barely keep from coming in your pussy anyway. I probably wouldn't last five seconds fucking you up the ass."

My brain spun hearing him say such vulgar things. He was so composed and calculating in the office; this was the unleashed version of him. When he shoved his dick back inside me, I decided I liked this version better.

I'd already reached what I thought was my limit on

orgasms. Two had been the most I'd ever been blessed with in one go. My body seemed spent until his hands fell onto my waist and he pulled me back on him, demanding more.

He slammed into me, thrusting, and . . . and . . . he was probably going to get me to come again, but he was going to have to work for it this time. The slide of his flesh inside mine wasn't like anything I'd ever had. It left me breathless and thirsty for more.

"Naughty girl," he scolded playfully. I glanced at him, but his eyes weren't on me. They were on Tara in the corner. She had her skirt pulled clear up to her waist and a hand moving inside her lace panties.

"Oh my god," I gasped. It was like someone had poured fire over me. It was so sexy.

"Listening to you come got her worked up," he said to me. "Do you like watching her touch herself?"

I couldn't take my eyes away. "Yes."

Logan drove into me harder and deeper, and I worried I was going to break rule three again without warning. But he slowed down and ground himself into me in a seductive move that teased.

"Will you take off your panties," he asked Tara, "and show us your pussy?"

She stood deliberately, her eyes hooded. She drew her panties down over her gorgeous legs and past her heels, stepping out of the lace one leg at a time. I expected her to sit back down in the chair but instead she stalked toward us.

I shouldn't have cared whether or not he was interested in her. Up until tonight I didn't think about Logan much. He was my boss and off-limits. But now it was impossible not to view this exquisite woman as a threat.

Her gaze wasn't on him, though. It was on me. She sat

on the table just above my arms, her hands slowly dragging the fabric of her skirt up. And up. And then she turned to us and spread her legs so they were straddling the table, exposing the bare skin of her sex.

"See how wet you made me?" she said, slipping a hand down into her glistening folds. It's not like I could look much elsewhere, she was only two feet from my face. "Have you ever been with another woman?"

I didn't have to answer her. I belonged to Logan tonight.

"Have you?" he asked, pressing deep inside me. My eyes all but rolled back into my head, and his perfect positioning made it hard to do anything.

"No." This was one of the boxes I hadn't checked on the willing list, although I'd considered it.

"Do you want to?" It came out casual, like he was asking something normal.

I couldn't give an answer because I didn't have one.

"Rule number two," he growled.

"I . . . don't know." I was drunk off the sex and power in this room. Power that was shifting my direction.

"Why don't you try and see if you like it?" she half-begged. The conflict between my conservative side and wild one left me disorientated. Logan's hand abandoned my waist to touch her knee.

"Come closer."

She smiled and did so, eager. "But just so you're aware, I can get in trouble if you touch me, sir."

There was nowhere to go when she lay back on the table and put her feet outside my arms. She smelled like coconut and vanilla. I was frozen, my head over her, hesitating. I wasn't sure if I wanted this, but my mind hadn't issued a "no" either. Not hearing the "no" made me want to try.

His hands gathered up my hair and he held it back, away from my face. He'd slowed almost to a halt so his thrust wouldn't send me face-first into her.

"Do you want me to tell you what to do?" he asked.

"I . . . yeah." My heart slammed against my chest.

"Put your tongue on her, start on the outside and work your way in, up and down."

I swallowed hard, closed my eyes, and leaned forward. I'd barely touched her, and she gave a huge sigh that encouraged me to really do it. My tongue trailed a path over her pink skin. She tasted . . . different. Good. When I reached her clit, she moaned and I felt Logan jerk inside me.

"Holy shit, that's so hot," his deep voice said. "Suck on her, then flick your tongue really fast."

She liked that, like, a lot. Her back arched off the table and then slammed down on it.

"Fuck, just like that." It came through her ragged breaths. "Right there."

Giving her pleasure gave me pleasure, and need wound a coil tight inside of me. Logan resumed a slow pace of movement that increased the tension. It felt like his dick went on forever when he pressed inside me. His hands cupped my breasts.

I felt her hand on my head, pressing me down on her. "Lick me harder."

I had to draw my mouth away from her to catch my breath and utter, "I need permission to come."

"Not until she does." He said it on a hurried breath, like this was taking its toll on him.

I dipped my tongue inside her and then returned to where she seemed to like it best. The coil got tighter when her hips moved in time with my mouth. Her hand wove into my hair, pushing Logan's away so she could grip a handful. Her moans rose in volume, matching mine. Closing in on breaking rule three again? I couldn't. I wouldn't. My tongue fluttered over her damp skin, urgent for her crescendo.

"Oh shit, I'm coming, I'm coming." Her body thrashed and her thighs clamped tight on my head, keeping me in place, holding me to her while she shuddered. Then her legs fell open and she stilled on the table, her breath slowing.

He'd slowed down too, of course, but I could feel him pulsing. He'd gotten very, very close.

Tara backed up and rose to sit, giving me a slow smile of satisfaction. It made my insides quiver knowing I'd pleased her. She swung her leg over and stepped down off of the table, her heels carrying her back to the chair, a deliberate and seductive sway to her hips.

Logan put a hand on my shoulder and the other on my waist, bracing me. He built a steady pace, faster and faster until I was wild. The only sound other than our gasps was the slap of our bodies together. The coil was so tight inside, strangling all thought except the need for release.

"Wait for me," he said.

"Shit, hurry."

Because it was happening now. I cried out, my hands balling into fists and wave after wave of bliss slammed into me. It was so intense it was painful, but seconds later I triggered his release because I could feel his spasms inside me. They prolonged the orgasm, and I was still coming when he collapsed forward onto my back, his hands gripping me tightly.

Neither of us moved or said anything. I closed my eyes, foolishly convincing myself I wouldn't have to face reality when they opened. I could feel his heart pounding in his chest. It was pounding as fast as mine.

He brushed my hair out of his way and feathered a kiss into the side of my neck, just below my ear. "I would have paid twenty for you."

My eyes popped open as he withdrew from me. He stepped back and I could hear the sound of him throwing something in the trash. Clothes rustled.

"Wait," I said, starting after him. But the straps painfully reminded me that I couldn't do that. "Logan." I craned my neck to try to see him. His zipper was yanked up and he shuffled backward, not attempting to button his shirt.

"Logan, wait," I pleaded. But he fled out the door, not looking at me. Abandoning me.

chapter SIX

His rapid exit sent me into an epic meltdown.

"Get these off of me!" I said to Tara, fighting the restraints.

"Is he really your boss?" She moved slowly. I could have opened ten Adobe programs in the time it took her to go to the hook and pull down the robe.

"Yeah, he's my boss. Can you go faster?" I tried to keep the edge from my voice.

She placed the robe over my shoulders and slowly undid the first restraint. I pushed her hands out of the way so I could do the other and shrugged into the robe, wrapping it around me as I fled for the door.

"Evelyn, you can't," she said quietly. "Let's go upstairs."

As soon as I made it to the hall, a massive man with a huge forehead was waiting, like a bouncer. He didn't say anything. He gave me a friendly smile and gestured to the stairs. Tara set her hand in the small of my back and urged me to go that way.

"Once a client's gone to the payment room, there's no more contact. That's for your safety."

I think I was numb with shock, on total emotional overload. When I blinked, I was back on that same couch in the lounge. Payton was already dressed.

"It was Logan," I said, still unable to make sense. How the hell did he know I was here? And how the fuck was I going to go into the office on Monday?

"Your boss?"

"Yeah," Tara said, "Her hotter than the surface of the sun, boss."

"You didn't tell me he was hot." Payton accused me with a look. "All you said was he was an asshole."

"I never said that, he's not—" Was I defending him? "He's good looking but he's my manager. And until tonight, I didn't think he liked me."

Tara had a wide smile. "Jesus, you should have seen the look on his face when he came in and saw you."

I couldn't even imagine. I didn't know him, but now I wanted to know everything about him.

Payton helped me get dressed. The bars were still open and she wanted to celebrate with a drink. I could barely focus on the simple task of pulling the dress on, how would I function in public? Adding to my confusion, Tara kissed me on the cheek and whispered a "thanks" before leaving, reminding me what I'd done.

Oh, god.

"I have to go home," I said to Payton as we started for Joseph's office.

She stopped moving, her face frozen in an expression I didn't understand. "You didn't like it?" Her voice sounded like a ghost.

I took a deep breath because it wasn't easy to admit. "I did, I'm just on sensory overload."

She collapsed into a chair at the edge of the lounge.

Panic rose inside me. I hadn't seen her look unsteady before. "What's wrong?"

"I'm fucking relieved, is all."

"What? That I . . . liked it?" It wasn't easier to say the second time either.

"Yeah, because now I know there's nothing seriously

wrong with me. That I'm not all fucked up."

Now it made sense. She hadn't told me her real reason so it wouldn't invalidate her test results. She'd endured a lot of guys calling her whore and slut over the years. Their judgment always seemed to bounce off her. But she had a strict Catholic upbringing, and maybe deep down she worried there was truth there. That she enjoyed sex and that was wrong.

"I did like it," I said, finding strength. "It was mind-blowing, the greatest sex of my life. I may have done some things I'm not sure I'll be super comfortable with tomorrow, but I'm not ashamed I enjoyed it."

Her smile was epic.

Joseph gave me a fat manila envelope in his office. Before he could ask—

"I'm sorry, but I don't think it's for me," I said. "But thank you for everything."

"You know where we are if you change your mind."

I followed Payton down the stairs, through the hallway, and into the now-empty holding room, where the black guy with the clipboard sat on the couch.

"You girls ready?" he asked, lumbering to his feet.

"Yeah," Payton said with a glowing smile. "How is it you're always the one who escorts me out, Julius?"

The enormous man beamed. "Just dumb luck, I think."

We went out the front door, and immediately I could sense something wasn't right. Julius spread his arms out, blocking Payton and me from someone.

"Evie," I heard him say. What the hell was Blake still doing here?

"I don't know you, buddy," Julius said to Blake. "You don't have no business here. And you," his head turned the opposite direction, "you I recognize, so you better get a move on. You ain't allowed to stay."

My gaze went in the direction of whomever Julius was talking to, and I quieted a gasp.

"Logan?"

"You told me to wait," he said, wearing a cryptic expression.

When I glanced between the two men waiting for me, it turned their focus toward each other. I could see the distrust on Logan's face. He'd recognized Blake from the picture, and after that exchange Blake must have assumed he'd been my client.

"Blake, stop," I yelled when he charged toward Logan. I ducked under Julius' massive arm and got in between them. Blake's face was raw anger and hurt, and even though I knew I wasn't responsible, I hated I was the cause of it.

Julius yelled at both the men to get back, to get fucking lost.

"I know them, it's all right," I said. "Payton, help me out."

"Get out of here," she yelled to Blake. "You had your chance, now run back home to your girlfriend who deserves way better than you."

"Fuck you, whore."

Payton looked smug. "Sorry, not enough money in the world."

Oh god, this was a mess. Logan watched the drama unfold, his eyes wary of the tall man fixated on me.

"Evie, are you okay?" Blake calmed when he stopped looking at Payton. "Let me drive you home."

I'd been in love with him for so long, and my broken heart thudded in my chest when I spoke to him. "No. Go home."

His face turned sour, a mixture of loss and anger. I watched him climb into his car and tear off, not looking at me again. My hand hurt because I'd been clenching the envelope full of money tightly, not noticing I'd gone all white-knuckles.

Julius didn't like it when I took a step toward Logan. "You sure you wanna talk to him? I can make him go away."

"Yes." Oh yes, I definitely wanted to talk to him.

He leaned against a midnight-blue BMW, wearing the black suit he'd worn when Player's had come in for an office visit, only this time there was no tie and two buttons had been left undone. I saw him through new eyes. My boss was stunningly handsome and powerfully sexy.

He'd parked several car lengths down from the club, and when I reached him, he stood.

"Who is that guy?" His demand was hushed, perhaps wanting privacy from Julius and Payton who watched from near the doorway.

"A friend," I said, then thought better of it. "I don't know, it's complicated."

"Come home with me."

I wished I'd had a witty comeback or biting remark, but my brain failed me. "What?"

He slipped his hand gently behind my neck and whispered in my ear. "That's rule number one."

Logan moved quickly, setting a hand on my hip to hold me, and dropped his head so his mouth could claim mine in a kiss. After everything in that room, this was the first time it had happened. It was so slow and seductive that I melted into it. Hands cupped my face, tilting my head to just the right angle so he could tease me with a hint of his tongue. He asked for more, and I welcomed it.

My hands followed his lead and circled his neck, and I pressed my body against his, wanting the kiss to deepen further. Oh my god, I wanted more. I wanted him.

"Come home with me," he commanded in his deep voice, one I couldn't disobey. I was too curious about his reasons to give any other answer anyway. Gravity pulled me to him.

"Okay."

He pulled the passenger door open, like he was a gentleman. I stared into the empty car then back to him. If I didn't get into this car, I wouldn't get any answers.

"I'm gonna go," I yelled to Payton. She flashed a gigantic smile and waved me off, then slipped her arm through Julius' and headed for her car.

There was a bottle of wine sitting in the passenger seat. I grabbed it and sat, setting it in my lap along with my purse and the envelope, and gave a nervous smile to Logan as he shut my door. *Oh. My. God.* What was I doing?

His car had a soft leather interior that I sank back into. The bottle of wine was cold in my hands, and the label had the same logo as the club.

"I guess this is a complimentary gift with purchase," I said when he slipped into the driver's seat.

"No, that was my purchase. You were the complimentary gift."

My pulse quickened. He started the car, put it in gear, and eased away from the curb. Once we were in traffic, he set his right hand on the bare skin just above my knee. I jumped, startled by how nonchalant it was for him. Casual, easy, yet dominating. The warmth of his skin gave me goosebumps.

We rode in silence, and it made me tense and anxious. I wanted him to talk, but he seemed content to study the traffic and act as if what we had just done had never happened.

"How did you know I would be at the club?"

He snatched the bottle of wine out of my hands and set it in the cup holder, then pushed everything in my lap to the floorboard.

"That," his hand glided to the inside of my knee and a few inches up from where it had been, "is definitely rule number one."

"In case you hadn't noticed, we're not there anymore."

"I paid for a night with you, and in case you hadn't noticed, it's night out." A half smile twisted on his lips. "You're still under my rules."

"No, I am not."

We reached a stoplight, and he turned a cold and commanding gaze my direction. "You're in my car, and soon you'll be in my place. My rules, Evelyn."

"I had no idea what I was agreeing to," I blurted out. This authoritative version of him chilled me and yet set me on fire. The dark timbre of his voice shot straight between my legs, made me weak with excitement. I ripped my gaze away from his and watched the traffic, the people gathered outside bars smoking and chatting in the warm August night. The car lurched forward when the light turned green. How was I supposed to get answers if I couldn't ask questions?

"What's on your mind?" he asked.

It was the first test. I didn't respond, curious to see what he'd do. Would he make good on his threat of punishment? He gave a sideways glance to me, and shoved my knees apart so he could put his hands on top of my panties.

"Answer me or I'll take you right to the edge and leave you hanging."

My mouth fell open so I could draw air into my lungs. I knew he could do it, and he certainly did, too.

"I'm wondering," my voice was breathless, "how this is going to work on Monday, if you'll go back to disliking me."

"You still think after what I just did, that I dislike you?"

His fingers moved and pleasure strummed through me. I issued a soft moan, and a hint of a cocky smile teased his lips. "I told you I thought about asking you out before."

"You really think people care that much about whether you get involved with an employee?" Crap, rule number one. His fingers pushed my panties to the side and touched me unhindered, making my hands clench around his wrist.

"They would if I promoted you." His fingers moved faster, torturing me.

"You're going to promote me?"

He slipped his whole finger inside me and I gasped. *Yes*, my body chanted, *yes*. The strength was gone from my hands around his wrist, but they remained, urging him to go faster, deeper, to give it to me exactly how I liked it.

"Do you like that? My finger inside you?"

I swallowed hard and nodded faintly.

"Tell me with words."

There was no oxygen in this car, so it was hardly audible. "I like it."

I was only marginally aware we'd turned from the street into a parking garage beneath one of the high-rises. As he drove down the aisle, my climax grew closer.

"Almost there," he said. Was he talking about his place or my orgasm? He parked the car and shut off the engine, then he had both hands under my skirt. I was panting. I clawed at him, pulling his head to me, and crashed my lips against his.

He allowed it for a moment. But then he completely withdrew from me, staying true to his word. Oh god, I was desperate. I felt like he was being cruel, and yet he'd forgotten an important detail. I didn't have use of my hands at the club, but I did now.

He grabbed the bottle of wine around the neck, pushed

open his door, and climbed out, not realizing I hadn't done the same. I shoved a hand under my panties, not caring if there was anyone else in the garage who could see me. After this crazy night, I was completely out of control.

He'd come around to my side to open the door for me like I was a lady. Instead he saw me touching myself. Heat flashed through his gorgeous eyes, but his face maintained its usual intensity.

"You are not going to break any more rules tonight. Certainly not that rule." He pushed my hands away and pulled me to my feet. "I told you, this is mine." He ran his hand between my legs, lifting my skirt with it, rubbing me for a moment. The independent side of me protested but the basic woman in me loved it.

I grabbed the envelope and my purse off the floor and followed him to the elevator.

"I think I prefer you naked," he murmured against my neck while we rode up to the forty-forth floor, "but this dress is a very close second." His fingertips skimmed over the bare skin of my back and drew a shiver from me.

His apartment was only a few doors down from the elevator, and when he turned on the lights inside, it made me angry.

"How much are they paying you that you can afford rent on this?"

The door shut behind him and his hands went to my hips, forcing me face-first against the wall.

"That was rhetorical," I said when his body flattened mine. He sank his teeth into the flesh of my earlobe. It was controlling, and hot. "I just meant your place is nice."

"It's not my place. I mean, it is and it isn't. I'm renting it from a friend who holds the lease." Hands caressed the curves of my body, holding me against the wall. "He's in

Japan for the next year and didn't want to lose the place, so his company pays half the rent and I pay the other. Otherwise, no, I couldn't afford it."

He released me and let me wander further inside.

It's not like the apartment was a penthouse, but it was spacious with an open kitchen where everything looked brand new. The living room was just beyond the granite breakfast bar, and the back wall was one seamless sheet of glass, floor to ceiling.

This apartment had the most unbelievable view of North Beach possible. Even at the dead of the night, I could see the outline of the lake and the marina.

"Wow," I said.

"I'm already dreading moving out. Nothing's going to compare." He set the bottle of wine on the counter and opened a drawer, fishing out a corkscrew. I saw wine glasses hanging underneath a cabinet and pulled them out, setting them right side up for him.

I studied his long fingers as he cut the foil. Not being allowed to ask questions made starting a simple conversation difficult, and he seemed to like the silence. I didn't. I could be smart about it; he usually responded when I made a comment or observation.

"I don't like not being able to ask you questions about how tonight happened."

"That must be frustrating for you." He uncorked the bottle, filled the glasses half full with the red wine, and passed me one. He was playfully smug about his rules.

I took a sip of the wine. It was dry and I didn't care for it, and when I set the glass down, a smile twitched on his lips.

"You don't like my twelve thousand dollar bottle of wine?"

"It doesn't taste like twelve grand to me."

"But I know you do."

I was nervous when he closed the distance between us and an arm went tight around my waist. His head dipped down to mine, and he kissed me, his mouth dominating and possessive. It sent my heart rate through the roof. Jesus, this man knew how to kiss.

"What are you thinking about?" he asked.

"I'm glad you didn't kiss me during negotiations."

His brown eyes were curious. "Why?"

"Because I would have agreed to your opening bid. Or I might have countered with a lower one."

He seemed pleased to hear that. He set down his glass and put his hands on me, lifting me up to seat me on the counter top. The granite was cold against my burning skin.

This next kiss was more aggressive. It dripped with lust and the promise of more pleasure as his hands skimmed over my thighs, working up. I set one hand on his defined jawline, as if I could steady myself by touching him, but it only made the room spin harder. I could feel control slipping away.

Logan grew hard between my legs, pressing himself against my center. His hand went to my shoulder and he guided me to lean back, to lie on the counter, his hand brushing over my breast as I went. But I only went back so far, staying up on my elbows.

He tugged my skirt to my hips, working it up slowly and methodically as he licked his lips, and gave me a view of the tongue that had me practically begging for him on that table. *Oh, fuck.*

"You want to watch?" He had a wicked look in his eyes.

The shy girl I had once been was nowhere. I'd destroyed her when I marched into Logan's office earlier this week. Who'd have guessed I'd end up here, enjoying my punishment?

"I didn't get to watch last time."

He didn't take my panties off. His fingers traced the seam just inside my thigh and pulled the fabric to the side. Then he bent down, set my legs on his shoulders, and kissed me right where I wanted him to. Logan's eyes fell shut like he was savoring me. He slipped his tongue through my flesh, used his hands to spread me open, and licked. Intense, delicious heat spread from it. It was addicting. *He* was addicting.

Watching him feast on me was exquisite torture. I had to fight for each breath when he opened his eyes and checked to see if I were still viewing the show.

"I'm going to come," I half-pleaded.

"No, you're not."

My elbows gave out, and my back was cold against the granite, Logan not relenting or giving permission. Need clawed inside me and screamed for release. I had to focus elsewhere. Fucking anywhere else. *Do not think about the tongue lapping at you.* My head fell to one side and I latched onto the first thing I saw.

A framed poster on the wall. It wasn't an artistic photograph or reproduction of famous artwork. It was an advertisement for a sports car. I'd worked with him long enough to recognize his style anywhere.

"When did you . . ." No, no questions. God only knows what kind of delicious punishment he'd give me right now. "I've never seen that one before. It's amazing."

He lifted for a split second to see what I was talking about, and his eyes softened with the compliment. "I did it right before you started." When his head dipped back down, I grabbed a fistful of his soft hair, tunneling my fingers through it.

It was like my praise lit a match inside him, for he was much more intense and urgent, somehow as desperate for the orgasm as I was. He put one long finger inside me and curled it back, quickly finding the spot that would send me tumbling out of control.

"Please, I need to. . ." I gasped.

"Say my name when you do it."

Pleasure slammed into me, burning across my skin, across every nerve. I jerked and my knee sent one of the wine glasses plummeting to the tile floor, followed by the sound of glass shattering.

I think I would have screamed his name regardless of his demand.

"You know, I have neighbors," he teased, releasing his hold on my panties, and they snapped back in place.

I fought to return to earth. "Sorry about the glass."

His strong hand closed around one of my wrists and he helped me sit up. "Don't worry about it, that's my fault for letting you come."

"For letting me . . ." Shit, phrase it as a statement. It was like some twisted version of Jeopardy. "You say that like you don't want it to happen."

His hand threaded into my hair and pulled back, tilting my head up to him. "I'd prefer it if you only came on my cock."

It could have been his words or the recent orgasm, but I shuddered.

"Would you like that?" His face was seductive and powerful. "To come on my cock again?"

I didn't have to do this; I'd made the money I needed to. I could leave the envelope with my name scrawled on it on his countertop since our business transaction was complete. I'd come home with him to get answers, but now I had a new goal. What he was asking . . . what my boss was asking, was if I *wanted* to sleep with him.

"Yes."

Oh, fuck, yes.

chapter SEVEN

He didn't clean up the wine or the broken glass. He ordered me to wrap my arms and legs around him so he could carry me into his darkened bedroom. He took one knee and laid me back on the perfectly made queen-sized bed, stepping away to slip off his suit coat and disappeared into the walk-in closet.

The light flicked on, and I rose to sit, watching him. Fingers worked the buttons of his dress shirt, cuffs first and then to the collar, and down. When it was peeled off and placed on a hanger, my eyes lusted over every delicious curve of his muscles. My brain-to-mouth filter stopped working. "Holy shit, you're gorgeous."

He blinked, like he was stunned. Surely a man like him had heard that or something similar before, but then again, I'm sure it's always nice to hear.

"I believe that's my line," he said. "Take off your dress."

Why did I like this? A man ordering me around was supposed to incur my fiery wrath. Instead I lifted onto my knees and obeyed, dragging the fabric up and over my head, tossing it aside so I was kneeling on the bed in only my panties, my breasts bared so he could fuck me with those fascinating eyes.

"When you came in on Wednesday," he undid his belt and stepped out of his pants, "I didn't recognize you until you sat down at your desk." He approached the bed, locking a hand onto my hip where the panties clung and began to ease them down. "I almost had to jack off under my desk after you left my office."

What? This side of him was shocking and exciting. "That would have been highly inappropriate."

He smirked. "Oh, you think so?"

While he was peeling my underwear down, I shoved a hand beneath his boxers and wrapped my fingers around his dick. Maybe it was a side effect from the straps at the club, but I loved the feel of him. I loved being able to touch, to feel him jerk in my hands, to get to tease him as he did to me.

"I want to go down on you," I said, not knowing where that came from. I mean, I liked doing that, but it wasn't something I usually announced.

"What a surprise," he said, deadpan. "I want that, too." He sat with his back against his headboard and discarded his boxers, his dick standing at attention. I'd already forgotten how large he was, and he must have noticed the concern on my face.

"What?"

"You're huge," I said, uneasy.

"This shouldn't be new information to you."

Oh, I didn't know he could be funny. "How am I going to fit that in my mouth?"

He froze. "Was that a question?"

"Nope."

I didn't give him time to react or think of a way to punish me. I slid down on the bed, opened my mouth as wide as it could go, and took him inside. His breath left in a hiss.

"Seems to fit all right."

I loved going down on men, loved knowing he wasn't thinking about anything else but what I was doing to him. I ran my tongue over the velvety head of his dick and began to slide him in and out. Controlling him this way . . . it was addictive.

I used my hands on him, squeezing one hard and pumping him when I took my mouth off for a moment. Then I kept my lips tight and shoved him back inside, making him groan. I sucked and flicked my tongue, doing everything I could to return some of the pleasure he'd given me, pushing thoughts away that this man held sway over my career. I didn't want to think about the repercussions of this night. He'd started it anyway.

Logan was different when he was in my mouth, under my power. He seemed scattered. Not his commanding self. And he was silent. Usually that's what I wanted, but not tonight. I could ask him what he liked to encourage him to talk, but that would violate a rule . . . Screw it.

"Do you like fucking my mouth?"

He was breathing heavy and it seemed like he struggled to process the question. An alarm must have gone off in his head because he hooked me under my arms and pulled me off of him. He brought me up, pulling one of my legs across his lap, positioning me over him.

"I like fucking your tight, little pussy better."

Holy fuck, the things he said. It was such a turn-on. He leaned in and my eyes fell closed, anticipating his kiss. I craved it, and just as the faintest hint of his lips touched mine, they were gone. I moved in, but he turned away. His hands cupped my head and held it tight so he could hover just a breath away.

He knew how badly I wanted his mouth on mine. "Don't break the rules," he warned. He put his lips on my neck and sucked. Hard. When he pulled back, he chuckled. "I cannot tell you how unprofessional I think hickeys are."

I tried to scramble off of him, but he held me tight.

"I'm joking," he said, "I didn't mark you. But I could do it other places."

There was a pulsing ache in between my legs. How did he mean? A hickey somewhere else? Another spanking, maybe this one less playful than the last time? The room felt like it was a thousand degrees. It was dark, but the moon outside was full and bright, and he'd left the light on in the kitchen, which streamed in through the open bedroom doorway. His eyes were warm and intense as they searched my face.

"You're going to hold back your orgasm because it'll be better when I allow it. So, I need to know when you're getting close."

"You seem to be pretty aware already." I was a little annoyed at how quickly he had command over my body.

"I want to push it a little further." He leaned over to the side table and opened a drawer, retrieving a foil packet. "Green means go, yellow means you're getting close, and red means stop because you're right on the verge."

"You want me to tell you to stop? Yes, that was a question, get over it."

He tore open the condom wrapper and laughed. "It's okay. Yeah, I'm trusting you to stop yourself. It'll be worth it, I promise." His hand moved between our bodies and he rolled the condom on. His hands were warm on my waist.

"I should probably tell you," I said, "that I've already had more tonight than I've ever had, so . . . it might not happen for me."

"I'm willing to try if you are." He urged me down so I pressed against him. He was right at my entrance and so hard. God, I wanted him.

"Okay." I swallowed a breath. Could I do this? "Green."

He pushed inside me slowly, lowering me down onto

him. Although I was already a little sore from earlier, it felt amazing.

"Yellow." It came out breathless.

"You can't just say yellow because it feels good." He gave me a devious smile. "We haven't started moving yet."

Then, he started fucking me. I say that because even though I was on top, he was in complete control. He kept one hand on my hip and guided my pace, his eyes locked on mine, while his other hand cupped my breast. His thumb brushed over my nipple, and I arched my back into his touch, enjoying the sensation. I filled my hands with his head, running my fingers through his hair. It was so soft.

"Kiss me," he demanded. How the hell could I say no to that?

The rock of our bodies together made our kiss spin out of control until it was aggressive and passionate, and I had to tear my lips away from him.

"Yellow," I gasped. This time he knew it was a real warning.

If he slowed down any, I couldn't tell. He had both hands on my breasts, squeezing them together and pressing me back enough so he could dip his head down to them and pull a nipple in his mouth. Oh shit, my nipple was like a hard knot and so sensitive I could feel every subtle caress of his tongue.

It came from me firmer this time. "Yellow, Logan."

Heat was pouring through my body and electricity danced down my spine. So when he nipped at me and thrust hard, it left me with no choice.

"Fuck, red."

All movement ceased and the only sounds were his steady breathing and my gasps. I sounded like I was drowning, and I felt that way, too. He pulled my face to his and kissed me. His tongue explored my mouth, inviting me to do the same. I did.

When the kiss ended, he leaned back and grinned.

"Green?"

"Green," I whispered against his lips.

Oh man, I was in trouble when his hips began to move again. I set my hands on his shoulders and fought him for control over the pace, but it didn't really matter. As long as he was sliding in and out of me, it felt too good. I forced myself down on him and widened my knees so I could take him as deep as possible.

"Yellow," he said, and I froze. A smile bloomed across my face, thrilled to learn this went both ways.

He let me ride him until I got to yellow, and then he took over again. He brought me all the way to red, where my thighs burned and my body begged for release. I didn't ask for permission; I knew he'd say no. My legs felt like jelly when he helped me off of him and rolled me onto my back.

He was on top, my breasts flattened under his broad chest. I couldn't believe this man, the one in the office a mere thirty feet from my desk, could be so damn good at what he was doing. I dragged my nails down his back the first time I got to red, and sank my teeth into his shoulder the second. It had been next to impossible to tell him red the last time, my body was clamoring for mutiny from my mind. He'd gotten to red for the first time and lifted himself up on his arms, his gaze on me beneath him. I watched the rise and fall of his chest.

"Please." I tried not to sound desperate. "No more."

He didn't answer me; instead he climbed off and turned me on my side so I was facing the large window, my back against his chest.

"You feel like you go on forever." I sighed when he slid into me. I closed my eyes, letting lose a tear of frustration.

"Are you ready? It's going to be intense," he whispered behind my ear. Like this hadn't been intense already?

I wouldn't be able to say it again, and it fell from my mouth broken and shaky. "Green."

His thrusts were slow and deep until I got to yellow, and then he put a hand on my hip and drove into me.

"Not yet," he said, slowing.

"No," I cried.

The hand left my hip, yanked my knee up, and pulled the leg back over him. So he could set his fingers on my clit. The moment he thrust into me, his fingers moved, touching me right on my core.

"Give me what's mine," he ordered.

Intense wasn't a strong enough word when it began. The pleasure was too much and it was painful, stealing my breath away when the sharp edge of the orgasm overtook me. And as the edge faded, the orgasm kept coming, wave after wave of it. He'd stopped moving, maybe to let me ride it out, but when all of my muscles clamped down on him, it pulled him along with me. His hoarse voice rang out in a long groan of my name as he thrust hard and deep.

That only made it better and so much worse. I think I blacked out for a second when he pulsed inside of me. The hand on my clit had slowed but not stopped, and I was so overly sensitive down there that my brain could no longer interpret the pleasure. It felt like pain.

"Stop," I moaned, still coming. Even the slightest touch from him made my whole body flinch and contract. "Oh god, please."

"Are you . . . begging me to . . . stop letting you come?" He couldn't catch his breath, even though his climax was ending. The hand was gone, and finally, the grip of the orgasm released its hold. My hand had a fistful of his comforter, and when I let my hand relax, he pulled out.

I half-laughed, half-sobbed into the pillow beneath my head. The bed shifted as he rolled, or collapsed onto his back. After a moment of rest, I heard him pull a Kleenex out of the box on the nightstand. He must have gotten rid of the condom.

"Are you okay?" He slipped an arm around me, turning my chin toward him. "You're shaking." His eyes were full of concern.

"Yeah, I'm good," I said. "Don't expect me to walk anytime soon, though. I need to lie here and die for a little while."

"Do I need to tell you how fucking amazing that was? Because it was."

"It was just okay for me."

He gave me a knowing look, his eyes gleaming. "I'll have to try harder next time."

Next time? I wanted to ask him what exactly he had in mind. But I couldn't. My body was too spent to risk anything and it would be morning in a few hours. I could ask him anything then. That is, if I was spending the night. Which I was going to need to do; I wasn't going to be able to stand for a while.

He curled me into his arms without saying a word. A strong hand brushed the hair on my neck out of his way. Logan kissed me there, and I passed out.

chapter EIGHT

I was in my boss's bed. Naked. The curtains on his picture window were open, and it was bright as day in the room. Day, not morning. Oh my god, what time was it? I rolled over and looked at his alarm clock. It was nine something. That wasn't so bad, but there was a very naked Logan Stone beside me, snoring softly. The one who'd mentioned he wanted to promote me. He looked good in a suit, but better like this. Peaceful, sexy . . . wait, no. Terrifying.

I forced myself to roll over and admire the other view in the room. Like the living room, it was floor-to-ceiling glass, and there were no buildings in between his and the beach. No one could see in here; no wonder he didn't shut the curtains.

I was sore from the blissful beating he'd put on my body last night. My arms ached from the straps, my abs hurt from holding my legs around him on the table. And the downstairs situation . . . painful, but totally worth it.

But there was no way we were going to be able to have any of those shenanigans this morning, and I suspected when he woke, that was going to be on his agenda. He'd kiss me and that would convince my body to want to endure it. I think his kiss could get me to do anything.

I sat up gingerly and rose to my bare feet, padding across the carpet to his side of the bed where my panties and dress were in a heap on the floor. I had no intention of leaving. I just needed a layer of clothes on for protection. To slow me down in case he woke and set his lips on mine.

My eye shadow and mascara had relocated to under my bottom lashes, and I wiped it away with my fingers, doing my best to not look like I'd had the brains fucked out of me last night. My hair was flat and listless. I could go get the hair tie in my purse I'd left on the kitchen counter.

Logan was still out cold. In the corner of the bedroom, there was a small, upholstered chair. A thought formed in my head. He'd wake eventually, discover I wasn't in the bed, and when he sat upright, I'd be waiting for him in that chair. Dressed, legs crossed, and holding the upper hand, ready to demand answers. I practically ran to my purse in the kitchen.

My idea must have distracted me from the sound of glass being swept up into a dustpan, so when I came out of the bedroom and she stood, we both startled each other.

"Good heavens," she exclaimed. She was a brunette with short hair, friendly eyes, and a few extra pounds around her waist. I'd guess she was probably in her fifties. She certainly wasn't his housekeeper – the resemblance was apparent. Logan's mother was cleaning up the glass I'd broken when her son was going down on me. I wanted to melt into the floor and disappear forever.

"You must be Logan's girlfriend," she said. "The one he refuses to let me meet."

Everything went cold and my mind went to war with itself, torn between anger and hurt. How could we have done all of that last night if he wasn't single? I hadn't been allowed to ask questions, but I had assumed I wouldn't need to ask that one. How could he?

"Oh." That was all I could say, when I really wanted to say, "Oh, shit." How was I going to explain I wasn't his girlfriend to his mom? She knew I'd come out of his bedroom. The dress I was wearing was not Sunday brunch attire. If I wasn't his girlfriend, then that made me the girl he was fucking on the side. Which, apparently, I was. My growing anger and embarrassment was getting to be too much—

"Yes," his voice came from the bedroom doorway, drawing our attention. "Yes, this is her."

The asshole had pulled on a pair of pants, and his eyes pleaded with me to play along. I let mine go narrow. Why should I do what he wanted? He had a girlfriend for that.

"Well, it's nice to meet you, Evelyn," his mother said to me, extending a hand. "I'm Susan."

Wait, what?

How did she know my name? It couldn't be coincidence. There weren't many women from my generation named Evelyn. I stared at her hand like it was alien, and then slowly shook it, trying not to be rude. When I let go, I turned to Logan and his face was blank. What the hell was going on?

"I gave you that key for emergencies," he said to her.

"You didn't answer your phone, and when I came in I saw the broken glass."

"We're fine."

"Well, can you hurry up then? We're already late."

"Late? What time is it?" His eyes searched for a clock. "Fuck."

She straightened at the obscenity. "Language, please. Will you be coming too?" She eyed my dress with concern.

"No," I said. It didn't matter what it was, all I wanted now was to get the hell out of there. "I need to get going."

"Wait a minute, let me get dressed and drive you home," he said.

Susan sighed and pinched the bridge of her nose. "I cannot miss another one of his meets. Are you going with me or not?"

There was enormous conflict in his eyes. "Yes, but I need a minute. Evelyn, can we—"

The whiplash from hurt and anger to overwhelming confusion and suspicion was crippling. I had to escape, to flee before I lost it. "Forget it, I've got to run. Nice meeting you."

"No." He stalked toward me but I snatched up my purse and glared back. I tried to make sure he knew it would be better to let me be.

"Oh, wait," Susan said. "I think this is yours? It's got your name on it."

She lifted up the fat envelope of cash, but I don't think she noticed her action wound the tension tighter between Logan and me. If I told her to leave it, that it was Logan's, would she take a peek inside? I grabbed the envelope.

He followed me to the door. "Please, wait, I need to talk to you."

"You can call me later." The scrutiny of his mother's gaze was heavy and I needed relief. I needed relief from his panicked eyes.

He couldn't ask me for my number if he wanted to keep up the charade that I was his girlfriend. So the idiot leaned in and tried to kiss me goodbye, but I anticipated this tactic. I shifted my head at the last second so his kiss fell on a cheek, and I hurried through the door before he could stop me.

⌘

My walk of shame was thankfully short. I turned my phone back on during the cab ride home and discovered I had a half dozen missed calls and eighteen text messages. Two were from Payton and the rest were from Blake. They ranged from apology to concern, and I deleted them. My head was a fucking mess.

The likelihood of Logan calling me was next to nothing. My cell phone number was too close to a Thai restaurant's, and last month I'd given up trying to explain to annoyed customers that they'd dialed wrong. I hadn't gotten around to updating my work file with the new number because weekend emergencies didn't happen in graphics.

By the time I was done showering, I'd replayed the conversation in my mind several times. What I knew for fact was he'd told his mother he had a girlfriend. After that, it was speculation. Either his mother didn't know my name and had seen it on the envelope, or he'd told her we were dating.

I was dressed and about to call Payton when my front door buzzed.

"Yes?" I asked.

"Evie, thank god you're okay," Blake's voice crackled through the intercom. "Can I come up?"

There was no putting him off, so I jammed my finger on the button. A minute later he was through my door, pulling me into his arms.

"Are you all right?" He crushed me against his body. "Don't you realize how dangerous that was? Going home with some random guy from that place?"

I pushed away from his embrace. "He's not random, he's my boss."

"Is that some sort of sex club term?"

"No," I snapped. "He's my boss. As in, the manager of the graphics department."

Blake's face contorted in a mixture of horror and confusion. "You know him?"

"Yeah." And no, not at all.

I folded my legs beneath me on my couch, and seconds later he joined me. He looked like he hadn't slept at all. I wondered what he'd told Amy, but didn't bother to ask. It didn't matter. His angry comment to Payton had shown me a side I hadn't seen before, and it was going to be tough to repair the damage.

"I know I shouldn't have said it when I did, but I'm not sorry I said it." Even with the exhaustion, he looked handsome. Just like the man I had been in love with until last night. "I love you." It came out just as forced as last time.

I leaned forward and cradled my head in my hands. "I can't deal with this right now."

My phone chimed with a new email. It wasn't my personal account, it was the office. It could only be one person. Typical form for his emails, it was short and direct.

I need your number, the one on file is incorrect.

I set my phone down on the coffee table and pushed it away. I decided to deal with the man sitting beside me first.

"If you love her, then go love her. Payton's right, Amy deserves a man who's honest with her. And so do I." My eyes ticked over to the phone, and then back to him. "If we were meant to get together, I think it would have happened for us."

"It's all messed up, I know. Tell me what you want. Do you still love me?"

"I seriously cannot have this conversation right now."

"Why?"

What the hell did he mean, why? Because I'd just had the most amazing sex of my life last night with a man who was fascinating. His comment about "next time" danced through my brain and tortured me.

"Last night was way intense," I said. "I haven't processed an ounce of it yet. But since you brought it up, I guess you remember New Year's Eve."

His expression softened. "I think about it a lot."

"Did you tell Amy about it?"

I knew his answer would be 'no' because it's not awkward between Amy and me. At least, not on her end, unless she's some sort of insanely gifted actress. I highly doubt she'd let Blake continue his friendship with me in its current capacity if she knew I was in love with her boyfriend.

When he didn't answer, I went to the door to show him out.

"I need you to give me some space right now. I'll call you later in the week."

When he didn't move, I worried he wouldn't go. But he sighed and came to me, his hand cupping my face. "We'll figure it out."

My phone chimed with another email, breaking the spell he had on me. I locked the door behind him when he left, and hurried to check the email. This time it was my address and:

I'll be there in twenty minutes.

I emailed Logan back, wanting to meet on neutral ground, in public, so I'd be less likely to murder him. Also, a place with no beds in sight.

I won't let you in. See you tomorrow, boss.

⌘

Getting ready for work is usually a chore. It's a battle to figure out what I wore recently so I'm not repeating outfits, and to make sure I'm dressing appropriately for the weather. It's only a few blocks from the CTA stop to the office building, but my day can be ruined before it starts if it's raining and I'm not prepared.

Today was difficult on a whole new level. I pulled on my

favorite bra and panty set, a baby pink one with tiny black polka dots, hoping it would make me feel like everything was okay and I wasn't about to endure the most uncomfortable day of work in my life.

I dressed in tan crop pants and a cream-colored blouse with glossy tan pumps, one of my newest outfits, which I accessorized with a coral-colored statement necklace. I try to dress the line between designer and business professional, and this is one of the few outfits I think pulls it off.

My pumps were tossed into my oversized purse right beside the envelope of cash I'd have to give to him. Maybe I'd wait until he went to lunch and put it on his desk, but that was a lot of money to leave in the open. I was sure he'd come find me anyway. There'd been no response to my email, and I found that a little scary.

I tried to read my book on the train ride in, but I kept scanning the same page over and over again and absorbing none of it. I had planned on coming in early, thinking I could get past his office door and to my cube before he was in, but I took too long getting ready and wound up ten minutes late. His light was on and the door open as I came down the hall. All I could hope was he wasn't in his office right now.

I breathed a sigh of relief when I found it empty, and that sigh died in my throat when I turned the corner into my cube.

"You're late," Logan said, his face dark.

I'd taken my time and selected what I thought was my best attire, and I had the suspicion he'd done the same. His steel-colored button-down shirt looked flawless against his tan skin, and I knew exactly where below his black pants the tan stopped. His tie was the perfect shade of gunmetal gray and for a moment I wondered if I could pull out my Pantone deck and find the matching swatch.

I set my bag down and pulled out my chair to sit. "Yes, I'm running behind this morning."

"Can we speak in my office?"

I wasn't going to make it easy on him. "Only if it's work related."

His expression didn't change in the slightest. "What else would it be?" He left me there, wordlessly demanding I follow. My blood boiled.

I remained in the doorway of his office as if that would keep him from trapping me there. He held up a frosted envelope — a job jacket with the design specs and guidelines.

"This is the GoodFood jacket. They want a complete identity rebrand," he said. "No green, the client was adamant. Modern, but not trendy or pretentious."

This was a huge job, and the fact he was assigning it to me temporarily let me forget about the awkwardness. "You're giving it to me?"

"You don't think you can handle it?" he said, maybe concerned I hadn't ripped it from his hands yet.

"No, I can. I feel comfortable taking on a project of this size." I took the jacket from him, disoriented when he didn't say anything. He wasn't even looking at me; it looked like he was scanning his email. How did he not want to talk about what happened?

"Did you need something else?" he asked, like I was hovering over him annoyingly.

Then I understood. This was another test, a game. He wanted *me* to initiate the conversation. Not a chance.

"Just to say thanks." My heels were silent on the carpet as I exited his office, a smile on my lips. This was a game I would win.

⌘

Getting the GoodFoods account couldn't have come at a better time. I worked through lunch researching the client and reading their complaints with their current branding over and over again, so I could address their issues in the best way possible.

I never saw him during the day. But at quarter to five, I got an email from Logan without a subject line, and I held my breath.

I need you to vectorize this logo for a client, and they need it ASAP. Since you were late, you can stay late.

When I opened the file, I cursed at the screen. It was a piece of crap image composed of ten different gradients and mesh fills. There was no way I could run a trace program on it. I'd have to redraw it from scratch, and it would take at least an hour. This was bullshit busywork. Punishment.

It's amazing how the office clears out at five minutes after five with people dashing to make their trains. I shoved my headphones on and got to work, jealous, but this was totally like Logan, and it was fair. I had been late.

I finished the logo in record time, my annoyance fueling me to the end. As soon as I was composing an email to Logan with the finished artwork attached, a new email appeared from him. He was still here?

Come to my office now and bring the envelope.

I dug it out of my purse and thundered into his office, slamming it down on the desk, startling him.

"Good night," I spat and turned on my heel to leave.

"Enough," he said, standing. "Close the door, we need to talk."

It's what I wanted, and yet I dreaded it.

He must have sensed my hesitation. "Let me sweeten the deal, then." There was an edge of unease in his voice. "Rules one and two apply."

I spun, incredulous. "How is that sweetening the deal?"

"Because they apply to me."

NINE

The door banged loudly when I closed it. I may have been a little too forceful in my eagerness. He wasn't allowed to ask me questions, but had to answer all of mine honestly? That did sound pretty fucking sweet.

"Lock it," he said.

"Why?"

He looked uncomfortable. "Because I'm hoping we're going to end up fucking in here."

Well, that was an honest answer, but I felt like turning the bolt on the door was agreeing to it.

"Better safe than sorry," he added.

I flipped the lock and sauntered over to the chair facing his desk, the same one I'd revealed my horrible mistake in.

"Why don't you take a seat?" I asked. Even though this was his office, I was the one in control. He lowered back into his chair, his gaze fixed on me. "Why do you look so nervous?"

"Because I don't know what questions you're going to ask."

"This was your idea," I reminded. "Do you have a girlfriend?"

A small amount of relief seemed to run through him as he sat back. "No, I don't."

A much larger amount of relief coursed through me. "Then why did you tell your mother I was?"

"My brother's getting married this weekend. My younger brother. She's convinced I'm not ever going to get married, that it's too late for me now that . . . I'm over thirty."

He loosened the knot of his tie and unbuttoned his sleeves, rolling them up as he continued talking. "She forbid me to show up at the wedding dateless, using that as an excuse to fix me up with someone horrible. So I told her I was seeing someone."

"And you picked me?"

"She asked me for a name, and I gave her yours."

I found that a little difficult to believe. "My name was the first one to pop in your head?"

A mischievous smile grew on his face. "Yes. I couldn't believe my dumb luck when she came in and dropped your name."

"What was your plan when you showed up dateless to the wedding?"

"I'd tell her that you broke up with me, and I was going to be too depressed to chat with any of the available women she wanted to unleash on me."

Okay, one major chunk of information sorted through, now on to the other one. "How did you know I was at the club?"

"Pass."

"I'm sorry, pass?"

"We'll come back around to it in a minute." When I opened my mouth to protest, he added, "I'm not violating the rule. It says I have to answer it and answer it truthfully. It doesn't say when I have to do it."

I don't know which I was more irritated about — the fact he hadn't answered, or that I hadn't known I could do that when his rules applied to me.

"Where did you get the money?"

"My 401K."

My eyes fell on the envelope sitting on the desk. Oh, god. I didn't pay much attention to investing, but my uncle was an accountant and had helped set up my account. The one thing he'd stressed was to not touch my 401K under any circumstances, because the penalties were steep. I'd only been working at the agency for two years, so what I'd accrued would have been wiped out if I'd tried.

So what this meant was Logan hadn't really paid twelve grand of his money for me. He'd paid even more.

"Why would you do that?"

He looked guilty. "Part of me felt responsible. I'd come to trust your work, so I had barely glanced at the proof you'd sent me." His eyes changed and turned warm and seductive. "A much larger part of me did it because I wanted to."

"Why?" I think I blushed.

"Because I thought you'd be amazing."

I don't know why I was nervous when he was the one being interrogated. "So, was I?"

"Didn't I make it clear that you were?"

My breath was gone for a half-second and then returned with the realization. "Wait, was that a question?" That meant he was supposed to have consequences, but my brain failed me. I couldn't come up with any kind of playfully torturous thing to do to him that wouldn't be torturous for me as well. "Answer my question. How did you know about the club?"

He looked a little disappointed that was all I'd come up with.

"Come here, and I'll show you."

I sighed and got out of the chair, taking three steps to get behind his desk when he stood abruptly and pulled me against him. "What are you—"

He silenced me with one of his mind-numbing kisses. It wasn't a delicate, soft kiss. It was an aggressive, controlling, devouring one. He'd slipped a hand behind my neck and the other was tight on my ass, pressing me against him. I struggled to stay above it, but I was drowning in him. Desire flashed white-hot through my body, straight to the center of my legs.

"You're not showing me anything I don't already know," I murmured between kisses, going back for more. The hand on my ass traveled to the front, dragging slowly up in the valley between my thighs.

The button to my pants was undone in a heartbeat, and he broke the kiss, turning me in his arms so I faced the computer.

"I need you to send an email," he said. His breathing was steady and controlled, but I was already hopelessly out of breath. He sat in his chair, making sure I understood he wanted me to stand, and he opened a new email compose window. I'd have to lean over him to do it while standing.

"Who is the email going to?" I asked, not moving.

"Evelyn Russell."

"You want me to send an email to myself?"

"Yes." His eyes were smug.

I gave him an exasperated look and bent at the waist, putting my hands on his keyboard. I typed in E and V and let AutoFill do the rest.

"What's the subject?" I asked.

"Computer Usage Policy."

I started to type when his hands closed around my waist and unzipped the zipper, yanking my pants down past my knees. The air on my naked skin was almost as shocking as the action itself.

"Hmm, I like these," he said, running a hand over the back of my pink panties. "Keep typing, please."

Because I'd only gotten three letters into "computer"

before turning to him in surprise. He'd rolled his chair back so he was directly behind me and his hands kneaded my skin, skirting the edges of my panties.

"What are you doing?"

"Dictating an email to you because my hands are busy."

I typed the rest of it, not bothering to put it in title case like I usually do, confusion making this easy task seem like brain surgery.

"Evelyn," he said, "You may or may not remember . . ." His fingertips brushed over the crotch of my rapidly dampening panties, making me jump. "You should be typing now."

I typed in a hurry, and when my fingers stopped moving, his started.

"—the company computer usage document you signed when you were hired." He rubbed the spot that was aching for him through the fabric. I tried to focus on the words and not what he was doing or the desire that was sinking its powerful claws into me.

"I'd like to remind you that your manager has monitoring software," he said. He tugged the panties to the side and exposed me to him, dragging his hand over my bare flesh. "And that your system should only be used for work related tasks."

What the hell was he talking about? I didn't use my computer for non-work things when I was supposed to be working. "I don't understand why—"

He buried a finger inside me and I moaned.

"I can't type when you do that." It felt so different at this angle, a new kind of pleasure. Plus I couldn't get over how incredibly hot and naughty it was, what we were doing right at his desk. Yet what he had me typing also had my brain confused and fighting for attention.

"You must find this distracting," he said in a low, sexy

voice. Then he returned to the tone for dictation. "You should not use your system to check personal email or social media, even during breaks." His finger drew back and then plunged into me again and again. "Type, Evelyn."

My fingers fumbled over the keyboard. I saw the red underline of a misspelled word and fixed it, all while he had my panties bunched to one side and fucked me with a finger. I was impossibly wet, and I knew his face was fixed on my ass right in front of him.

"Thank you for your understanding, Logan." As soon as the words were gone from his mouth, he leaned forward in his chair and put his tongue on me.

"Oh, shit," I cried. My legs shook when his tongue caressed me. The need that gripped my body threatened to break me.

"Send it," he whispered, barely taking his lips off of my skin. I clicked the button, but remained as I was. There was no way I was going to stop him, but my goddamn brain wouldn't shut up, and the distraction was keeping me from getting where I wanted him to take me.

"I still don't understand."

"I saw the club's logo on that email the owner sent you, and I was curious who designed it," he leaned back and peeled my panties down to my knees. "I thought you might be freelancing, so after you left my office, I watched your computer."

I had forgotten he had those capabilities. I'd thought I was safe since it was my personal account and I hadn't said much in the email. "There wasn't anything in the email, though."

The warmth of his face returned. His tongue slipped inside me, and then, like he'd done at the club, it drifted further to the spot that brought me pleasure but also made me uncomfortable. Dirty and wrong, but felt so good.

"Stop, I can't think when . . . you're going down on me."

"I don't want to stop." He locked his hands on my hips and licked me front to back, drawing a shiver from my body. "You'd said you were getting the money Saturday night, and the owner said to bring the contract with you on Saturday." He shoved two fingers into me, filling me as his mouth sucked.

"All I had to do," he continued, "was email the guy and say you'd referred me to him. He spelled it all out for me."

My hands balled into fists as the fracture in my brain widened.

"What did you think when you found out?"

"I was excited you were . . . *are*," he corrected, "interested in that kind of thing. But I was worried about you, and pissed off. I almost gave you the money on Friday to stop you. But if I gave you the money, shouldn't I get something in return? I've wanted you for forever. So I could give you the money, get what I wanted, and have you never know it was me."

"What?" My hips moved subtly with his rhythm, asking for more. *Forever?* I was getting close. Was I supposed to tell him yellow?

"I wasn't planning to take off your blindfold."

He couldn't see the shocked look on my face. It was hard to imagine it now, in retrospect. What if he hadn't? I'd have gone to work every day completely oblivious.

"Why did you?"

"I didn't like you not knowing it was me, and I figured I was safe from a sexual harassment complaint once you were begging for me to do this."

The air left my lungs when he stopped talking and shoved his face into my pussy. I arched my back, and with the confusion finally sorted out, I came in a heated rush, collapsing on the cool desktop, electricity washing through every inch of my body. For a moment, the only sound was my heavy breathing.

"You're supposed to only come on my cock." His voice was wicked. The wheels of his chair squeaked as he rose, and there was the sound of his belt and zipper being undone. I was still recovering when a condom wrapper tore open.

"If I could, I'd ask you if you want this." The head of his dick slipped between my folds, teasing me. It was a question framed as a statement. He was already doing so much better than I did.

"Yes. Do you?"

"Fuck, yes." He wasn't as gentle this time when he pushed inside me.

"Whoa," I gasped in discomfort. "Slower."

"Sorry," he whispered, freezing. He held still and let me slowly back myself onto him until he was as deep as he could go.

"Move," I half-commanded, half-begged.

He did as I asked, easing himself out and then back in at a luxurious pace. Here, on his desk with all the lights on and my panties around my knees. His hands roved over my body, slipping under my shirt to cup my bra-covered breast.

"Take off your shirt," he said.

I tore it up over my head, and he made a noise of appreciation when he saw the bra. I had wanted to talk to him in a place safe from beds, but somehow when I dressed this morning, I knew it was irrelevant. I was going to let him have me again if he could explain himself adequately. So I'd worn the sexiest lingerie I owned for him.

He filled his hands with my breasts, the pads of his thumbs skimming over the sensitive flesh just above the low-cut cups.

"You should ask me what I'm thinking about," he urged.

Oh, right. I'd forgotten about that perk. "What are you thinking about?"

"That the cleaning crew has a key to my office and will be here soon."

I had been expecting something sexy and that definitely wasn't it.

"So I'm going to fuck you hard and fast," he continued. "Feel free to come as many times as you like."

That was better. He drove into me, thrusting harder and harder with each pass until I was breathless and frantic. My fingers clawed at the desk, seeking something to hold onto, and found the edge out before me. I curled my hands around it as he grabbed a fistful of hair at the base of my skull.

He pulled back, hard. It wasn't painful, but it made me crazy with lust. He put his lips on the side of my neck. This made me channel my inner porn star. "Do you like my tight pussy?"

"I fucking love it."

Oh, shit, he was going to make me come. His furious thrusts sent my hipbones banging into the drawer of his desk, but I didn't care. All I could think about was the release that threatened and the blood rushing in my ears. But if that's all I could think about, what about him?

"What are you thinking about now?"

He hesitated.

"Rule two, Logan."

"I'm thinking about how you'll react if I do this." He licked the pad of his thumb and slipped it between my cheeks, pressing down on my other entrance. This felt dirty, but not as bad as what he'd done with his mouth. Naughty. Taboo.

I was curious. Payton enjoyed the anal stuff. She wouldn't say that if it weren't true.

"It . . . feels good," I admitted.

He jerked inside me like my willingness turned him on. He pounded into me, and slowly he increased the pressure until he could slip his thumb up to the first knuckle into my ass. It was shocking and foreign, and made me tremble.

"I want to know how that feels," he said between breaths. "If you want me to go further."

Honestly, I had no idea. I was so close to going over the edge, I felt scattered. "I just want you to make me come."

"I can do that," he said. His other hand slid to my waist so he could shift the angle of my body to one where I could feel all of him at once, both inside and out. I slapped a hand on the desktop, dragging it squealing down. *Oh shit, oh shit, oh shit. . .*

This orgasm outdid the first. It was fast, but intense, and bliss rolled through me.

He didn't slow down like he had the other times; he kept up his driving pace. His breath became louder, labored, and short, as his thrusts were more frantic. He was as hard as a rock inside me, filling me. I could sense he was so close, and I wanted him to lose control like he made me.

"Are you going to come?"

"Fuck, yes. Right. Fucking. Now."

His body drove into me a final time, and then he was moaning again and again. God, listening to him made my insides quiver, and the feeling of him pulsing inside me was like nothing else. He made me believe no other man could satisfy me.

He caught his breath before I did, and he fell back into his chair. His hands pulled me so I was sideways on his lap.

"We should probably get dressed." He lifted my chin and kissed me softly. "I want to have dinner with you."

"Do the rules apply?"

"Until we leave my office."

I gave him a coy smile. "We can order in."

"It's too hard to have a conversation without questions."

That was true, and we hadn't really had one. "Okay, what did you have in mind?" I climbed off of him and pulled up my panties and pants, as he got rid of the condom and sorted himself out.

"There's that stir-fry place, have you been there?"

I stop mid-search for my blouse and looked at him. This time my brain was working, so I reached behind me and unclasped my bra, letting the straps drop down to my elbows, and then fall to the floor.

"Oops," I said with a straight face.

It's not like my breasts were anything spectacular. They were fairly average, maybe slightly larger. But he was a man, and men like pretty much all breasts. I sat on the desk and let him gaze at them, and when he reached out to put a hand on one, I pushed it away.

"No touching, you broke a rule."

He smirked. I resumed getting dressed as he finished zipping up, and realized my window of getting answers out of him was closing. So if there was anything I wanted to know that he'd be reluctant to reveal, I needed to ask it now.

"How many women have you slept with?"

He shut down his computer and sighed. "I hope you're sure you want to know."

"I am."

"It's probably close to thirty."

I had asked, but I frowned. God only knew what Payton's

number was. I'm sure it was more than thirty, but my number was so low. "Would you like to know my number?"

His eyes widened with surprise. "Yes."

"Five."

His gorgeous eyes went even wider. "I assume your number doesn't includes me."

"It does." I slipped my shirt on and checked to make sure everything was back in place. "Why are you single?"

He had just undone the knot of his tie and his hands paused. In fact, his whole body went motionless. "Pass."

"You can't pass again." I rolled my eyes. His gaze was shockingly intense and sobered me. It stole my breath.

"It's because I'm not interested in being in a relationship right now." He resumed movement, but his whole body was tense. This was the question he was nervous about?

"Why?"

His expression turned sour. "Relationships are about compromise." His expression set into an authoritative one. "And me? I don't do compromises."

No, definitely not. But still . . . "That's not a real answer."

"So I broke a rule. What are you going to do about it?"

His challenge was startling and my brain was utterly blank, so I did my best to make sure it sounded strong. "I'll think of something."

TEN

We were seated right away at a table near the door. Even for a Monday night, the place was busy. We'd both taken our bowls with our names written on them to the buffet and piled them with meat and veggies, and deposited them by the cooking station that held a team of men hovering over woks.

"We've done this backwards," he said as we made our way back to our table. "Sex, then dinner, and afterward I'm going to ask for your number."

"What if I don't give it to you?"

"I'm going to insist, for your file." His expression was serious, but there was playfulness in his eyes.

"Let me see your phone."

He passed it to me and, as I plugged my number in, a thought occurred. What exactly did he need it for? I set the phone down, and when he leaned across the table to retrieve it, my hand trapped his.

"What do you plan on doing with my number?" I asked.

"Call you?"

"For what?" My voice dropped to a hush. "Sex?"

His eyebrows pulled together in confusion. "I was under the impression you liked doing that with me."

"I do." I released his hand, confused myself.

"Evelyn." He took a measured breath and his face was strikingly intense. "I think we're past the point of being shy about what we want. So say it."

He was right, but it was still difficult to put into words,

especially after what he'd just confessed in his office.

"I'm not built to do that outside of a relationship. I'll need it to be . . . more."

There was no reaction from him, sending my heart plummeting into my stomach. His pupils focused in a discerning look, evaluating me.

"Pretty sure I told you, I'm not interested in that."

I pulled air into my lungs, unsure how to proceed. "I understand, but I'm not interested in casual sex."

"Did that feel casual to you?"

There was that sparkling Logan personality I was familiar with. "You know what I mean."

"So, this is, what? An ultimatum?" His voice was harsh. "I'd advise against it. I don't react well to them."

This conversation was on a downward spiral. "It's not an ultimatum. All I'm telling you is I can't sleep with a guy who's sleeping with other people."

His mouth dropped open, and snapped shut a half second later. "I understand. I won't do that."

I blinked my skeptical eyes at him.

"What you're asking for is not unreasonable," he said. He fell silent for a long moment, as if considering something. "I'm not interested in a relationship, but I am interested in you. I can be exclusive to that."

Was he trying to turn my brain into spaghetti? What did *that* mean? "You'll be . . . ? I don't get it."

"You won't have to share me, and I don't have to share you."

God, he really didn't want to put a label on it.

"We need to discuss how it's going to work. It could be difficult at the office, and then there's the issue of your promotion."

"Why's that an issue? I've been there long enough, half the people already think I'm a senior designer."

There was a flash of something in his eyes, and then it was gone. "Yes, that's true. But we still have the problem of critiques. Are you going to take it personally if I say something negative about your artwork?"

I had to be smiling. "Um, no, boss. I'll handle it like I always do. I'm plenty used to it."

"What's that mean?"

"Come on, I've endured your morale-boosting critique sessions for a year now. I've got a thick skin." Our server presented our food to us, and I nodded a 'thank you.' "You don't have to worry about sending me home in tears."

"I've never done that," he scoffed.

He didn't know? "Not me, but remember that first proof on the cupcake ad Jamie did last month?"

He made a noise of disgust. "I'd prefer not to."

I gave him an expectant look, waiting for him to get it.

"I made her cry?"

It came out before I could stop it. "You can kind of be a dick."

He pulled his shoulders back, like I'd shocked him. Yet, he was too arrogant or stubborn to hear it. "No, I'm not, I'm honest."

"Yeah, brutally honest. It's one thing to say someone's hard work isn't their best. Maybe not even good. It's another to say it looks like total shit."

"I'm not going to sugar coat it. That cupcake ad made me want to stop eating food altogether." He jammed his fork into his dinner. "You think what I say is bad? You should hear the feedback I get from some of our customers. And you know what it's like, everyone with a license for Photoshop thinks they're a designer."

I'm sure it was true, that he'd heard much worse things. "Yeah, I know, but you can get your point across without so much edge. We think you get off on it."

"We?"

I wasn't sure how much I should tell him, but if it would make a difference, I had to try. "I'm not the only designer who thinks that."

His shoulders rose and fell and there was defensiveness in his eyes. "Who else?"

"I'm not naming names."

He scowled. "Give me a number."

"I don't know. Maybe twenty."

"That's half the fucking department," he said.

"I wasn't meaning to ambush you with this, maybe we shouldn't talk about work stuff."

"No, it's fine." Although his tone said it was anything but. "Tell me, then, how you would have handled Jamie's critique."

I barely remembered the ad, but the look Logan gave me was piercing, and somehow I knew if I didn't come up with something, he'd use it to prove his point.

"I'd have told her it was cliché and expected, maybe to sit with a designer that has a totally different aesthetic and see what their approach would be. Jamie's stuck in a rut," I said. "I don't think she's going to figure out to stop putting drop shadows on everything until you actually tell her."

I was sitting across from a wax figure; I don't think he even blinked. Had I really shocked him? Wounded him?

He swallowed, slowly returning to life. "She probably would have reacted differently to that." He said it like it was painful to admit, and I was grateful to be seated when it happened. Perfect Logan Stone had admitted a mistake.

"You were different last Monday. Better," I said.

"I'd been late to the meeting."

"Oh, right. You must not have had time to prepare because of your massage." I couldn't help but get the dig in.

"I was prepared, but since my massage therapist was in a car accident and showed up twenty minutes late, I had to keep the critiques brief and on schedule. I'd already wasted enough of everyone's time. No one really cared what I had to say after that."

"Oh." It had been true. "You could have tried apologizing."

He gave me a tight smile. No, that wasn't his style.

"Okay, let's forget about that," I said. "I promise I won't hold a grudge if you want to be honest with my work. That's separate from . . ." I gestured between us, ". . . what this is."

"What this is," he said, "is against policy. That's why we're not going to tell anyone about it at the office."

That kind of went without saying to me. "I understand. I'm not really close with anyone there anyway." In fact, Logan was now the closest friend I had there.

⌘

When dinner was over, he drove me to my place and parked on the street.

"Can I come up?" he asked.

His apartment had been immaculate, which I hadn't found surprising. He was a control freak at the office; I assumed that bled into all aspects of his life. Certainly his sex life, not that I was complaining. However, my place was a disaster. It was always a disaster.

"I didn't exactly make the bed this morning. Or clean up the clothes explosion." Or do the dishes from dinner with Payton last night.

"So, that's a no?" The brown eyes were surprised.

"No, but it's . . . not like your place. Do you get claustrophobic?"

He gave me a wary look. "I don't think so. What level of messy are we talking about? Do I need to report it to FEMA?"

When I ushered him inside, he understood. My studio apartment was cramped. The kitchen was one row of cabinets and appliances on the right. I had a bistro table in the center, and along the back wall was my sitting area.

I'd left the door open to my closet, which sat adjacent to my bathroom. He didn't seem too bothered by the mess, but he could tell right away something was off.

"Where's your bed?"

I gave him a sheepish look. "It's in the closet."

It was easier to show him rather than explain. I pushed the door open further and pulled the string on the light. The walk-in closet was surprising large for such a small place. Just large enough to fit my twin-sized bed.

He laughed and then sobered, probably thinking about the two of us on it.

"You start every day coming out of the closet."

"You think you're the first one to make that joke? I've heard them all already." I slipped off my shoes and pushed all of the clothes I'd tried on this morning into a pile so there was room to make our way to the couch. I'd made it halfway there when arms circled my waist and turned me into his kiss. This one was less aggressive. Almost sweet, but it got to me all the same. He lowered us both to sit on the couch as the kiss grew intense and spiraled out of control.

"I can't keep my hands off of you," he said. I could relate. His soft lips left my mouth and journeyed down the side of my neck until he found the perfect spot where my pulse was racing for him.

"You won't hear complaints from me." There was something about him that made me say whatever was on my mind, like he disabled my mental filter. It was strange and exhilarating. "I love the way you touch me."

He gave me a wicked smile. "You do, huh?"

His strong arms locked around me and lifted, pulled me over him so I was straddling his lap, staring at the dark eyes that studied me. He leaned his head back on the couch and looked up at me, looking back down at him. His hand brushed my hair away and gently pulled me into his kiss.

It wasn't like any of the others he'd given me. This kiss was tender and slow and filled with heat that threatened to consume me. It stole my breath and made me lightheaded. My heart pounded so fast, I could hear it loud in my ears.

"Someone's knocking on your door," he said, breaking through my fog. It hadn't been my heartbeat; it was a fist banging against wood. I didn't want to move, but the knock came again.

"Evie," Blake's muffled, raised voice came from the hall.

What the hell? I had told him I would call him later in the week, what happened to giving me space? I groaned and climbed off of Logan, and my kiss-weakened legs carried me to the door.

"Someone let me in downstairs," Blake announced as he came in. "I left her." He spun to face me, oblivious to everything around him, including the man who rose to stand from the couch. Blake's face was wild and chaotic, and he looked . . .

"You're plastered. Did you drive over here?" I demanded.

"No, I took a cab. Did you hear me? It's over with Amy. I told her everything, I told her I love you. How you told me . . ."

Oh, no. "Stop talking, Blake—"

". . . that you love me. It's always been you, Evie."

Blake's back was to Logan, but I could see every ounce of unease in Logan's face. His dark look toward Blake was adversarial.

"That was months ago," I announced so Logan would hear. "It isn't true anymore."

"What? What do you mean, it's not true?" The chaos in Blake's eyes ratcheted up another level, bordering on anger. "You just, what? Stopped loving me all of a sudden because I tried to keep you from making the worst mistake of your life?" He took a step toward me, looking broken. "You could have gotten hurt, or raped, or sick."

"It's not like that there," I said.

Logan quietly advanced on Blake, who remained oblivious.

"I don't care what it's like there, I only care about you."

Six years of want in me quivered to hear it come from Blake's lips, all while staring at the man over his shoulder, and it threatened to tear me apart. Blake's hands seized my waist and hauled me up against him, and in his drunken state it wasn't gentle. I slammed into his chest and immediately struggled to get free from his sudden embrace.

"What kind of man pays that much money to sleep with a woman? I'll tell you, the really fucked up kind."

"I don't think we've met," Logan said.

"Jesus Christ!" Blake stumbled away, releasing me, knocking one of my kitchen chairs sideways. The moment Blake's alcohol-hazed mind recognized Logan, his gaze went to me, white with shock.

"Blake, this is Logan."

"Her boyfriend." There was no hesitation from Logan,

and my brain went deaf with surprise.

"Your what? I thought you said he was your asshole boss."

Logan looked amused. "Yeah, I'm that too."

Blake composed himself, pulling his shoulders back. It's not like Logan was small, but Blake was tall and cut, and his size was physically intimidating. If Logan was nervous, none of it showed. He was calm and cool, and very much in control, the opposite of Blake.

"Isn't it enough what you did to her at the club? You're blackmailing her to be your girlfriend too? You're a sick bastard."

I watched as Blake's hands rounded into fists, and all of the hair on the back of my neck stood up. I'd never seen a true fistfight before, and sensed I was closer than I'd ever been to witnessing one right this second.

"He's not blackmailing me," I said. "*I* asked him."

"You . . . ? Did you not just hear me say I left her? For you?"

"Remind me when I asked you to do that?" I snapped. "That's right. Never."

Blake's expression changed to one of disbelief. "This is what you wanted."

Maybe a little part of that had been true once. But now? "No, it's not. I told you, it's too late."

He didn't look like he believed a word of it, but he stood there with his eyes unblinking for a moment. "So, we just go back to being friends?"

"Yes."

"I don't think it's possible."

"We've been friends for, like, six years. Why can't—?"

Blake's expression changed and hardened. "Okay. Amy kicked me out, so I need a place to crash."

"Not going to fucking happen." Logan's voice was

authoritarian and terrifying. His dark eyes were fixed on me, waiting for my confirmation.

"Figure it out, Blake," I said. "Call one of your other friends or get a hotel room."

The taller man gave me a sad smirk before he went for the door. "It's not too late for us. We've waited a long time. I can wait a little longer until you figure out this guy's not for you."

He didn't slam my door when he left, he simply pulled it closed behind him, not even uttering a goodbye. Logan's gaze burned into me.

"Can we pretend that didn't just happen?" I asked, not meeting his eyes.

"Yes. Why don't we go back to my place?" His voice was light but I could hear the edge beneath it. "I've got an adult-sized bed I'd like to do very adult things to you in."

His joke broke the tension and I looked at him, grateful. Only, I don't think he was joking. It was hard to tell with him, when he was half-serious and when he was entirely serious.

"Yeah, I'm sure no one will think it's weird that you're driving me to work tomorrow morning."

"There's an L stop two blocks from my place."

I didn't want to feel like I was sneaking into the office. I'd gotten ready this morning, not knowing what was going to happen between us, and this was about the last place I'd thought we'd end up.

"No, not tonight."

"All right." He looked disappointed and then it morphed into something I didn't recognize. "Do you have plans this weekend?"

"Uh, I don't know." His expression made me nervous. "Why?"

"My brother's wedding."

Breath caught in my throat. "Are you asking me to go?"

"Yes."

"With you?" God, was my brain even on right now? "Like, as your fake girlfriend?"

A half-smile crept on his face. "As my real girlfriend. If I'm doing this relationship thing full-out, I should get the perks that go along with it."

I'm sure my face filled with surprise. Or maybe panic. I barely knew him, and going to his brother's wedding was like throwing me in the deep end. Not to mention I was still reeling from the concept that Logan Stone was now my boyfriend.

"I can always make up an excuse for you to miss it," he said. "Now that my mom believes you're a real person, she'll leave me alone."

"Are you in the wedding party?"

"I'm the best man."

A thousand thoughts went through my head. I would undoubtedly meet his entire family. He'd have wedding duties that would probably have me on my own most of the time. But, dear god, Logan in a tux.

"Yeah, I guess I can do that."

After declaring we were in a relationship, it felt weird to be standing there, staring at each other and not touching, and I must have force-quitted my filter. "I thought you weren't interested in . . . compromises."

He gave a sort of bitter laugh. "Well, your tall friend made an impression on me. Specifically when he grabbed you." Then, Logan's gaze hardened. "I won't be doing any compromising, though, Evelyn. Let's be clear. I spent too much time doing that."

"That's why you're single?"

"I'm not single anymore."

"Logan."

He stalked toward me, cupped my face, and kissed me. My knees melted. No, my whole body melted into him. How did he do that?

"You realize refusing to answer only makes me more curious," I whispered.

His lips on mine weren't sweet. They were persuasive and sinful and demanding. "Be curious a little longer."

"You can't kiss me," I blurted out, pulling back. "Not until you answer the question you passed on. That's your consequence for breaking the rule."

He gave me a predatory look that made me nervous but thrilled, and my heart beat faster.

"You may think you're being smart, but you're going to cave before I do." It came out as arrogant as he usually sounded. "Take off your clothes."

The smile froze on my face. "What?"

"You heard me." His hands unbuttoned his shirt and it fell open, showing me that glorious chest I wanted to drag my fingernails down. He pulled one sleeve off and then the other, folding his shirt and tossing it onto the couch.

There something about a gorgeous half-undressed man with an expensive watch on one wrist that is undeniably appealing, and there was one currently standing in the center of my apartment. His fingers undid the clasp, and he set the watch on his shirt. So neat and tidy. His fingers went to his belt.

"You're falling behind," he said.

His power was goddamn fascinating, and I was a slave to it.

My hurried hands undid the clasp on my necklace and set it on the kitchen counter, which was the closest flat surface I could find. I stumbled back a few steps to snap off the light, so only the bulb in the closet lit the room. Not that it mattered, he'd thoroughly seen me naked, but it felt more intimate somehow when the room was darkened. The shirt went up over my head, and I tossed it on the pile.

"No, leave that on," he said when I reached behind myself to undo my bra.

He removed his shoes, socks, and pants and added them to his neat pile. All he had left was a pair of black boxer briefs that made want to drool. I undid my pants, which fell to the floor, and I simply stepped out of them, leaving them wadded there.

"I want to clarify," he said, brushing a finger over my lips, "I can't kiss you here. But everywhere else is allowed. You will let me kiss you here." The finger drew a line down my neck, down into my cleavage, and over to trace the top of the cup of my bra. "And here." The finger traced down my stomach. Further until it touched my center and made my mouth drop open. "And certainly here."

How did he do that? One simple touch and I was falling apart. My need for him was insatiable.

"Correct?" His finger dipped down the front of my panties and touched me.

"Yes," I answered.

"You're already so wet. Do I turn you on that much?"

"Yes." God, truer words had never been spoken.

"You know it's mutual." He used his other hand to take mine and set it on top of his dick straining against the cotton of his boxers. He was so hard. It was powerful, knowing I did that to him. And with that power, I knew what I wanted to do. I put my hands on his hard chest and eased him the three steps back to the couch.

Last time I'd gone down on him, it had lasted all of a minute. Tonight I wanted to see just how disoriented I could make him while I got to be in control. He allowed me to push his shoulders down, and he sat in the center of my worn but comfortable couch. I knelt between his knees and pulled his boxer briefs down, setting his massive dick free.

"Are you going to suck my cock?"

"That was the plan. Is that all right?" I touched it to my lips and looked up at him.

His face was determined. "If you don't mind."

I rolled my lips over my teeth and slid him into my mouth, enjoying the response that got, the sharp hiss of breath from him.

"Fuck," he whispered. His hands pushed my hair back to give him a better view. I tried to take him as deep as I could, and as I drew up, I sucked hard, hollowing my cheeks. This earned me a whole slew of profanities, but they were all encouraging.

"You've got a dirty mouth, boss," I said.

"Stop talking and focus on your task." Again, no clue if it was a half-joke or completely serious.

I started slowly, just my mouth and suction, and graduated to moving my tongue around, licking him from the base all the way to the ridge beneath the head. His hand not holding my hair back was splayed out on his thigh, and I watched his fingers curl into a fist and then flex back out.

That was what I wanted. That tiny signal that maybe I could make him feel as out of control as he made me. I wrapped my hand tight around the part I couldn't fit in my mouth and dragged my grip up, then back down, following with my mouth. It took no time for his dick and my hand to be coated in saliva.

He took shallow, quick breaths, watching me through hooded eyes. "Yeah, just like that." Over and over again I moved, sometimes twisting my grip or letting my teeth ever so gently skim over him.

"Fucking shit," he groaned. "Do you have blowjobs . . . on your résumé . . . under special skills? I'll give you a recommendation." I wanted to laugh or flash him a smug smile, but his hips moved to match my pace, urging me to go faster. I did, and his breathing grew more uneven and desperate.

"Evelyn, fuck, you have to stop."

I wanted to hear it and kept my grip moving on him. "Why?"

"You'll make me come."

I used the most seductive voice I had. "Maybe I want that."

But the power I held over him wasn't as great when I was using my hands, and I could feel it slipped back to him.

"That's not what I want." It was almost a growl from him. "Stand up."

I was independent and strong, and raised not to take orders from anyone. Yet, his orders made me shudder, made heat pool in my body, flowing toward the junction of my thighs. I put my hands on his knees and raised myself up so I stood between his legs.

His hand went to the pocket of his pants nearby, fishing out a condom packet and tearing it open. I watched long fingers expertly roll it on. He slipped his hands around my waist, dragging his tongue on the skin just above my panties. Fingers slipped under the fabric, easing one side down over my hipbone, and his hot mouth followed.

"Logan," I whispered. Hearing his name on my lips did something to him. Like it snapped the control he had on himself, if only for a second, but it was so worth it to see him come undone. His hands yanked my panties down.

"Come here," he said, snaking an arm behind my back and pulling me down on him, one leg on either side and his dick right at my entrance. "I want to be inside you."

Yes, I wanted that too. I lowered down on him, taking just the tip in, and I had to bite my lip. Would my body ever get used to him? His hands were on my hips, but helping to hold me there, not pressing me down on him.

While my body was adjusting, he set his face in the crook of my neck and began kissing me, working his way up. Toward my mouth, where he knew he wasn't allowed. I took another inch inside, gasping against the protest my body made.

It always felt so good, that first time he was completely inside me and, wanting to prolong it, I continued to move an inch at a time.

"Fuck, you're making me crazy." It rang out on his tortured voice.

His lips wandered over my cheek, over my chin, the base of my throat. Everywhere but where I wanted them and denied them.

As usual, Logan Stone was right. I was going to cave long before he did. I wrapped my arms around him, setting them on his shoulders, and sank down all the way. Pleasure was immediate. The grind of my body against his created a sharply focused need, growing more acute when he guided me up and back down on him. Again, and again.

"Oh my god," I murmured, my head falling onto my arms banded on his shoulder.

I felt his fingertips skirt across my back, releasing the bra clasp, and slip the straps off my shoulders.

"I want to see all of you," his voice was hushed. Tender.

I uncrossed my arms and let him pull the bra hurriedly

away, the straps tangling briefly on my arms as they went. I think he'd had plans of another marathon session with lots of dirty talk, but apparently I'd changed his course simply by uttering his name. This wasn't fucking.

It was something else completely.

His hands were everywhere, caressing me, stroking me, making me tremble. I moved faster on him, my mouth planting kisses on his neck, sucking on his earlobe. His soft hair was in my hands when he locked his mouth around my nipple, swirling his tongue and using the slightest hint of teeth.

I pulled his head to mine, trying to put my lips on his, but he turned away from it.

"I'm not going to break your rule," he said, his voice broken. His eyes were intense and spoke volumes. He wanted that connection as badly as I did.

"Please?"

"No."

"Then make me come," I pleaded.

"I can do that." His hand drifted between our bodies, touching the hard knot just above our union. His other hand wrapped on the back of my neck, holding me to him so our foreheads were touching, our lips only a breath away. He watched me intently, gauging each tiny reaction to what he was doing, watching my cues so he could send me over the edge.

"Yes," I gasped, "Yes, oh my god, yes."

Pleasure exploded inside me, radiating outward. I writhed and bucked on top of him, his hands holding me to him as I trembled through my orgasm.

"Fuck, Evelyn." He was coming, pulsing and throbbing inside me, his hands so tight on me it was almost painful. My head rolled forward, resting on his heaving shoulders.

"I didn't know you were close," I said, catching my breath.

"I always get really close when you come."

I lifted my head up and glared down into his face.

"Why," I asked, "did we wait so long to start doing this?"

An enormous grin spread on his face. It was good I'd already come, because the sight of it probably would have made me.

"I guess you're not upset I took the blindfold off, huh?"

ELEVEN

Tuesday morning I passed by his office without turning my head to see if he was in. His light was on and his door was open, and I knew eventually I'd see him. I'd decided on my train ride in that this would be another game. Who would be better at pretending we didn't have nasty, dirty sex in his office or crazy-passionate sex on my couch yesterday? I was determined it would be me.

Before leaving my place last night, Logan had casually told me that as his girlfriend now, rule three was always in effect. Even if he wasn't around. So if I wanted rub one out real quick before going to sleep, I'd have to call or text him and ask permission.

I'd laughed, but of course, he wasn't kidding. My second response was to tell him the rule applied to him as well. The joke was on me when I got my first-ever text message from my boyfriend at ten minutes after midnight, an hour after I'd fallen asleep.

> Thinking about you going down on the girl at the club. I need your permission.

I hadn't thought this through. He was a guy, which meant he was going to be blowing up my phone every time he jerked off, which I knew guys did frequently.

But . . . I kind of liked it. Knowing he would always have

to think of me whenever he was close to coming. I gave him permission last night, but what would happen if I said no next time, denied his orgasm? Would he drive right over to my place and demand I give him what he wanted? What would happen if he said no . . . to me? Oh, shit, this was going to be fun.

I heated my lunch in the break room and was working on the GoodFood business card design when my phone chimed with a text message from Logan.

I guess lunch is out of the question.

Can't. Need to get a first proof to my boss by 5.

Sounds like he's a real slave driver.

Yeah, he loves telling me what to do.

You love it.

I chuckled to myself. Yes, I did.

At four-fifteen I retrieved my proofs of the GoodFood rebrand from the color printer, and marched them into Logan's office.

"Do you have a minute?"

He looked at me like he couldn't remember my name. Always the actor.

"Proofs?" He cleared the paperwork on his desk to make room for them.

This was our first test on whether or not we could keep our personal feelings compartmentalized. I set the sheet down on the desktop, my eyes watching his. He scanned it quickly.

"Thank you so much for wasting the ink in the color printer." He shoved the proof back at me, displeasure verging on disgust. He thought this was a joke. I held my face steady and pressed my lips together, and the color drained from his face. "This is a real proof?" In his shock, his gaze went back to the artwork and searched for something redeeming. He came up empty.

"Evelyn, this is terrible."

My face widened into a smile. "I'm sorry I wasted the ink, but I had to know you wouldn't hold back." I put the real proof down on top of it.

He looked pissed-off. And relieved. "You've worked with me long enough, you should know I don't do that. Not here."

I felt my face flush.

He evaluated the proof critically but said he liked the direction I'd taken with it and sent me back with some changes he'd like to see before presenting it. I'd been at my desk less than a minute when I got his text message.

> You're going to pay for that.

> Family in from out of town for the wedding so I'll be busy the next few nights. I'll call you later.

I took the train home. I was turning into a full-on addict around him, so some space might not be a bad thing. God help me, I cleaned my apartment. I actually hung clothes up and put the dishes away, which did make the place seem a little bigger and distracted me while I waited for his call like a desperate teenage girl. At nine forty-five I changed into a tank top and cotton pajama pants, brushed my teeth, and climbed into bed, the phone beside my pillow. I wasn't a morning person in the slightest, which meant I had to force myself into bed early so I could tolerate waking up at six thirty.

Maybe it wouldn't be so bad now that I'd see him every day.

His call came right at ten o'clock. "Hey, sorry, dinner ran really long." He sounded like he was walking.

"It's okay," I said. "You're just heading home now?"

There was the sound of a car door slamming shut and the engine starting. "We're going to need to get our story straight."

"What?"

"They asked a lot of questions, like how we met, how long we've been together. If you want kids."

"Interrogated you, did they?" I hoped he could hear the smile in my voice.

"You think they won't do it to you? Think again. Yours will be worse."

"So what did you tell them, boss?"

"I tried not to lie," he said. "I told them we work together, but I didn't mention I was your manager. I said we've been dating a few months. Okay?"

"It's fine, I guess." It's not like we'd never met before this past Saturday; we'd been working together for over two years. "What about children? Do I want them?" I loved that he was forced to reveal this information, because everything about him screamed he wouldn't give it up easily.

"Yeah," he said, "you do. Which reminds me, are you on the pill?"

"Yes." Why was he asking? "Did something happen last night that I—"

"No, no. I wanted to ask how you'd feel about maybe not using condoms."

"Oh." I didn't know how I felt about that. It wasn't something I'd done before. Didn't he say he'd slept with thirty women before me?

He must have sensed the question in my hesitation. "I'll get tested and prove I'm good, even if you want to keep using them."

"I can do the same."

"You don't need to do that," he said quickly.

"No, it's only fair."

"No." His voice was tight. "I've already seen your test results."

Of course, at the club. What smart man would drop twelve grand without checking the quality of the product? "Right." Since he couldn't see my face, I cringed a little.

"Hey, whatever you're comfortable with, I am too."

The idea of having nothing between us was appealing. "If you can show me it's safe, I guess we could try it."

"I'd like that a lot. You will, too." His voice sounded like sin.

My hand wandered down to the silk tie at the waist of my pants, toying with it. "So, tell me about last night."

"What about it?"

"We had sex twice yesterday. Wasn't enough for you?"

He made a noise, sort of like a laugh. "It was, trust me. But when I got home, I saw the bottle of wine from the club, and even after I'd put it away . . . I got really fucking hard thinking about it."

I shuddered and undid the silk knot keeping my pants closed.

"Which part?" A wicked smile curled on my lips. "Be specific."

"Where are you?"

"In bed." I heard a car horn honk in the background, signifying he was still stuck in traffic.

"You mean, in the closet. Ironic, don't you think, given what you did to that girl at the club?"

My fingers crept inside my panties. "That wasn't exactly my idea."

"No, I suppose it wasn't. But, shit, it was so fucking hot. Are you touching yourself?" He asked it like he already knew the answer.

"Maybe."

"Naughty girl. I wish I could come over right now and help."

I stifled a moan when my fingers circled, teasing myself. "Why don't you?"

"It's late, and traffic's a bitch. You'll have to wait until I can do it right."

My fingers moved faster, becoming slick in my arousal, and I didn't bother to quiet this moan. I closed my eyes, wanting to listen to his sexy voice. Hearing him without seeing him was a lovely reminder of our time with the blindfold.

"You should probably stop now," he said, hushed. "I won't give you permission to come when you ask."

"What?" My hand stilled. "Why?"

"Because of how awful that first proof was," he said. "You're okay to enjoy yourself, but don't break our rule. I promise you, I'll know if you do."

"Bullshit."

"You're welcome to test me."

He was infuriating and intoxicating, and I loved every second of our back-and-forth. I pulled my hand away and tied the pants closed, my body muttering a protest.

"Fine," I said. "I stopped."

He chuckled. "Good girl."

⌘

The rest of the week dragged. Getting to see Logan at work but not afterward was torture, and today, Friday, I didn't see him at all. He had to use the day as vacation to help with last-minute wedding preparations and drive out to Arlington Heights to pick up his tux. We'd talked every night, but as Friday drew closer, those conversations were later and shorter.

He'd refused me all goddamn week, and yesterday I'd barely kept myself from breaking the rule. I was beginning to hate this, and when he asked permission to come himself, I told him to fuck off. He hinted I was only making it worse on myself.

I'd gotten approval, from him of course, to leave work early at four and take the blue line out to Arlington Heights. I changed awkwardly in the microscopic and filthy bathroom on the train into a gray and yellow sheath dress with yellow heels.

He was waiting against his BMW at the Arlington Park racetrack, which was right on the other side of my train stop, wearing a gray suit with a black shirt beneath it, made casual with two buttons open. We didn't say anything to each other as I walked toward his car and he straightened. He opened the passenger-side door for me, and then buried his face in my neck, kissing me there since he still hadn't answered my question from Monday.

"Missed you today at the office, boss," I murmured.

"I bet. Did Jamie get any work done?"

"I'm sure she put in as good of an effort as usual."

When he was this close, I could smell his subtle cologne, and it made my knees go weak.

"You have no idea," he whispered in my ear, "how good you look to me. I suggest you get in the car before I bend you over the hood."

When I looked in his eyes, I was sure this was not an empty threat.

Paper crinkled underneath me when I sat, and I pulled it out, scanning it. My mouth went dry. He got into the driver's seat and gave me a coy smile.

"That copy's yours, for your records." He feigned seriousness.

I folded the test results once, twice, and then once more, sliding it into my purse. My face felt like it was on fire. Bare-back, I believe the term is? That's what his test results had cleared him for.

Like the night he'd taken me to his place, once the car was in gear, his right hand went to rest comfortably on my knee, his hand just under the edge of my skirt. I liked it, but it was a thousand degrees in his car and the heat of his hand wasn't helping.

"I should probably warn you," he said, reading my mind and rolling up the windows, turning on the air conditioning, "my family may be a bit overly excited to meet you."

"Why's that?"

"I didn't bring home too many of my past girlfriends, so taking you as my date gives the impression things are pretty serious between us."

Weren't they? He'd paid a rather large amount of money to have me. I knew how he meant it, though. There may be lots of personal questions as his family tried to discern whether or not I was worthy if Logan decided I was The One. It's exactly what my aunts and uncles did to my past boyfriends.

Oh my god, I bet Logan would have them eating out of the palm of his hand in no time.

"Should I be nervous? Because, don't worry, I am." I was dreading facing Susan again.

"Don't be, there's nothing to worry about. Worrying is strictly my mom's territory, she's got that covered for you. Now, I like Hilary a lot. But her family?" he said, referring to the bride. "They're fucking crazy."

He gave me a quick course in family history. The groom, Nick, was two years younger than Logan. Their parents had married young and divorced when Logan was ten, and four years later his mother had remarried. Logan's half-brother, Garrett, was a junior in high school.

The relationship between Susan and Logan's dad was cordial, according to Logan. His dad hadn't remarried, but had a live-in girlfriend.

As soon as we'd parked by the picturesque church, he ran around to open my car door for me and took my hand. I hoped he thought it was the warm weather that had it sweaty. I found mass-introductions terrifying, and I was horrible at remembering names.

We'd only made it up a few steps outside the church before it began. It was a parade of faces and handshakes, and then I was deposited in a pew beside a cousin who'd been charged with one of the readings. I had no idea if she was from the bride's side or Nick's, but she was friendly and charming, and I was pissed at myself for insta-forgetting her name.

Nick didn't look a whole lot like Logan. He was handsome in a wholesome, boyish way, less of a hard edge. I watched him joke with his groomsmen, looking completely at ease. Excited, like he couldn't wait to get married.

Hilary was petite with a huge mane of curly hair and big eyes, and she seemed physically unable to look anywhere else but at her fiancé. They were hands-down the most adorable couple I'd seen.

Occasionally I'd catch Logan's eye and give him a small smile. I couldn't wait to see him standing beside his brother tomorrow. Was there anything more romantic than watching two people pledge their love to each other? It wasn't like I was going to turn into a pile of mush about it; I wasn't much of a crier. But it would be hard not to fall under the spell of the day, just a little bit.

When the rehearsal was over, I waited until she was free and then went to Susan.

"Hi," I said in my friendliest voice, "I'm sorry I was so rude before, when we met—"

"Oh, honey, don't be silly, you were fine. I'm sorry for barging in on you two. It was nice to finally meet you. I was beginning to think you weren't real."

I felt a hand on my back, and Logan appeared at my side, and soon after I was whisked away to meet the rest of his family involved in the wedding. We sat with his father and his girlfriend at dinner, who both seemed like nice people. His father was a man of few words, and often I felt compelled to fill the silence when neither of the Stone men would. To my delight, and I suspect Logan's horror, there was a slideshow of the bride and groom, pictures of them growing up and when they first started dating.

"Nice shorts," I whispered to him when there was a soccer photo of him and Nick. He couldn't have been more than eight, and apparently, his hair hadn't always been perfect. But in this picture it was perfectly adorable. He'd been a cute kid.

There was one later in the show of Nick and Logan, in athletic apparel, flushed and sweaty, each with medals around their necks that boasted they'd finished last year's Chicago Marathon. Even after running twenty-six miles, he still looked amazing.

"When's your next race?" I asked. "In case I wanted to come, or, you know, sit at home and feel like a sloth."

He gave a slight smile. "The marathon's October eleventh."

I pulled out my phone and put it in my calendar.

When dinner was over, we mingled for a little while longer, and then said goodnight. Most of Nick's family lived in Oak Park and were heading back toward the city like we were. Traffic wasn't bad for once, and we chatted about the rehearsal dinner.

"I didn't get grilled by anyone," I said.

"I think that will be tomorrow. We're sitting with my mom's family." His hand brushed a little further up my leg. It sent shivers up my spine and made me reconsider the plans I'd made for us to meet Payton for drinks. You'd think it had been three years since I'd been with him and not three days.

We stopped at my apartment to pick up my overnight bag. Yesterday Logan had asked me to stay with him at his place tonight. He'd booked a hotel room for tomorrow, teasing we were going to try to out drink Hilary's Irish Catholic family. Two days with him, non-stop. It was too much and too soon, but I didn't care. I suspect this was the true reason he'd denied my orgasms. He wanted to ensure I'd agree to it because I was too desperate not to. Plus, I think he was worried I would make him late.

"What the hell happened here? Did someone break in and clean your place?"

"No, this is your fault for telling me no all those times I asked for permission."

He flashed a smile and then looked at his watch. "I assume we don't have time to get in the closet."

I laughed and got hot at the same time. "No, we don't."

He helped me load my overnight bag in his car, and this time, when I was seated in the passenger side, his hand went to my knee and dragged upward, carrying my skirt with it.

He made a noise of disappointment when his fingers brushed the silk edge of my panties. "I was hoping you weren't wearing anything under your skirt."

I raised an eyebrow. "Sorry, not when I'm meeting your family."

"That's done now, so take them off and put them in the glove box."

I blinked at the challenge, momentarily stunned. My hands went under the dress and I pulled them down slowly, the damp fabric running over the skin on the inside of my thighs. I wouldn't have thought this was sexy, but I liked the idea that part of me would be in his car.

The compartment clicked closed and his fingers were on me. Sliding in me, circling where I was aroused. I was instantly out of breath and my hand latched onto the leather-wrapped door handle.

"This," he said, fucking me with his fingers, first one and then another, "is where I'm going to put my cock tonight. Would you like that?"

"Yes," I gasped and opened my legs wider to give him

better access. His windows were tinted, but still, anyone in an SUV who got close could look down and see what he was doing to me.

"Do you want me to make you come?"

"Fuck, yes," I moaned. His fingers pumped in and out, building to a furious pace.

"Use your hand too, since I can't use both of mine. Help me get you off."

I was eager to obey the command. My left hand rubbed my clit while his fingers slammed inside me, making my grip tighten on the door. The need took hold, forced my hips to match his rhythm while I touched myself shamelessly. I probably should have been worried about his focus being on the road, but . . . shit. I felt completely out of control. A willing slave to the desire for him, that built, and built . . .

"I need permission—"

"Yes," he said. "I can't wait to come inside that pussy."

The realization that that was going to happen was his final push to send me over the cliff and tumble into an orgasm that was like a bite right on my center. I cried out and shoved his hand away, overly sensitive to his touch, shuddering on his leather seat.

He parked and turned the car off, turning his focus to me, watching the aftershocks of my orgasm rock my body. I closed my eyes, letting the blood rushing in my ears quiet some. I was surprised to see him still sitting there, watching me. He'd always moved so quickly to get my door.

"Is everything okay?" I put a hand on his cheek.

"I just need a minute, is all." For his massive erection to go away. "I don't think you realize how much I like watching you come."

"Probably not as much as I like you doing it. You're pretty

good at it."

He leaned forward and kissed me on the cheek, just to the side of my lips. Frustration was immediate. I missed his lips on mine.

"I give up, Logan. Please, kiss me."

He had a look like it was a bittersweet victory, and his eyes went clear. "Tomorrow. If you're a good girl." He threw open his door and rounded the car, leaving me stunned and full of anticipation.

⌘

Payton could wear anything and look good. She had on a low-cut ivory sequined top and black tuxedo jacket, paired with jeans that looked like they'd been handcrafted for her. She spent hours in the gym every other day, and it showed.

Logan was attracted to her. Just about every person in the bar was, and it wasn't a big deal. I was used to it. I appreciated Logan's attempt to not stare at her full breasts that were teasing out of the top of her shirt.

"You paid big money to sleep with my girl, here," Payton said.

"It was well spent," he replied.

A smile grew on her face. "So I've heard from both Evie and Tara."

He glanced at me, confused. He hadn't heard that name before.

"Tara was the woman in the room with us," I said in a hushed voice. I wasn't ashamed of it, but still not comfortable saying it out loud.

"She had nice things to say about you, Logan." Payton toyed with the straw in her drink. "Very nice things to say about Evie."

"Can we, like, not talk about that?" I shifted on my feet in the yellow heels that were amazing and torturous.

"Nope," she said, setting her sights back on Logan. "First threesome for you?"

My mouth hung open and I had to make an effort to shut it. I hadn't asked him that when I had the chance. And now I realized there were a whole bunch of other questions I should have asked. When he'd lost his virginity. Craziest place he'd done it. How many girls had let him go in the back.

"Yeah, but it wasn't really what I'd consider a threesome."

Payton nodded. "Because you couldn't touch. Yeah, that's extra. Like, double extra."

"Does that happen a lot?" he asked.

"No, usually if it's a three-way, the guy brings in his girlfriend or wife. Paying for one girl's expensive enough."

She finished her drink, and Logan signaled to the bartender she wanted another, and his hand fell to rest on my hip, his arm around my back. The bar was getting crowded, and I liked being pressed against him, almost in a possessive way. I was his.

"I'm curious," Payton said, "why did you ask Tara to stay and watch?"

He gave her a tight smile, and I could sense his shields were getting ready to come up. "How far are you planning to go into my sexual preferences?"

"As far as you'll let me."

"I asked her to stay because I thought she was hot. I was hoping she'd want to join in."

The bartender set down a new drink, but Payton ignored it. Her gaze was fixed on him, serious. "You're lying."

She'd always been so good at reading people. Even the perfect actor Logan Stone didn't have her fooled. From the sharp inhale of breath, I could tell he was off-guard. He didn't like being called a liar, even if it was true.

His dark eyes never glanced my direction as he spoke. "Fine. I asked her to stay because I wasn't sure I could go through with it."

chapter TWELVE

This was truth that he'd hesitantly revealed.

"Because you were my boss?"

He finally looked at me and his face was a mess. "Because I wasn't planning on taking off the blindfold, so I wasn't sure I could be that guy. The one you were forced to sleep with to fix a mistake that was as much mine as it was yours."

The guilt he carried over my mistake was crushing. Still crushing him. I never wanted to kiss him more than I did right then.

"That mistake brought us together," I whispered in his ear.

He blinked, stunned, and realization slowly washed over his face. The hand on me tightened subtly.

Payton looked pleased and snatched the drink up off of the bar. "Keep that in mind, Logan. I am the human lie detector, so don't bullshit my girl."

"Understood."

"Did you like performing for Tara?" She waved to a guy across the way from us, who shot back a, *"Who, me?"* look. She nodded, motioning for him to come over. "Would you want to do that again?"

Logan and I exchanged a look.

"Why are you asking?" I said.

She shrugged. "Tara said you two together were, like, the hottest thing she'd seen." The guy she'd waved over was working his way through the throng of people. "I want to watch you two fuck."

Logan had no response. He turned to me with those same stunned eyes.

"Payton," I said, "I'm not comfortable with that."

"Why not?"

"Because I'm not sure I'm comfortable with anyone watching, and you're my best friend. That's . . . it's just too weird."

Again, she shrugged and tousled her hair when the guy walked over.

"Do I know you?" he asked, a curious smile on his face.

"No," she replied. "Wouldn't you like to?"

⌘

I had warned Logan during the drive into the city that Payton was direct, and sexual, but even this request had shocked me.

"That was interesting," he said, holding the bar door open for me as we left.

"Yeah." And embarrassing. "I'm sorry."

His face was completely serious. "Why? Didn't you think it was flattering?"

My best friend wanted to watch us. Awkward, yes. But flattering? "I don't know, I guess."

He looked amused. "Don't worry, I'm perfectly happy without an audience."

I walked beside him, desperate not to appear I was limping on the shoes. He fumbled with his keys, and when the door was unlocked, he didn't open it. Instead he pressed me back against it. His lips brushed over my neck and sparks shimmered through my skin, electricity showering down on me. My hands went inside his jacket and around his waist, holding his hard body against mine. But it wasn't enough.

"I want you," I said. In fact, I might have purred it.

"Hope you don't mind if I drive fast then."

No, I didn't. I put my hand on his lap as he drove, high above his knee, the side of my pinky finger against his semi-hard dick. What type of sex waited for me in his apartment? Whatever kind, it was sure to be intense. It didn't seem like Logan was capable of having mediocre, run-of-the-mill sex.

On the elevator ride up, his mouth was hot by my ear. "Where are your panties?"

I flushed under his victorious gaze. I'd left them in his car, forgotten. "You know where they are, boss."

He dropped my bags just inside the door and didn't bother with any lights, which only made the view out the window more unbelievable. I was drawn toward it and the orange-yellow line of the streetlights on Lake Shore Drive. Arms circled me from behind and pressed me forward. Further until I was up against the cold glass.

He didn't say anything, not that he had to. His body pressed into me, molded to mine, his hips surging forward while hands pulled me to arch back into him. His teeth nipped at my ear. His mouth feathered kisses lower. I fogged the glass with each staggered breath I took and enjoyed the rush to be right against the glass, forty-four stories up in the air.

It was a back zipper on the dress, which I felt him draw down ever so slowly, like he was going tooth by tooth. Fingers slipped under my bra band and it went slack, undone. But he wasn't so much undressing me as he was getting clothes out of his way. Moving them to the side so he could slip his large hands inside the dress, sliding them over my skin, caressing my back.

My palms were flat on the glass by my chest, so when his fingernails raked gently down my skin, I tried to push off. I was already insane for him.

"No," he said, one hand pressing my shoulder back into the glass, while his hips moved, insinuating that he wanted to fuck me right here, right like this. His dick was hard against my ass, pressing into me.

"Keep your hands on the glass."

My feet were killing me. The strap across my toes bit into my flesh, but I followed his orders, and he rewarded me by pulling one shoulder of the dress and bra down and then the other so they were bunched around my waist. My nipples were tight and hard, and he skimmed his fingers over one before rolling it between his thumb and forefinger, pushing it forward to kiss the cold pane of glass.

I made a noise of satisfaction and desperation. I didn't want foreplay. That's what the last three days had been. I whimpered and a belt unbuckled. His zipper was undone. Air was cool on my ass cheeks when he hiked the skirt of the dress up to my waist, so the whole dress was bunched there.

Without words, he used his body to show me how he needed me to be to best bring us together, pulling my lower body away from the glass and leaning me over.

I was dripping wet between my thighs and he took full advantage. His dick slipped between the hollow of my legs, rubbing himself in my wetness, getting himself ready to take me. His soft skin against my slick skin, with no latex between us, made me tremble.

"Are you okay with this?" he asked, his subtle movement teasing me. "No condom?"

"I've never done that before, but, yeah."

He blew out a long breath, and then positioned himself so he could press into me, pushing slowly. My eyes were closed and my arms crossed on the glass, my forehead resting on them.

"Holy fuck," he whispered. "Something that feels this good should be illegal." And he wasn't even inside me all the way yet. My body wasn't as resistant as before. It was hardly uncomfortable.

I could feel everything, every inch as he advanced in me.

"Does it feel good?"

"Yes," I gasped. "Oh my god, more."

I moaned and bit my lip when he pushed all the way in, his skin against the skin of my backside. Just having him inside me was like setting the roller coaster cars on the track, climbing up that first big hill. His hands were on the dress at my waist, holding it in place. He seemed to be holding himself in place.

"Are you ready?" he asked.

Ready? Ready for –?

A sound of immense pleasure welled up from deep inside me when he withdrew and then slammed back into me, deeper than he'd been before. All of him touching me inside and out.

He fucked me, harder with each thrust until I couldn't breathe. My legs shook, my eyes rolled back into my head. It'd never been like this before. My cries of pleasure swelled as my orgasm approached like a freight train. I had to put my hands flat on the glass again to steady myself as he drove into me.

"I'm going to . . . " my panicked voice said. "Oh, shit . . ." I knew I was supposed to do something, but I couldn't think what. The next thrust would be the one to get me there. That was all I could think of. But every thrust only took me higher.

"Yes, Evie," he said. "Come for me."

He pushed so deep inside me I screamed. At least, I

think I did. My climax gripped me. It made my ears go deaf. My forehead was against the glass where beads of sweat had made it slippery. The muscles inside me flexed over and over again, and I rode the remainder of the orgasm out on him.

"No," I heard him groan. "No. Fuck." His hands were tight on me, clamping down on my waist. Who the hell was he talking to?

Himself. Because he was coming. Once he'd gone too far to pull himself back, he gave up fighting and pumped his dick in and out furiously, until his body seized.

"Fuck, Evie, fuck . . ."

The throbbing inside me was strong, a series of jerks followed by a rush of heat as he shot into me. The sensation was so unexpectedly hot, I quieted a moan and dragged a hand down the glass Titanic-style.

"I don't remember . . ." I gasped, ". . . giving you permission."

"Yeah, well, maybe don't scream when you're coming all over my cock."

I turned to look over my shoulder at him. I don't know where the playful words came from. "Hey, don't blame me, asshole. It's not my fault you don't have any self-control."

Genuine shock on his face morphed into a hard look, and I gasped. *Oh, no.* He pulled out of me suddenly. *It had been a joke—*

His hand came down so fast I heard the smack before I felt the sting of his fingers on the flesh of my backside. Heat all but incinerated me.

"I have plenty of control," he whispered, rubbing where he'd just struck me. "Maybe I just won't let you come anymore. Would you like that?"

I simultaneously felt relief and concern. He wasn't mad

about the asshole comment. In fact, he looked like he enjoyed it. But I absolutely believed he'd make good on his threat if he needed to.

"No, I wouldn't," I replied.

"I thought so."

He helped me to stand up, the dress falling to my ankles. Feeling had returned to my body and now my feet screamed in protest. I put a hand on his shoulder to steady myself and bent a knee to undo the strap, but his arms went around my body and lifted me off of my feet. He carried me a few steps to the couch and set me down, bending on a knee so he could undo the tiny buckle holding the suffering shoe in place.

He had a weird, bashful look on his face. Guilt.

"What is it?"

"You wanted to take these off before we started and I didn't let you." When the shoe was slipped off, he rubbed the sensitive flesh beneath it gently, and went to the other one.

"You knew the shoes were hurting me?"

He nodded. "But doing it like that," he gestured to where he'd pressed me against the glass, "we needed the extra height."

I choked a laugh. "I'll survive. You, on the other hand, broke one of your *own* rules."

"I did. I have an idea for a consequence, if you want to hear it." He scooped me up into his arms and lifted me from the couch, lumbering with me toward the bedroom.

"I'm all ears." He set me in the center of the bed and stepped back, undoing the cuffs of his dress shirt.

"Since I couldn't follow the rule, you don't have to next time."

Interesting. But . . . "You can do better than that."

"All right. The rest of the weekend." He pulled his shoes

and socks off, and stepped out of his pants so he was as naked as I was. I smiled in acceptance. He'd said it begrudgingly like this was a huge concession, and I relished it.

"I wouldn't have pegged you for a cuddler," I said when he slipped into the bed. He was on his back and pulled me up against him so my cheek was on his shoulder. He was warm, and his cologne smelled amazing. Like a man. His hand went to my knee and pulled it over his thigh to tuck me around him, our damp skin sticking together.

"You're surprised I want to have a beautiful, naked woman draped on me?"

"Not when you put it like that, no."

I put my hand on his chest and let my fingers wander, tracing patterns over his heart. He turned his head and brushed his lips over my forehead in a kiss and then sighed.

"It's getting late," he said in a hushed voice, "and we've got a long day tomorrow."

"I know," I said. "I just like touching you. Feel free to fall asleep."

"So you can steal my virtue? No thank you." His arms tightened on me. "Sleep. You can have your way with me tomorrow."

⌘

I woke early and alone, and called out to him but got no response. I yanked the sheet off the bed and wrapped it around myself, then roamed into the kitchen to discover the note he'd left for me there.

"Gone for a run, be back by seven forty-five. Diet Coke in the fridge."

Years of working together had taught him I didn't start my day with coffee, but with a silver can of soda. I cinched the sheet tighter at the cold from the fridge, retrieving the can, and when I shut the door I glanced into the living room.

The clothes we'd dropped in there were gone. He must have hung them up while I was sleeping. There was a spray bottle of Windex with a towel folded over top, from where he'd cleaned the glass. What a little neat freak he was. It brought a smile to my face when I wondered if he got turned on cleaning the smudges we'd put there.

I popped the top on the can and took a sip when I heard the door open behind me.

"It's fucking hot out there," he said.

I almost dropped the can when I turned to face him. He had on a pair of shoes and shorts, but no shirt, and a black armband that carried his iPhone. Sweat rolled down his flushed face and dripped from his tanned and toned chest. He pulled a bottle of Gatorade from the fridge and drank while undoing the Velcro of his armband, and then set it on the counter.

I just stood there, awestruck, as he finished the entire bottle. He tossed it in the recycling bin, pulled a water bottle from the fridge, and turned his focus to me.

"I'm sorry I had to go out, but I have to stick to my training schedule." He took a breath, looking concerned. "You okay?"

"I'm just trying not to drool."

A smile broke on his face. "I'm a sweaty mess. You're the one wearing nothing but my sheets. Take them off."

"Why?"

"Because I'd like to fuck you in the shower. If you don't mind."

Sometimes I think he said things like that to catch me off-guard, but I loved throwing it right back at him.

I dropped the sheet to the floor. "I guess we could do that."

There was a crunch of plastic as his grip tightened on the bottle.

chapter THIRTEEN

This was another first for me. It's not like the showers in my college apartments were spacious or remotely sexy, and the shower in my place now barely had room for one.

I stood awkwardly in the semi-hallway between his bedroom and bathroom, watching him toe off his shoes and toss his socks into a laundry basket. In one swift move, he yanked down his shorts and boxers and added them to the basket, his feet falling heavily on the floor as he moved toward me.

It was bizarre, this feeling of nervousness I had, and I shook my head as if that could shake the sensation from my body. He'd seen me naked plenty, and I'd been up close and personal with his anatomy. Yet there was sunlight flooding every inch of his apartment and it was like a spotlight on every flaw in my body. He looked at me like they didn't exist. He gave me a gaze filled with pure, unadulterated lust.

This man desired me like no one else. My feet moved backward into the bathroom so I wouldn't break his gaze. I had blinders on; nothing else existed.

"Are you running from me?" he asked, when I backed up with a thud into the wide glass door of his shower.

"No. I like looking at you. I like how you look at me."

Logan's shoulders lifted in a deep breath and his eyes softened. *Whoa.* He liked hearing that. A hand reached out and took my wrist and silently asked me to step forward, so he could pull the door open and start the water.

It rained down from the ceiling in the large, subway-tiled

glass enclosure. I'd never thought of describing a bathroom as sexy, but this room was full of sex, and not just because he was standing in it.

"I should probably warn you, we don't really have a lot of time. I know traffic's going to be bad on 90."

"So, you're telling me no dilly-dallying? Let's get right to the sex?"

He had an enigmatic smile. "Something like that." He pulled the door open again. "Ladies first."

I stepped in and under the water, wiping my hair back out of my face. It was hot. I took another step further into the spacious shower to allow him to get in. Instead, his body crushed me flat against the tile, his defined chest in my back.

"It's going to be hard, and fast, and rough. If you want to stop, tell me," he commanded.

All of the air left my body in an instant. He wanted it rough enough we needed a warning? He flipped me around to face him and leaned me back into the tile wall, water pouring down the intense expression on his face. He had one hand stroking his dick and the other buried between my legs, his thick fingers teasing me.

I wasn't sure my body could go from zero to sixty, but I was already turned on at the sight of him. The way his hand touched and rubbed me, caressed me . . . it took no time for the ache to build to fever pitch.

"Do you want my cock?"

I nodded, already too drunk with desire to find words easily.

"Say it."

"I want your cock," I said on a broken, shuddering breath.

"Where? Here?" He shoved a finger inside me, unapologetic. His face was shocking and dark, like a predator and I was his cornered prey. "Beg me for it."

I swallowed, not really sure how to do that. "Please, Logan."

"Not good enough. Make me believe."

The water ran into my eyes and made him blurry. His fingers moved in a wicked sequence, touching me outside and then plunging inside. Each time he repeated it, my need and agony grew.

"Please," I cried, "please. I have to have it. I *need* it."

"What do you need?"

"Your cock." I trembled, out of control and falling apart. "I need what only you can give me."

His nostrils flared in approval. Then, the predator descended upon me. Hands went to the insides of my thighs and urged them apart, lifting one of my knees up so it was hooked over his forearm. His hands braced himself on the wall and he bent his knees so he was at just the right angle to impale me in one swift move.

I gave a sharp hiss at the invasion, my body not used to his size so suddenly. I wrapped my arms around his neck, having to hold on when he fucked me. It was just as he'd said it would be. Hard and fast. My body slammed into the wall from his thrusts. The sound of us colliding over and over again was just loud enough over the shower.

The water running off of him was salty with sweat and I licked my lips, tasting it. Tasting him, since we hadn't kissed. The hand not holding my leg up abandoned the wall and locked onto my breast, squeezing so hard it was right at the edge of pain.

But it was so fucking hot. Not just the shower, but what he was doing.

I should have been upset by this. That there had been no requests or apologies. No compromise. This was all about his pleasure. I was a prop, a doll for his command.

Yet, I loved this. Surrendering completely to him, allowing him to take exactly what he wanted. Letting him yank my other knee up around him so he held me up, pinned to the wall, and could drive into me harder, crashing my back against the unforgiving tile. I arched, pressing my breasts against him, letting my wet body slide against his.

"This pussy is mine," he growled. "No one else has been inside it like I have."

God, the stuff he said. I was grateful we were in the shower, because it sent a rush of liquid desire straight to my center. This feral, alpha-male version of Logan was scary and thrilling and I was drawn to it. Eager to submit.

"This pussy is yours," I repeated back to him, and he made a sound of pure satisfaction. My orgasm came out of nowhere. By the time I had an inkling of it, I was already in the throes, past the point of no return. Electricity jolted down my spine. I gasped when I came, moaning in his ear, over and over until it subsided.

He dropped my legs and pulled out of me, no warning or explanation. His rough hands whirled me around, putting me it the same position I'd been in last night, my hands flush against the tile. He didn't have to tell me to keep them there. I had no choice unless I wanted him to literally bang my head into the wall.

His furious pace created a slap between our bodies.

"You like it when I fuck you hard?" he asked.

"Yes." I was panting, much like I'd done that night on the table. One week ago. It felt like a lifetime had passed since then. The air was thick with steam, and I felt like I was breathing in water, drowning in it.

He put a hand in my hair at the nape of my neck and

yanked, bending my head back toward him. It hurt this time. It was awkward and made me feel powerless. Dominated. So of course I enjoyed it. This was why he had warned me? A little hair pulling?

No. It had more to do with the hand that was in the small of my back, drifting lower, closer to his body inside me. Sliding into the crevice between my cheeks. My heart was already racing, threatening to explode, and I started to shake when he pressed his thumb against my entrance there. Just the feeling of him was shocking and confusing like last time, and just as pleasurable. He increased the pressure, and started to invade me.

He hadn't slowed down a beat on his thrusts, but my thoughts were firmly focused on the finger working deeper inside me, a burning and uncomfortable sensation. Usually off limits. But, fuck, it turned me on. I shouldn't like it. But I really fucking did. He pushed in deeper until I think his thumb was as far as it would go.

"You like that, dirty girl?"

My throat closed up, and I couldn't nod my head because of his hold on my hair, but, holy fucking shit, I did. I shouldn't. It was so wrong.

"I bet you do. I bet you want more."

The burning sensation was gone and then shifted. He slipped his index and forefingers inside. I held my tongue that wanted to tell him to wait. I could do this.

"I'm going to fuck you here." Before I could respond, he added, "Not right now, but soon as you're ready, I'm going to fuck this tight, little virgin ass."

For effect, his fingers moved slowly, in and out in contrast to what his dick was doing. It wasn't really uncomfortable. My body relaxed to his movement, and the first wave of enjoyment washed over me. But it was million degrees in this shower.

"It's okay to like it," he said, as if reading my mind, the one that was in total panic. I clawed at the wall, shaking apart. Oh god, I was going to come.

It was going to be loud.

"I'm . . . going to . . . scream." Each breath was a giant struggle.

"Go ahead."

He released my hair. His hand dragged up my neck and curled around my face until his palm was firmly covering my mouth. So my scream fell against his skin, muffling it somewhat but it still echoed in the vast space, and it set him off as well with a whole tirade of dirty words and jerky thrusts as he came. Most of what he said I couldn't understand; I was busy trying not to collapse. The orgasm had been epic and gave me shaky legs, and his hand remained around my mouth, making it almost impossible to breathe.

He removed his fingers from me, but as soon as I'd come, I wanted them gone. My body felt overloaded. His hands closed around my waist and pulled me upright and back against him, so he was holding me from behind. I couldn't catch my breath. Where was the air?

"Are you okay?" he asked with a decent level of concern. I tried to nod, but it only made me dizzier. The water falling around me looked . . . wrong. It was falling much too fast. I couldn't—

Black.

"Evie!" He peered down at me, his face terrified. What the hell? He had me cradled in his arms and he was kneeling on the floor of the shower.

"What happened?"

He squeezed me, hugging me tightly to him. Crushing me. "Jesus, you scared the shit out of me!"

"Logan, stop. How did we end up on the floor?"

He relaxed his hold, and his head over mine shielded me from the falling water. When he smoothed a clump of wet hair back off of my face, I could see the subtle shake of his hand. "You passed out."

I looked away because his panicked face was devastating. I tried to sit up, but his arms were reluctant to release me.

"I'm okay. I just got really hot."

He helped me move across the floor, positioning me so I was sitting against one of the walls, and he threw open the shower door. He stormed through it, abandoning me there with absolutely no words. I stared out the glass, dumbfounded. How could he just leave?

He was back a moment later, naked, dripping wet, a water bottle in hand. *Oh.* He stepped back in and turned the water temperature down so it was just barely warm, then knelt beside me, unscrewing the top and offering the bottle. When I took it, he sat back from me and ran a hand through his dark hair. He looked horribly unsettled.

"I'm sorry," I said.

He stared at me with disbelief. "I'm the one who did that to you. My body core temp got messed up from coming into air conditioning after the run. I had no idea the water was too hot."

"I'm okay, really." I took a sip of water, already feeling almost normal again. "You need to stop looking at me like I'm dying, it's freaking me out."

He was unconvinced. When I tried to stand, he put his hands on my shoulders and stopped me. I wrapped my hands around his wrists.

"I'm fine," I said, "and we don't have time to hang out on the floor of your shower."

Appealing to his practical side worked, although he looked uneasy about it. I let him help me up and pretended not to notice how intently he studied me.

"Shit," I grumbled. "Is that the only shampoo you have? I don't want to smell like a guy."

He barely said anything else to me during the shower, except to tell me to finish drinking all of the water in the water bottle. He had to get out of the shower a second time to dig under his sink for a half-empty container of hotel shampoo.

I tried to get him past what had happened, a simple mistake. But he couldn't let it go.

I hurried getting dressed, trying to recover lost time from my fainting in the shower. I didn't want him to dwell on it more than I suspected he already was, or for him to have to come up with some excuse for why he was late.

I could hear it now. *"Sorry I'm late, Nick, on your special day, but I was busy fucking my girlfriend in the shower so hard I made her pass out."* I'm sure that would go over well.

He was dressed in jeans and a simple black V-neck shirt, sitting on the bed, his phone in hand, although he wasn't paying attention to it. He was still sulking, and I wasn't having it.

"I want to talk about the shower," I said, sitting beside him on my knees on the bed.

"Which part? When I suffocated you, or when I gave you heatstroke?" His voice was filled with self-loathing.

"I want to talk about the man in there."

"It won't happen again." It was hushed. Ashamed.

"Why not?" I put my hand on top of his on the bed. "Couldn't you tell I loved it?"

He looked gorgeous, even when he was visibly confused

and conflicted. "Evie."

"I'm not saying I want it like that every time, but I love never knowing how you're going to come at me," I said. "You're kind of an adventure, boss."

He came up off of the bed and put his hands on my waist, drawing me to him and kissing me chastely on my forehead. "Are you ready to go?"

"As soon as you go back to treating me like you were before, asshole," I said with a wide smile I hoped reached all the way to my eyes.

He took a breath. "All right." His face softened and turned playful. "I want to take off your clothes and taste that pussy."

My mouth fell open. "Do we have time?" I asked, hopeful.

"No, I'll take a raincheck though."

⌘

Having a steering wheel under my hands was foreign. It had been ages since I'd driven. Because I was nervous about traffic, and driving Logan's car, and the whole meeting-his-entire-family thing, I left with plenty of time. For once in my life, I wasn't late. I parked behind the church with an enormous white steeple and did a final check of my makeup. I hadn't seen Logan since I dropped him at his brother's hotel room this morning.

There were friendly smiles when I joined people heading into the church, but no faces I recognized until I spotted him. He was huddled up with the other groomsmen by the interior doors. Holy mother of god, he looked amazing. A black tux with a simple black bow tie, James Bond style. He must have sensed my arrival because his head turned toward me.

Logan's gaze started at my rhinestone strapped sandals

and worked its way up, lingering on the royal blue, one-shoulder dress that matched my eyes. He spent an indecent amount of time staring at my chest. He liked what he saw. I understood. It took an iron grip on my self-control to keep my indecent thoughts from seeping onto my face, or out of my mouth, as he approached me.

"You look amazing." He kissed my cheek.

"I believe that's my line."

"Come on, I've got a seat for you beside Chelsea."

Chelsea. That was the friendly cousin's name I had chatted with during the rehearsal. I slipped my arm into Logan's, and just as we crossed through the interior, Garrett passed me a ceremony program. It was beautifully understated in design, and Logan to a tee.

"Don't critique me too hard," he said. "Hilary was rather specific."

"No promises."

As stated, Chelsea had an open spot beside her that I slid into, giving her a smile. She looked nervous, rereading the weathered piece of paper in her hand that had notes written in the margin. I admired the program while the string quartet began the processional.

Sometimes weddings seem to last a lifetime, and others seem impossibly short, and this one fell into the latter category. Hilary looked stunning in her antique lace dress. Her wild mane of hair had been styled back into a soft up-do with a cathedral veil pinned beneath. And while Nick was a handsome groom, my eyes were glued to the man on his left.

Despite her notes, Chelsea zipped through the reading in less than a minute. It was a big wedding, and I could understand why she'd been nervous. The kiss at the end was just like Nick and Hilary – adorable. He kissed her much too quickly, so she went back for seconds, drawing chuckles from the guests. Logan found me after the recessional, introducing me to some aunts and uncles, and nice people I had absolutely no hope of remembering.

"We've got pictures now," he said. "I'll come find you as soon as I can when we're done."

"I'm fine. I've got Chelsea to latch onto," I joked. Although, not really.

I waited until the parking lot drained of cars and then drove the ten minutes to the country club. Cocktail hour had already begun in the garden behind the ballroom. Servers with silver trays offered various hors d'oeuvres, and a line had formed at the open bar. Chelsea spotted me and waved me over.

More family to meet, and the questions began now. *How did you two meet? How long have you been together?* And my personal favorite, *How do you feel about kids?* Yikes. I had to remind myself of the lie since it had been an actual week. Even with the lie, two months dating seemed a bit soon to be prying into that.

I worked my way through the line beside Chelsea to get a rum and Diet Coke.

"It was a disaster," she said about her reading. "Did you understand a single word?"

"You enunciated really well."

"Aw, you're sweet, but you're not a convincing liar." Chelsea laughed and swirled her drink.

We stood off to one side of the garden where the perfume from the rose bushes clung heavy in the air. It was a beautiful day, although hot. Logan must be sweating up a storm in that tux, which of course made me think about when he'd appeared shirtless and drenched in sweat this morning.

"What the hell?" Chelsea muttered under her breath. She turned to me, panic streaking her face. "Um, maybe you should—"

A woman approached us, staying on the path so she wouldn't sink into the soft grass, her slender legs extending above stiletto-clad feet. She was oblivious to the effects of the sun, not a perfectly-styled hair out of place. It was like looking in the mirror, only one that reflected back the complete opposite of what I was. For instance, I was an inch shorter than average with thick thighs, whereas she was tall and rail-thin. Blonde, with a model pouty face that men seem to find so appealing. She looked like she was maybe thirty. Picture-perfect.

She gave Chelsea a smile, but it was cold and unfeeling.

"Wow, it's been a while." I'd known Chelsea all of three hours, and I could tell this was strained.

"Yeah," the blonde said. I don't think she was capable of sweating. Like it was beneath her. "How have you been?"

"Good. And yourself?"

The blonde's flat smile continued. "I've been great."

"Good for you. I'm a little surprised to see you here." Chelsea's voice was uneven. "And I can think of some other people who might be surprised, too."

The blonde gave a tinny laugh. "Susan invited my parents, but my dad's sick. Nick's practically family to me, so, here I am." Her dusty green eyes turned to me. "I don't believe we've met, you must be from Hilary's side."

She held a manicured hand out to me for a handshake, which I took. Her cold hand was soft like silk. How the hell was she cold in this heat?

"Actually," I answered, "I'm Logan's girlfriend. Evelyn Russell."

The hand froze, tightened on mine while her gaze flew to Chelsea as if demanding confirmation. All Chelsea did was take a long sip of her drink, and the blonde's eyes returned to me, narrow and assessing. She let out a strange noise, a bitter laugh like she'd just heard the most ridiculous thing in her life.

"Nice to meet you." It sounded like pure bullshit. "I'm April Kelley." Those words came out weighted. It was revealed as a seemingly recognizable name, although I hadn't a clue.

"Nice to meet you, too," I said, giving her a blank look that wiped the smile from her face.

"How long have you and Logan been seeing each other?"

"A couple of months."

April had a bizarre expression. "I hadn't heard he'd started dating again." Her voice fell down an octave. "But it's not like we talk these days."

Every cell in my brain screamed that she was one of Logan's ex-girlfriends. It wasn't surprising, her cold and distant personality was similar to his at times, although I think she was at level: expert. She was stunningly beautiful. They must have made a gorgeous couple.

Chelsea's reaction told me I had to tread lightly. The break-up between them hadn't gone well. I wondered immediately who had ended it. In my experience, you can come out just as wounded when you're the one who breaks it off, so it was too hard to know from her thinly-veiled contempt if it was his doing.

"Well," Chelsea said, "I'm glad to hear you're doing good, April. We should probably go mingle with my family. Some of them came up from Florida, and I don't get to see them often." Chelsea gestured back toward the swarm of people by the bar. "Evelyn?"

"Okay," April said. She smiled like the Cheshire cat, as if aware she'd sent Chelsea running. "Nice meeting you."

"You, too," I responded, hurrying to keep up with Chelsea.

I waited until we were well out of earshot, but Chelsea beat me to it. "I'm so sorry about that," she said. "That had to be really awkward."

"Yeah, probably, except I still don't know who she is. She's one of Logan's exes?"

Chelsea's mouth dropped open. "He didn't tell you?"

"No, tell me what?"

"She's not one of his exes, she's his *only* ex. They were together for twelve years."

FOURTEEN

Twelve freaking years. That's not a relationship, that's a marriage. He spent twelve years with that calculating woman. Was that why he was the way he was? Had she trained him to be such a tidy, neat freak?

Oh, god.

Was that why he was obsessed with controlling me in the bedroom?

I finished my drink and snatched a bottle of water off one of the trays of a server who passed by. It solved the problem of my cottonmouth.

"No," I said. "He's never mentioned her."

"I cannot believe she came, she's got some balls on her. Logan never told us what happened between them. But whatever it was, it was bad because suddenly April's name was like Voldemort's – she who shall not be named."

"When was this?"

"I dunno, a while. Maybe three years ago."

Things came into focus. If I'd invested twelve years in another person, only to have it fall apart, I'd be hesitant to get back into a relationship too.

"He's not going to like that she's here," Chelsea added.

"Well, what's a wedding without a little drama?" I responded in a humorless joke.

A text message came from him a few minutes later, telling me pictures had run long, but they were in the limo and on their way. I was composing a response to warn him about

April, when an elderly couple approached. Logan's cute grandparents wanted to meet his new girlfriend. Knowing what I did now, his earlier comments made more sense. Was I really only his second girlfriend? I pocketed my phone out of courtesy and beamed a smile to them.

Was his family as confused as I was about Logan choosing me as a girlfriend? I don't think April and I could be more different if I tried. Two minutes into the conversation, I felt a warm hand on my hip and Logan appeared on the other side.

"Hi," he said. "Evie, do you mind?" He pointed at the water bottle in my hand. I passed it to him and watched him finish it. He chatted with his grandparents for another minute, and then the staff was asking for the wedding party to line up for announcements.

"I'll see you inside," he said, giving me a squeeze and following the rest of the bridal party toward the entrance.

I wanted to tell him, but really, what good would that do right now? I followed the herd of people moving into the elaborate banquet room, picking up my seating card. Thank god Nick and Hilary had opted for a sweetheart table so I could sit beside Logan.

The bridal party's announcement was thankfully short and our table filled, first with his mother and stepfather, then Garrett, and finally Logan. The maid-of-honor didn't sit, she went straight to the microphone and began her toast, which meant Logan would be up right after.

"Are you nervous?" I asked him. I had forgotten about this duty, and hadn't seen him practice. He didn't reach into his jacket to pull out notes.

"I'm fine," he whispered back, cool as a cucumber.

The maid-of-honor gave a toast that was more of a roast of her sister, throwing out comments about how thrilled their parents were to have Hilary off the payroll. Hilary was a good sport about it, and Nick seemed to think it was hilarious. The sister ended it on a sweet note, and we were clinking glasses. Logan kept hold of his champagne and stood, moving to take the offered microphone from her.

"Some of you might not know the real story on how Hilary and Nick met, and if you two don't mind, I'd like to share it now."

Nick and Hilary exchanged a nervous smile with each other.

"The story that they tell is while they were in college, Hilary and her friend Katie were walking home from the library late at night, and discovered Nick. He'd lost his wallet outside just a few minutes before, and asked them to help him look. While doing this, Hilary stepped off the curb and twisted her ankle, and Nick had to carry her back to the dorm. They didn't find his wallet, but they found each other instead."

A smile twisted on his lips, and I took a deep breath. Seeing him stand up there, all eyes on him yet so comfortable, was intoxicating.

"It's a nice story, but they leave out some critical details." His smile grew into a grin, while the nervous one on Nick's lips started to fade. "Nick didn't lose his wallet. He'd seen Katie and Hilary getting ready to leave and devised the 'lost wallet' story because he wanted to get her number. Not Hilary's, but Katie's."

You could hear all of the heads turn to face Hilary, to see if this was a revelation. Her smile said it wasn't.

"Hilary wasn't about to let that happen. She'd had her eye on my brother from the moment he got to the library, and so she made a story of her own, a not-really-twisted ankle. That allowed her to hang on my brother for the next twenty minutes, and I think after the first ten he was in love with her."

Adorable.

"So, I want to toast to the new Mr. and Mrs. Nicholas Stone. To finding each other," he said. Then, his eyes zeroed in on mine, as if speaking directly to me. "To doing *whatever* you have to, to get what you want."

It was like he'd just poured lava on me.

"Oh, I almost forgot." His eyes turned playful. "They were both fall-down drunk. The Library is the name of a bar on campus."

I think people chuckled. Maybe Hilary scoffed at this being revealed. All I could think about was the meaning in his words. Susan leaned over and clinked her glass of champagne against mine when I held it up.

Logan didn't sit down. He pulled the glass from my hand and set both of ours on the table, took my hand, and tugged me from my seat. I followed him out the door, down a long hallway.

"Where are we going?"

He didn't answer because I didn't think he knew. We wandered through an empty bar and then into a darkened office that looked like it wasn't in use. He shut the door and pressed my back against it, his face an inch from mine.

"I'm over your rule." Before I could respond, he set his mouth on mine.

Yes. Oh my god, yes. His kiss was filled with so much longing I gasped against it. His soft lips teased, his tongue slipped into my mouth to stroke mine, and it eased a moan from me. Then, he began to use his hands. One slipped behind my neck to hold me into his kiss while the other closed on my waist so the rest of our bodies could touch.

"Logan," I tried to get out more between kisses, but the week spent without had made us both hungry to make up for lost time.

"Hmm?" he mumbled. Lips returned to mine, greedy and insistent. Demanding my participation, which I was all too ready to give. My hands clung to him. I wanted to sink inside his skin, to rip his jacket off. To ball my fists in his dress shirt, wrinkle it, and pull it up so I could slide my hands beneath.

He wouldn't like wrinkles in his shirt. That was the thought that made me go cold. "I have to tell you something," I said. "April Kelley is here."

"What?" He'd heard me because he'd gone rigid. "How?"

"She came with her mother."

He straightened, stepping away, and the desire inside me complained when the heat of his body was gone. His face hardened and soured, layer by layer.

"Did you two talk?" His voice was cold.

"Not really, Chelsea pulled me away."

He ran a hand through his hair. "What did she say?"

I gave him a rundown of the brief encounter and repeated what Chelsea had told me. "Twelve years?" I asked. "You started dating when you were—"

"Fifteen."

They'd been kids. "Can I ask what happened?"

"We weren't right for each other."

Wasn't that ultimately the reason all couples broke up? There had to be so much more to the story. How had it taken them twelve years to figure that out? Logan's face was a total fucking enigma. He seemed to be studying me, and I could sense I had to tread carefully. Now was definitely not the time to go investigating into his backstory.

"Okay. I liked your toast," I said, hoping it sounded as

sincere as I meant it.

He blinked as if stunned at my topic change. Then, he looked pleased. Yes, I was willing to accept another non-answer from him. The pads of his fingers skimmed over my neck, up to cup my face in a hand. He dipped his head to brush his lips across mine.

"Yeah?" he said. "Thanks." He left his warm hand on my jawline. "Look, I know you probably want to talk about that—"

"It's fine. You can tell me about it later, when you want to."

A stunned Logan was so different from any other version. He'd expected me to push, but that wasn't my way. I had no problem with compromise.

His kiss now was on fire but over too soon. "I have ideas of doing things you'd call highly inappropriate to you right now. But . . ."

"We have to get back."

He nodded. "I'd like to hold 'highly inappropriate' for later. Does that sound agreeable to you?"

"Yes." I matched his pretend serious tone. "That's acceptable."

⌘

During dinner he had one hand on my knee beneath the table, at times in a dangerously inappropriate spot. I think he liked the blush he drew out of me whenever it crept too high and I had to shift in my seat to guide it back to my knee.

This wedding was one motherfucking powerful aphrodisiac. During Nick and Hilary's first dance, I'd turned in my chair to face the dance floor and Logan's arms slipped around my waist, pulling me to lean back into him. He kissed my bare shoulder right where it met my neck, and I had to bite my lip. Heat sizzled down my body, through every nerve until it reached between my thighs.

The next dance was the bridal party, but the newlyweds let the party choose their own partners. I was on my feet and in his arms a moment later.

"You dance, boss?" I whispered.

"I can slow dance like an eighth-grader, yes." His hands settled in the small of my back and my arms slid around his shoulders, and we turned slowly in a circle to a sweet love song, our feet shuffling beneath us. As we finished a rotation, there was a scowl painted on April's pretty face.

I don't think of myself as a particularly petty person, but I'd finished my glass of champagne and was feeling catty. I curled a hand into his soft hair and turned his face to mine, pressing my lips to his.

He was as into putting on a show as I was. Yet, I'd forgotten how good kissing between us was, and how it had been denied, so it flared wildly, deepening. A hand threaded through my hair and his tongue tasted mine.

"Stop showing us up," Nick joked.

I hadn't realized we'd stopped our eighth-grade dancing, or that the bride and groom were right beside us. And now April's seat was empty.

Besides being fans of booze, Hilary's family tore up the dance floor. It was a massive pile of sweaty bodies, young and old, shaking it to classic wedding fodder on the hardwood. Logan didn't dance, nor did either of his brothers. They seemed content to stand in a semi-circle and critique the crowd, each with a drink clasped in hand.

Since he didn't dance, Logan had no problem farming me out to other men in his family. Uncles, cousins, and his grandfather, who turned out to be the best dancer of the bunch. It was getting late, and I was tiring, dancing with a drunk cousin who wobbled unsteadily, when I glanced over and saw him deep in conversation.

Nick and Garrett were gone. It was just Logan and the blonde, his one and only ex.

Whatever they were talking about, neither of them looked too happy about it. I fought the urge to go and interrupt. But when Blake had shown up drunk at my apartment, Logan had been understanding. I could do the same.

The deejay announced the next song would be the last, and a slow, haunting love song filled the room. April turned away from Logan and thundered off, his gaze moving to me. He approached and held his arms out, wordlessly asking me to dance.

"I didn't even come close to out-drinking Hilary's family," I remarked, my forehead against his neck, fighting the urge to ask about her.

"Are you even buzzing?"

"No, I was too busy," I scolded. "You could have warned me that you don't dance."

"If it helps, you're a big hit with the family."

That did help.

"I stole a bottle of champagne from the bar," he said, "I thought we could have a glass back at the room before I claim my raincheck."

My pulse jumped. The image of his head between my legs, my fingers tangled in his hair, flashed in my dirty mind. What kind of Logan was I going to get tonight?

It worked out that I was able to drive, because the shuttle to the hotel was full. He couldn't drive. Even though he'd only had a few drinks, he admitted he rarely drank.

"I got that all out of my system in college, and it's not good for training," he said when he climbed into the passenger seat of his own car.

I couldn't tell he was impaired, but since I hadn't had a drink in hours, it wasn't a big deal. The hotel was just down the road, but he glanced over at me at one point when we were stopped at a long light, a weird look crossing his face.

"You don't like me driving your car," I said with a wicked tone. Such a control freak, and I loved it.

"Maybe, but it's not personal. Why are you smiling?"

"Because I like watching you squirm, boss." For effect, I shifted into neutral and revved the engine. Oh, he really didn't like that. The minivan beside me looked at us like we were idiots.

"Think I can take them?" I teased.

"Maybe think about the fact that there could be consequences to your actions." It was another joke that might not be a joke at all. "Think about what I might do to punish you." There was a gleam in his eye that stole my breath.

The hotel room was about what I expected. A king-sized bed dominated the room, opposite a wardrobe that concealed a TV and mini-bar. As soon as our luggage was in, he went to get ice for the champagne. I sank down to sit on the edge of the bed, undid the straps on my heels, and let my tired feet rest flat on the floor.

What the hell was this feeling in my stomach? Was I . . . nervous?

Things were different now, though. The revelation left me spinning. He'd only been in a relationship with one other person. Sure, he'd slept with way more people, but I'd had five times as many relationships as he had. Who exactly was the more inexperienced one now?

"I'm torn," I said when he returned with the bucket in hand, "on peeling that tuxedo off of you and making you leave it on."

All I got was a seductive smile. My insides quivered. Skilled fingers undid the foil and cage on the cork, then put a towel over the top and popped it.

"Not the first bottle of champagne you've opened, huh?"

He poured the bubbling liquid into a glass and offered it to me. "No, it's not."

It wasn't all that cold, but it still tasted divine. He poured himself a glass, but didn't join me on the bed. He leaned against the desk and took a few sips, watching me, curious.

"What is it?" I asked.

"I'm just wondering how much longer you're going to go without asking me about her. I'm impressed you haven't, but then again, I'm finding new, impressive qualities you've got every day."

It was both sweet and dirty. A compliment with a sexual skew on it.

"I told you that you can tell me what you want, when you want to."

His eyes warmed and then went serious. "April and I were together for so long, momentum took over. After we made it through the first year of college, we were stuck on a one-way street." He took a sip of his drink, but his focus never left mine. "Our families went on vacation together, everyone was pressuring us to get married, even though we already felt like we were married. We *fought* like we were married." He said it hesitantly. "I don't like to fail. I thought I could make it work."

My breath caught. I knew all about that.

"April wanted everything to stay the same. To live in the suburbs, to hang out with her family on the weekends. She likes to be in control, to have routines, to be organized.

Everything always her way."

"Uncompromising," I whispered.

He gave me a bitter half-smile. "When I took the job in the city, an hour commute each way, after she'd told me not to . . . She was furious. There was an ultimatum."

The memory spiked of how he'd said he didn't respond well to ultimatums. I felt like it was okay to ask, like he wanted me to. "Which was?"

"Get down on one knee or get the hell out of her life. I don't think she expected that to go the way it did. When it was over for me, it was *over*. I cut her completely out. Twelve years gone, like they meant nothing, and . . ." he struggled to finish, "that hurt us both."

I couldn't even imagine. I'd had a few bad breakups, but to burn twelve years? Both of them would carry scars from it.

He set his drink down and shrugged out of his jacket, hanging it in the open closet by the door. His fingers undid the tie at his neck, and then left it open when he returned to his champagne.

"Since we're doing all this sexy talk about exes," he said, "Can I ask about the guy at the club? The one who showed up at your place?

"I told you, he was never my boyfriend."

"But there's more there."

"Blake and I've been friends for years, and occasionally one of us would want more, and it always worked out that the other person was unavailable."

"He said he loved you and that you told him you loved him." His rich brown eyes evaluated me.

"I did, on New Year's Eve when I was wasted and lonely."

"Was it true?"

Why did it matter? "Maybe. Yeah, but it's not true

anymore. I think he only said it to stop me from going into the club."

"I'm glad he wasn't able to." Logan's face was intense and had a gravity I couldn't resist.

"Me, too."

He moved to the air conditioner and turned the temperature down so the unit kicked on, blowing cool air on us.

"You think it's warm in here?" I was kind of cold.

"I don't want to get you too hot again," he said. "And I'd like to take my time being highly inappropriate tonight, if that's all right with you."

I felt my face heat. "I'll allow it."

But he moved back to where he'd been leaning on the desk, rather than coming to me. "Good. Strip."

The temperature in the room rose. My breath quickened with his command. I stood on my feet and finished my champagne, setting it on the end table with a quiet thud. My hands went to the side of my dress and dragged the zipper pull down painfully slowly, my gaze fixed on his.

"The lights?" I was more curious than worried. The glass of champagne seemed to go straight to my head

"We'll leave them on."

I pulled the strap off my shoulder and the dress came down, exposing my bare breasts. I pushed it over my hips and it fell, the satin lining caressing me as it went. There was a steady rise and fall of his shoulders as his gaze wandered over my curves. I had on a simple pair of black cotton panties. Without a boyfriend for the last two years, sexy lingerie hadn't made the budget.

He went to the far side of the bed and pulled down the comforter so only the sheets were left before returning to his spot. "On the bed, now."

What did he have planned? I gathered the pillows up in a pile and sat on the cool sheets with the pillows at my back.

"I want to watch you touch yourself."

My breath caught. "You do, huh? Where?"

"Wherever you want."

I started with my breasts, because honestly, I knew he wanted a show. If this were for me, a private-alone-time kind of thing, I'd head straight downstairs. I filled my hands with the weight of my breasts, my nipples already tight and hard from the air conditioning and his inescapable gaze.

My fingers danced over the soft, bare skin, and I teased myself with a pinch, pulling the nipple away and letting it snap back. The eyes on me were heavy. I could feel every move they made, especially as they followed my hand that drifted lower. All the way down until it touched the black cotton.

He sat there, leaning on the desk and drinking the remainder of his drink casually as my fingers continued. I opened my legs wider, bending my knees as my hand explored. I stayed over the panties, rubbing myself until a moan broke free from my lips. I wanted this to be his hand touching me, not my own. But before I could say that—

"Pull them to the side. I want to see how wet you've made yourself."

I swallowed an enormous breath. His words were such a turn-on, was it possible I could get off just from the stuff he said? I wasn't wet from what I was doing, it was from his commands. My fingers hooked around the side and pulled the fabric away to expose myself to him.

He exhaled and made a sound of appreciation. "Take those off and make yourself come."

"What?"

"I want to see how you do it, so I know exactly how

you like it."

I didn't mind touching myself in front of him, but that? It was so *private*. "You know how I like it."

"I'm sure there's room for improvement."

I doubted it, but slipped my fingers under the waistband and took them off, dropping them over the side of the bed. I was totally naked for him. My knees fell to part when my fingers went down over my mound to touch were I was slick and hot.

It felt different when he was watching. The pads of my fingers rubbed and circled, sending pleasure sizzling across my nerves. I closed my eyes and enjoyed myself, listening to his heavy breathing over my own.

"Do you only use the one hand?" He asked it hushed, like he didn't want to disturb me.

I nodded, keeping my eyes closed. Oh my god, I was embarrassingly wet.

"Do you finger yourself or just rub your clit?"

"Why?" It was hard to focus when he asked me questions. "Are you taking notes?"

He chuckled, and then there was another noise as he shifted. I opened my eyes. He'd undone his pants and had a hand inside them, stroking himself, although I couldn't see.

"How is that fair?" I kept touching myself lazily. "You get to watch and I don't."

His long fingers unbuttoned his shirt. He removed it, hung it on the back of the chair, and then his pants were off, folded on top.

"I believe I'm naked, sir." I rose an eyebrow at the fact he'd left his boxers on. He grinned so widely that I froze. "What?"

"The last time you called me that was when you had a blindfold on. I liked it."

That wasn't surprising that he had liked it. That implied authority as if he were my master. He was anything but. Sure, I took commands from him, but I was smart enough to know I held plenty of power over him. He was touching himself because of what I was doing. My effect on him.

His boxers were yanked down and his dick sprang free, hard and straight, and he wrapped a firm grip around it.

"You're so fucking sexy," he said, his gaze fixed on my fingers that were stirring faster and faster, building in intensity. I moaned and relished the compliment. He stood and came to me, his hand on top of mine, stopping it so he could put his own hand there.

My moan of satisfaction turned to frustration when he stepped back. He'd run his hand between my legs to get it wet, to give himself lubrication as he jerked off.

"Logan."

"The sooner you show me, the sooner you can have me."

Well, if that wasn't motivation, I didn't know what was. I didn't normally use two hands, and the one stayed on the outside. It never felt as good as the real thing to me, but if it could speed me along, I was all for it. My other hand walked down to join the first, then further until I could insert my finger as deep inside me as it would go.

There was a sharp intake of breath. "Imagine that's my finger inside you."

"Why do I have to imagine?"

"Go at the pace you want me to fuck you." His hand slid back and forth on himself, his knuckles white.

I did as he told me, and lying there before him, doing something I'd never let anyone else truly see, I let go. I closed my eyes and imagined his finger inside me, taking me up and up, climbing closer to the peak.

"I could watch you do that all night."

No, he really fucking couldn't. Not after this morning.

"Oh god, I'm coming," I cried.

My hands moved furiously, fingers pumping in and out. My back arched, and I cried out and collapsed back into the pillows. My orgasm hadn't subsided before he was on the bed. He knelt between my legs and ran his dick on me, drenching himself in my orgasm. Then he pressed inside me, and the second orgasm, the one that piggybacks, roared into life with this sudden connection. I threw my hands around his shoulders and clung to him, convulsing. Pulsing. Throbbing.

He moved slowly, stroking me from the inside, prolonging the enormous pleasure until it ebbed.

"Not that I'm complaining," I whispered when I had my breath back, "but what about the raincheck?"

"Don't worry, we'll get there." His devious expression gave me another aftershock.

He grabbed a handful of pillows from behind me and tossed them aside, so I was flat on my back, him up on straightened arms. He moved, grinding his hips into mine. Electric shocks flashed through my sensitive body.

His handsome face had that seductive smile on it. "I want your hands."

I dragged them down his arms, loving the feel of the strong muscles beneath his flesh. He took my hands in his, lacing our fingers together, and pressed them above my head, holding them to the mattress. He leaned forward and brought our lips together.

My eyes would have gone wide if that was possible, but it wasn't. They closed under his silent command. Under the power of this kiss. Tonight, Logan wanted to make love.

He withdrew almost completely and then sank back into

my body, which welcomed his every gentle intrusion. I drew a line on his lips with my tongue, begging to taste him.

"Yes," I whimpered. "Yes."

He hadn't asked me a question, and yet I'd give him whatever he wanted. I shifted to meet him, eager. Drowning in my desire for him and in the passion of the moment. It'd never felt this good. It could have been hours or just minutes, I lost all track of time when his mouth was on mine and he was moving deep inside. I writhed beneath him. My soft cries of pleasure were muted by his unrelenting kiss.

He stilled and shifted over me, withdrawing and trailing kisses down my chest.

"Where are you going?" I demanded, even though it was obvious. I wasn't one to usually turn that down, but now? It was cruel torture to tease me with his lovemaking and take it away. His fingers spread me open to his intimate kiss, and I jerked up onto my elbows.

"Logan, please . . ." I cried. My hand curled under his chin to try to bring him back to me.

"You don't like this?" His deep voice rumbled from in between my thighs. He fucked me with his mouth, his tongue fluttering on my flesh and heat raced outward from it.

"Oh!" I moaned when he pressed his face into me, nuzzling me and causing me to collapse flat on my back. I was utterly conflicted. His mouth was indecent and, holy shit, I didn't want him to stop. Yet I worried that when he returned he'd change, he'd adopt a new style. He'd have a new way to satisfy me, and I didn't want that.

"Come back to me," I said in a breathy voice. "Make love to me."

He lifted his head in startled surprise, so I seized it and pulled him up. His hard body slid over mine. His wet lips returned to my lips, and he nudged me with his dick, slipping into me with a groan of pleasure.

In the pit of my stomach, desire tightened like a vise.

His hand was warm and tight on my hip and his other held my face to his kiss. Longing for each of us to reach our end poured out, seeping everywhere, blurring the lines for me. What I'd asked him to do was dangerous. The romance of the wedding, the glass of champagne . . . It all had a powerful, drugging, manipulating effect.

"Open your eyes." This demand from him sounded much like a plea.

His dark, beautiful eyes were hypnotic. I fought the swell of pleasure that threatened to consume. He eased a hand behind my knee and guided me to open my legs wider, to lift the knee high around his waist. It was so he could bend a knee, and the hand on my hip slid under my body, tilting me so I could feel everything. His chest dragged over my hardened nipples, edging me closer to overload.

"I can't stop thinking about you," he whispered, his eyes watching mine.

I stayed silent, unable to form thought. Every second I remained beneath him, fighting to drag air into my body and keep my eyes open, forced my climax closer and closer until I felt like it was on top of me and not him. The glide of his body in and out of mine became too much.

My skin was covered in goosebumps, but I wasn't cold. He'd set me on fire. Every inch of his skin covered my skin, and it was tingling the moment before my orgasm descended on me.

"Logan," I cried out, digging my nails into his flesh.

Oh, holy, fucking shit. The explosion inside my body rocked my foundation and threatened to tear me apart. He kept moving. Which meant the damn thing kept getting better and better, changing and intensifying.

He was hard as steel inside me while the tongue in my mouth was softer than velvet. Things were out of control now and I let it take over. I jolted in his arms and broke the kiss, moaning shamefully loud when I finally reached what I thought was the peak, until he jerked. His whole body seized, pouring into me in spurts, every one better than the last.

He slammed his lips over mine roughly, but I'm not sure who exactly he was trying to keep quiet, because he'd grown loud when I had, matching my intensity. He slid inside me so deeply on the final thrust it might have hurt, but I was too lost in ecstasy to care.

We lay still for a long time afterward, and I could feel his heartbeat slow to a normal rhythm with our chests pressed together. He rose onto an elbow and brushed my hair out of my eyes, then kissed me deeply.

"So, yeah . . ." he said. "That was the best orgasm of my life."

The corners of my mouth turned up in a smile. "I'm familiar with the feeling." I'd been cringe-worthy loud. "Please tell me none of your family is staying on this floor. Or in this hotel."

He laughed and rolled onto his side, folding me into his arms. "I'd tell you that you shouldn't have said my name, but I love it when you do. I love it even more when you're screaming it."

FIFTEEN

He woke me up by running his hands over my waist, down a hip, pushing the sheets out of his way. I was on my side, facing away from him.

"What time is it?" My voice was heavy with sleep.

"A little after nine."

"Did you already get up and run?"

"No," he said, spooning me. "It's a rest day." His hard dick pressed into me.

"I was resting," I murmured. "You don't feel like you want to rest."

He slid his dick between my thighs, nudging me. "I'm still in bed." He kissed my neck and his tongue worked upward until it traced the edge of my ear. His hand closed around my breast, massaging me before venturing down.

"Do you want me?" His fingers slipped in my folds.

It was a ridiculous question, of course I did. He knew it was true since I was already wet for him. "Yes."

There was little foreplay. He buried himself inside, taking me from behind. I laced my hands on top of his and clung to him as he held me, fucking me slowly. But this wasn't going to be lovemaking this morning, I could tell right away.

"I want you to be totally quiet when you come," he said.

He'd just told me last night that he loved it when I screamed his name, so . . . "Why?"

"In case I want to do something like this to you someplace public."

The shiver down my body flooded me with warmth. "Where?"

"Nowhere," he teased, "if you can't stay quiet."

It was like he threw himself into second gear, and I gasped. His hand, with mine still wrapped over it, moved so it could rub right above where we were joined.

"Ssh," he whispered. "You can be quieter."

I loved a challenge and forced myself to eat my moans of pleasure. When I was successful, he took it to third gear, and I squeezed down on the hand that touched me.

"Yes, Evie." His hushed words made me bite my lip. "I have to make you come hard to make sure we'd be safe to try it. What if I want to fuck you in the back seat of my car during your lunch break?"

Great. Now I was going to be turned on thinking about the parking garage beneath the office. I eased my grip on him, breathing heavy. His thrusts became harder, urgent, but he stayed quiet too. The slap of his skin against mine and the faint squeak of the mattress frame were the only noises over our labored breathing. I could tell he was close, because I was close.

"Are you going to be quiet for me?"

My eyes closed so I could focus. "Yes, sir," I said, knowing it wasn't exactly fighting fair by saying that.

He inhaled sharply, like he was mutually pleased and displeased. The hand was gone from me, and wet fingers shoved into my mouth. "Suck these off."

The dick flexed inside me when I closed my lips around them, tasting myself. I sucked on them hard, and the moan escaped my lips before I realized what happened.

"Come on, you're not even trying." The fingers returned to my clit, rubbing me furiously. Almost as furiously as he pounded into me.

I clutched at the sheets, clawing at them, finding something to cling to.

He took short, shallow breaths. "Better."

I pressed backward, meeting his thrusts while managing to stay silent. The desire swelled and sank its claws in, taking hold. I pressed my lips together and arched my back, my legs squeezing shut tightly so I could ride the orgasm with him deep inside. A whimper was the only sound I couldn't contain as he hurled me over the edge into bliss.

I was deathly quiet even when my insides were screaming.

"I knew you could do it. Now it's my turn," he said.

It only seemed fair to make it difficult for him. "Are you going to come hard in my pussy?"

"You know I will." His words rolled over my skin, sinful.

I needed something else. "Your cock feels so good inside me."

That only earned a slightly deeper breath. I'd have to find something even dirtier, and I went with the first thing that popped in. Something I should have thought about before it was out of my mouth.

"I want you to fuck me in the ass."

He froze. "Now?"

"Um . . ." I searched for a way to backtrack. Is that what I wanted? He'd certainly said he did yesterday, and I had liked what he'd done in the shower. There was a reason it had been the first thing to come to mind. I knew eventually I was going to let him have me there. I was going to want to try it. He was so good at everything else, how could he not be good at that? My lips trembled.

"If you want to, we . . . could try it," I said, and then held my breath while I waited for his response.

He resumed fucking me at a steady pace. "I do." His hand had moved to hold tight on my hip, and now it moved again, abandoning me. I glanced over my shoulder to see him slide his thumb in his mouth and then down behind my back. His hand parted my cheeks to touch me, his wet thumb probing.

"You want me to put my cock in here?" He put pressure on my asshole.

I tried to sound confident. "Yes."

His body shuddered beside me with anticipation. "I'm afraid this will have to do for now, you dirty girl." He slipped his thumb just inside. "I need to get a few things that might help. I want you to enjoy it your first time."

A mixture of relief and unexpected disappointment coursed through me. Just like signing the contract, once I had agreed to it, I'd gotten a thrill of excitement about doing something that should have made me terrified.

His dick continued to slam into me while his thumb penetrated further. I was crazy and frantic. He took huge gulps of air as his orgasm neared. The hand was gone from inside me. It grabbed my waist and yanked me back into him so the warm skin of his chest was against me. A quiet sigh came from him and then, as he came, he sank his teeth into the back of my neck.

Painfully. It made me gasp.

The teeth were gone instantly and his mouth moved over the bite mark I was sure he'd left there.

"Are you okay?" he said, quiet and strained. "I didn't mean to hurt you."

His arms went around me in an embrace, and I hooked my hands on his forearms. "I'm okay."

"Apparently you're better at that than I am."

"It seems like we both passed your test."

He turned me in his arms, revealing the amoral expression on his face. "You won't have to be quiet tonight."

"Tonight?" Good god, he was a machine.

His kiss drugged me. "Come over to my place for dinner. We'll try whatever you want to."

I swallowed a breath.

⌘

He dropped me off at my place, walking me to the front door of my apartment building. Such a gentleman, who had less than gentlemanly intentions for later. He wouldn't tell me what "supplies" he needed to get when I'd asked on the car ride back into the city.

As I fished my keys out of my purse, he put a hand on the small of my back.

"Evie." His voice was odd. Uneven. "Thanks for going with me yesterday."

I froze into a statue under his intense gaze. I'd never seen him look unsure before. His eyes drifted from mine to look vacantly through the glass entryway.

"It was hard seeing her again," he said. "But it would have been a lot worse if you weren't there."

"Oh." The keys in my hand stabbed me as I clenched them into a fist. It was shocking seeing him with his walls down, even just a little. "You're welcome."

Logan's admission flooded me with warmth, knowing I'd helped ease an uncomfortable situation.

His sincere eyes met mine. "I had a really good time."

"Me, too." It barely made it out of my mouth. He closed the distance between us and claimed me in a kiss that was full of passion. It was over too quickly, but I think that was his intent. To leave me hungry for more, to come back to him ready tonight.

"See you later," he said with a smirk.

I spent the afternoon paying bills and submitting bids on a freelance design website. Occasionally someone would accept my bid and I'd increase my income that month by a few hundred dollars. It was helpful in keeping my head above water.

At four, I decided to stop putting it off any longer. I flopped down on my worn couch and called Blake.

"I wasn't sure I was gonna hear from you again," he said. "I'm glad you called. I wanted to apologize, but I wasn't sure if calling you would make things worse."

"How are you?" I asked.

"I feel like a fucking idiot. I don't really remember a whole lot, except that I was beyond wasted, I made an ass out of myself, and . . . I think your boss was there?"

"My boyfriend," I corrected. "His name's Logan."

"Oh, yeah." The line was quiet for a moment. "Is he a good guy, Evie? Because—"

I sighed. "Don't get judge-y on me."

"I'm not. I want to make sure he deserves you." He sounded sincere.

"I think so. He . . ." I wasn't sure what kind of conversation I could have with Blake now. We used to feel comfortable talking about anything, and now it was painfully awkward. "I like him."

"Okay, well, that's good."

Calling him hadn't been a great idea. I struggled to find something else to say. "Where are you staying since you and Amy called it quits?"

It was deathly quiet. Had the call dropped out? I looked at the screen on my cellphone, and it said we were still connected. "Blake?"

"She took me back."

Oh, did she? I shouldn't have cared. I had a boyfriend I'd just spent the weekend having all kinds of sex with. Blake was my friend. Shouldn't I want him to be happy? Despite all that, it got under my skin.

"Oh." That was literally the only thing I could say.

It made me wonder what exactly she'd been told. If I'd found out the man I loved was running around telling another woman he loved her, I certainly wouldn't be taking him back. Maybe Amy was more forgiving and understanding than I was.

"I told her about New Year's Eve, and how I panicked outside that place and tried to stop you—"

My face heated with anger. "You told her what I did?"

"No, not really. I told her that you were doing something risky for money. She assumed it was like a medical thing."

"Great." The way Blake had described it, it also could have sounded like I'd taken up selling drugs.

"I told her how confused I was, and she said to leave and don't come back until I'd figured it out."

"So, you got sloppy drunk, came over, got rejected, and went back to her."

"No. I got sloppy drunk, came over, got rejected, and sobered up. Then I made my choice. I asked her to marry me."

Once again, I shouldn't have had the reaction I did, but shit, I'd been in love with him. My heart raced in my chest. "And she said?"

"No. Ask her again later, like she was a Magic 8 Ball, or something."

"Are you okay with that?"

"Yeah. I love her, Evie."

"Good." My voice was tight. "I've always liked her."

"Can you do me a favor and apologize to Logan for me? I can't remember if I took a swing at him, or if I just wanted to. I was a fucking mess that night."

Eventually the tension eased when we talked about other things, and he dropped the second bombshell on me; he'd called Payton and apologized for what he'd said outside the club. She'd failed to mention that to me when we'd gone dress shopping. Why?

We hung up and I lost track of time, and before I knew it, it was six. I was supposed to be at Logan's at six thirty and, what a shock, I was going to be late. I sent him a text, letting him know I was on my way from the back of a cab. I should have taken the bus, but this was faster.

My brain again felt like spaghetti. I'd woken up in Logan's arms this morning after making love last night, so why the hell was I thinking about Blake? As the cab turned off of Lake Shore Drive, I succumbed to my anxiety about what I'd offered this morning, and that cleared out my brain quick. The thrill and tension returned, wrapping its fingers around me until I was gripped tightly.

I knocked on his door, and it swung open a moment later. He was on the phone, but gave me a smile and stepped back to let me come in.

"Okay," he said to whomever he was talking to. "Evie just got here so I need to get off." His eyes were wicked with innuendo. "Yeah, will do." He said goodbye and hung up, shoving his phone into his back pocket. Hands rested on his hips and he glanced me up and down, curious.

"You changed clothes." There was playfulness in his words. "Why?"

What does someone wear on an occasion such as this?

Whatever it was, I did not own it. I knew because I had searched every inch of my closet. I'd changed into a pair of jeans and my black open-toed pumps with a black tank-top. Over that I had a sheer heather-gray shirt with an asymmetrical neckline that hung off of one shoulder.

"This kind of felt like a date," I said.

His eyes warmed and the corners of his mouth twitched into another smile. He hadn't changed from this morning, but he still looked damn good. The navy blue t-shirt hung close to his lean form, and below, faded jeans and bare feet.

"Are you ready to eat?" On the stove, a pot boiled, sending tendrils of steam into the air. The smell of garlic was faint but delicious.

"You cook, boss?" I had assumed we'd order out.

"I can make a few things that are edible, yes."

"It smells good. What is it?"

"Pasta."

"Okay." I set my purse down on the counter, which he picked up and put in the entryway closet. "You realize that pasta is a vague descriptor?"

"Pasta, with meat. Does that help?" His face was unreadable.

"I, like, have no idea if you're kidding. It's impossible to tell with you sometimes."

He smiled, amused. "Chicken pesto and penne pasta."

"I'm allergic to pine nuts."

His grin froze. "You are?" His gaze went to the skillet beside the boiling pot where I could see the chicken sautéing in the pesto sauce.

It was kind of fun to watch him derailed, but I didn't let it last too long. "No, not really."

Oh, I could see in his eyes that he both did and didn't

like that. He came to me and leaned in for a kiss, and at the last second pulled away, denying me.

He hadn't lied; the meal he'd cooked was good. It wasn't some special family recipe or anything crazy-fancy, but it was good. Of course it was. He seemed to be good at almost everything.

We chatted about random things, movies and music, discovering where we had similar tastes and teasing when we found the other person's likes didn't match our own. The sun's journey had brought it low in the sky, and the room was full of warm, amber-colored light.

I tried to help clean the dishes, but he'd rather do it himself. He was so particular. When the last item had been put away and his kitchen had returned to full order, he set his attention on me. The air in the room was thick and difficult to breathe.

"Did you," I asked on a hesitant voice, "get the supplies you needed?"

"Yes." He went to the freezer and pulled out a bottle of some sort of golden liquid, setting it on the counter.

Tequila.

"Seriously?" I asked, kind of annoyed.

He gave me an indecent look. One that said he wasn't joking. Two shot glasses appeared from somewhere, and there were lime wedges in a plastic bag pulled from the fridge.

"These are your supplies?"

"There are other supplies in my bedroom." His face was abruptly serious. "I think this will help you relax and like it, but . . ." He struggled to put what he wanted to say into words. "I don't want to take advantage of you. I don't want you to do something you don't want to, or just because you think I want to."

I stared at the bottle where condensation was already frosting the sides. I understood what he was saying. "Don't worry, boss. If I don't like it, you'll hear about it."

He unscrewed the cap and poured us each a shot. I picked it up in one hand and readied the lime in the other.

"Well then, bottoms up," he said, straight-faced.

I knocked mine back and bit into the lime, my eyes shut tight as the liquid burned down my throat. "Ugh."

He raised an eyebrow as he poured a second shot for me, amused at my lightweight, girly reaction.

"I should warn you, me and tequila usually aren't friends in the morning." I slammed the second one, making an even louder noise of disgust this time. "One more should do it," I said, holding out the glass for him to fill.

He took a breath like he was debating it, so I grabbed the bottle from him and poured it myself. The deep brown eyes studied me as I struggled to get the last one down without gagging.

I felt like I had to explain. "I don't like to fail either."

Hands were on my hips, drawing me close against his chest. "You can't fail at this, Evie. If it doesn't work out, it doesn't work out. That's all it would be."

His head bent so his lips could brush mine, and ignited the desire inside me like lighting a matchstick. I filled his mouth with my tongue, desperate to get started. But he could sense my anticipation, so of course he wanted to draw it out.

"Go into the bedroom." His command was on a hushed breath, but authoritative all the same. "Take off everything except for those shoes and wait for me on the bed." He feathered a kiss into the side of my neck. "Wait for me on your hands and knees."

His embrace was gone in an instant and I almost fell over.

He left me standing there with my mouth hanging open, so he could clean up the glasses and put his "supplies" away.

"Go, Evie," he said, firm.

SIXTEEN

My heart raced as my shoes clip-clopped their way into the bedroom. As I stared at the bed, nervous waves traveled through me. I could do this. The tequila would help me through. I pulled both shirts over my head at the same time and cast them on the chair in the corner, the one I had hoped to interrogate him from a week ago. My clothes came off quickly; shedding them was easier than my trepidation. I slipped the shoes back on once my jeans were removed.

I walked across the bed on my hands and knees, unsure of what to do now. He hadn't given me any directions other than to wait. I positioned myself so when he came in, he'd see my round cheeks waiting for him, and so I could look out the window. The rose-colored light bounced off the nearby, shorter buildings, reflecting the sunset on the water of Lake Michigan.

I waited.

And waited.

There was no sound from the other room, forcing me to think about what was going to happen when he finally came in. Would we go straight to it or would we mess around first? He'd said he had more supplies in here, but the tops of his dresser and nightstand were bare.

As I waited, I got tipsy off of the tequila and the situation. Totally naked, well, other than the shoes, waiting for him like a servant. It made me insane and needy and so fucking turned on.

"Logan," I said, loudly. "Are we going to do this or what?"

Bare feet. I'd forgotten that without shoes on, he could move around without making much noise. He set his palms on my hips and drew me backward. Backward onto his face.

"Oh, shit," I mumbled. His tongue licked me, circling where I was swollen and aching for him.

"Your pussy tastes even better than it looks." His intimate kiss was invasive and mind-numbing. More. I wanted more. The tequila was kicking in now, and I rocked my hips against his face, positioning myself exactly how I wanted it.

"Do you want to see the other supplies I bought today?" As soon as the words were out of his mouth it returned to me, fucking me.

"Not if you have to stop doing what you're doing," I moaned.

There was a chuckle, the same half-laugh I'd heard when I called him sir at the club. A drawer squeaked open and he rummaged around, but his mouth stayed on me, thank god. I was getting close to my first of what I hoped would be several orgasms tonight when he started tossing items down on the bed beside me.

A bottle of lube. Batteries. A simple white vibrator still in its plastic package.

Leather handcuffs.

"We don't have to use all or any of it, if you don't want to."

My brain was foggy with lust. All I could focus on was the tongue lashing at me, the mouth sucking at the knot between my legs. His hot mouth made its journey to the back, and I exhaled loudly.

"Do you own a vibrator?" The tongue slipped down, plunging into my entrance.

"I haven't had a boyfriend in two years," I said, "and I

live alone. I could have just brought mine."

"Maybe I want you to have your own here, so I can use it on you whenever I want."

In my drunkenness, I laughed. That's the kind of relationship we had; I'd have a spare vibrator at his place before I had a spare toothbrush. As soon as the laugh was out, he eased a finger inside me and I grew serious. The finger moved deliberately and unhurried, even as I writhed on the bed, eager to find release that was only a breath away.

"Shit, don't stop," I said. It was crazy the command he held over my body.

Why the hell did I say anything? Of course he did exactly what I didn't want him to do. His hand was gone and I heard him straighten.

"Get over here. I'm going to fuck that dirty mouth you've got."

I turned over my shoulder to see the dark, nasty expression that waited for me. I scrambled over the bed and rose onto my knees. My hands flew to his belt buckle and hurried to undo it, and then the fly of his jeans. He didn't help me. Instead he shed his shirt. His hands pulled me from the bed. A second later the jeans and boxers were bunched at his ankles.

"On your knees," he ordered in a dark, powerful voice.

In a second, my knees were buried on the plush carpet. I would only allow him to do this. To put his hand on my head and push me toward his crotch, demanding I give him pleasure. Fuck, it was hot. I opened my mouth and took the damp head of his dick inside, rolling my tongue over the ridge. I slipped it in further, sucking until my cheeks hollowed out.

"Look at me when you're sucking my cock."

I shuddered at his words and obeyed, opening my eyes to look up at his handsome face—

The hand not holding my hair back was holding his cellphone.

I drew my mouth away. "What are you doing?" Although it was obvious he was taking video.

"Do you have any idea how fucking hot it is watching you go down on me?"

The brown eyes left the small screen in his hand to lock onto my gaze. If I had a problem with it, he expected me to say so now. Maybe if I'd had less to drink I might have cared, but I didn't. I could always make him delete it when I sobered up, and the idea of this video in his phone . . . I liked it.

I locked a firm grip on the part of him that had no hope of fitting in my mouth, flicked my gaze back up to him, and tried to give the greatest blowjob I'd ever given.

"Fuck, yes. You like the way that cock tastes?" he groaned, glancing at the screen and back to me. I moaned my approval. Once again, I put on a show. I shifted angles, I tried to keep my hair out of the way, and I ran my tongue down the length of him. Then I opened to his magnificent dick and let him pump it in and out of my mouth.

"You're so gorgeous with your lips wrapped around my dick."

I sucked at the soft skin covering a steel bar of flesh. He was doing surprisingly well, or else my inebriation made me sloppy, because he didn't stop me or seem to get all that close like he usually did. Perhaps the phone had him distracted. "I'm going to fuck that pussy, Evie. And then I'm going to fuck that ass."

I moaned again, his dick vibrating in my mouth. There was a mechanical chime, signaling the video was shut off and he tossed his phone onto the bed, where it slid to a stop near the center. This meant he had plans of using it again, otherwise he would have put it on the dresser where it would have been safer, but out of reach.

His hands hauled me up to stand and our kiss was raw and wild, driving our naked bodies together. He felt hard in all the right places, and my hands were drawn to him like a magnet. I wasn't allowed to explore for very long. Rough hands turned me and shoved me down so I was bent over, face down in the bed. I was nervous and excited when his hand closed around my wrist and pulled it gently behind my back. Breath came and went in shallow bursts.

"Are you interested in these?" he asked. His naked body pressed against me, skin against skin. He had my wrist held in one hand, and the black leather cuffs with a metal clasp connecting them in his other. I fought against my desire and aching need, forcing myself to focus on his question. I liked being restrained; the night at the club had shown me that. But what about—

His breath was warm, washing over me. "We'll take them off before we get to the new stuff."

I nodded a wobbly head. "I'm game, boss."

He loosened the buckle on the leather and eased my hand inside and then closed it tight. When he reached for my other wrist, I moved away. His eyes went wide with concern, thinking I was scared or had changed my mind, but then he saw the teasing smile on my lips.

His hand captured my wrist easily, buckling it roughly. Then it was done. My arms were secured behind my back. I arched up off the mattress, stretching my arms behind me to touch him, but as soon as my fingers touched skin, he put a hand on my shoulder and pushed down gently. With nothing to stop me, I fell forward onto my stomach.

"Stay just like that, naughty girl."

His long fingers grabbed the batteries and packaged vibrator, and I had to lift my head and turn it the other direction to see him disappear out the bedroom doorway. It was a nice view of his naked ass, but it was gone before I could fully appreciate it.

A drawer opened. There was the sound of plastic being cut open, followed by the faucet running. His large frame reappeared in the doorway, sliding batteries into the vibrator and screwing the cap back on. With a turn of his wrist, I heard the soft hum as he tested it and then turned it back off, satisfied.

It wasn't very long or thick. Logan was calculating and he'd selected this vibrator for a reason. Maybe he didn't want me to get addicted to it, to make sure his dick was more impressive and I'd crave it over the vibrator. If that was his reason, it was ridiculous. How on earth could I ever want a piece of plastic over him?

The vibrator fell onto the comforter beside me, and he set his palms on my shoulders. Warm, damp hands trailed down my biceps, past my elbows, down until they were on the cuffs. Further, onto my ass. Down the backs of my thighs, and knees. This gentle touching, seemingly innocent while I was cuffed and waiting for him to please me, was making me insane.

"Fuck me," I said, edged with desperation.

He feigned reluctance. "Oh, all right."

His dick pressed against my entrance, stretching me as he intruded. I exhaled loudly. "It feels so good."

"When I'm inside you?" He pushed deeper until he was buried as far as he could go. "I agree."

The orgasm that had threatened before lurked in the shadows, and when he established a casual tempo to fuck me, the orgasm stepped onto the scene. It almost kept me from noticing he'd picked up his phone and started recording again.

I was going to have to watch the video at some point. The concept of him sliding his dick in and out of me while my hands were pinned behind my back . . . Hot. His hips thrust into me faster, slamming against my rear and beckoning the orgasm to come closer.

"Logan," I cried out.

"Come for me. Come on my cock."

"I'm . . . coming, oh shit." Pleasure slammed into me with each of his relentless thrusts. The alcohol lowered my inhibitions enough that I didn't care how loud I was being or the fact that he was videoing such a powerful orgasm.

Eventually he slowed to a halt, but it had nothing to do with letting me recover and everything to do with the bottle of lube he scooped up, not breaking our connection. My heart raced, pounding like a hammer in my chest.

"Let's see how you like my supplies," he said. The phone landed with a soft thump up on his pillow, and I turned over my shoulder to watch him uncap the small clear bottle with a baby blue top. He held it high over me, letting it drip . . . Drip . . . Drip . . . and it ran down my crack.

"Oh my god," I murmured into the comforter. My cheek flattened the fabric beneath it and I shut my eyes, enjoying the sensation. Holy shit. He returned to fucking me, and the lube continues it slow, silky, wet path down between us, and further down between my thighs.

The only downside was it made a rather unsexy suction noise, but it was interrupted moments later by a hum. His arms were around me, one hand exploring the bare skin just in front of our union, and the other bringing the vibrator closer until he could set it against me. The vibration teasing my skin was sinful. My whole body sang.

"Oh my god," I repeated. My brain emptied and I couldn't find anything else to say.

"You seem to like that. But what if I do this?"

The vibration began to travel. It drew a path over my hip, around the curve of my body until it was barely below the small of my back. He traced the tip of it down between my cheeks, using a hand to pull one to the side.

My breath caught in my throat. That was why he'd bought a small one. He wanted to use it *there*. He circled the rosy ring between my cheeks, my whole body vibrating.

"Do you want the handcuffs off?"

Already my arms were beginning to feel uncomfortable, but I shook my head, unable to speak. Anticipation made it impossible. He stayed inside me, unbelievably hard but unmoving. I closed my eyes shut tight, and felt pressure. More pressure and the burning sensation that was becoming familiar from the times he'd crept inside. I bit my lip. My body wanted to push back against it, to expel the intrusion. Yet the indecent side of my brain whispered to wait. To let him show me something new.

"How much is it in?" I asked.

"About an inch."

What? It felt like a foot. He pushed a little further, and I inhaled a deep breath.

"Does it feel better when I do this?" He began to move it back and forth, easing it almost out and then in.

"No, not—"

Wait a minute. My body stopped fighting as much with the movement, and as the vibrator gained ground, so did the concept that this could be pleasurable. "That's . . . it kind of feels good."

"Do you want me to go deeper?"

I could do this. Hell, I could like this. Every small pass he made was more enjoyable than the last. "Yeah."

It continued like this, an inch at a time until he had worked all five inches in and out of my ass. He didn't move fast, and he watched me intently for any signal to stop. I wasn't going to stop him. The complete fullness in my body wasn't like anything I'd experienced before.

"Do you like it?" His voice was a whisper.

"I . . . do."

"Good."

Ever so slowly, he withdrew his hard dick from within me, like he wanted me to focus on the vibrator alone. It continued to move. Continued to feel better and better. He knelt behind me, his mouth working its way up the back of my thigh until it was buried in my pussy.

I sighed at the feel of his tongue parting my lips, and the sigh increased to a moan when he increased the tempo. Each stroke in and out, every pass of his tongue catapulted me closer to going over the edge. If the vibrator felt this good, what about him inside me? Plus, I wanted him to get equal pleasure from what we were doing.

He could tell I was close and must have read my mind. "Is this enough for tonight? Or do you want to try it?"

"Let's keep going," I blurted out.

SEVENTEEN

The mouth left me and the vibrator turned off, but stayed deep inside me. I heard him stand, and when he went to the nightstand, I saw him wipe my arousal off of his lips. What was he doing? He opened the nightstand drawer and retrieved a condom.

"Why do you need that?"

In the fading light, he looked glorious. Delicious. I blinked my sluggish, tipsy eyes at him when he picked up his phone and snapped a picture. Naked in high heels, handcuffed and a vibrator inside me. The phone fell back onto the bed, ignored as he opened the condom and rolled it on, disappearing behind me.

"I'm going to need all the help I can get lasting." The words came out slightly embarrassed.

He set one hand on the small of my back. The vibrator retreated, and I scrunched my face in displeasure, not enjoying the moment it was pulled out. The hand on me moved to my wrist. The clasp holding the handcuffs together clicked and the tension was gone as he released me.

I walked my trembling hands forward over the soft, satiny fabric of his comforter, stretching them out in front of me. Needles danced over my skin as feeling returned to my arms. His skin was against mine from my backside all the way up to my shoulders; his body enveloped mine. What? Was he shaking?

I shot up on my elbows, turning to look at him.

"What's wrong?"

The eyes watching me were full of concern. "I don't want to hurt you. You have to tell me to stop if that happens. Not like the shower."

I softened, reached a hand behind his head and pulled it close to mine. "You won't hurt me." I kissed him tenderly and he answered it back. And then I let the tequila take control for a moment. "Now stop being a pussy and do it."

I don't know what kind of reaction I was hoping for, but there wasn't one. Like this moment wasn't playful and he wasn't going to rise to the bait. His fingers trailed down my back, through my cheeks where I was slippery, and when they found what they were looking for, his sheathed dick was right there.

"Ready?" he asked, hushed.

I nodded. He nudged, pressing into me. But everything was so tense, and I was trying so hard not to shake apart, that I wasn't allowing him a chance to enter.

"Take a deep breath," he whispered.

When I did as asked, he moved at me more aggressively, pushing much harder, and—

"Fuck!" I spat out, fire and stabbing pain were he'd gained entrance. My jaw tightened and my hands gathered loose fabric up, clenching it into fists. My body was not pleased, but I kept a lid on it.

"It'll feel better when I start moving," he said.

"Then start moving," I groaned through my clenched teeth.

"I have to get deeper to do that."

My discomfort made me short-tempered. "Then do that, but go slow."

Technically, I'd just asked for it, but his dick moved further inside and I tried to get away. The bed kept me from moving off of him and he gained further. The burning and stretching was bad. He was too big. I was going to fail at this, just like I'd thought. How could someone find this remotely enjoyable?

I was a heartbeat away from telling him to stop, when he retracted a tiny bit and then eased back in. Like with the vibrator, his movement calmed the resistance.

In.

And out.

In, deeper this time.

"Fuck, Evie, fuck . . ." The pleasure-soaked words spilled from his mouth, and it distracted me from my discomfort further. He liked it. Knowing I gave him pleasure was such a turn-on, just like when I went down on him. His hands kneaded my flesh beneath them.

One slow thrust at a time, displeasure faded and gave way to a new sensation. Enjoyment. Satisfaction. I wasn't failing. Every movement was success, a little victory, and that allowed me to start to find pleasure. It was taboo and forbidden, and I was doing it.

"Does it hurt?" he asked.

"No." It wasn't a lie, it didn't hurt now.

He sighed, his body relaxing as it was flooded with what I assumed was relief. "Can you take a little more?"

More? I reached a hand behind me and my breath left in a frustrated burst. He was barely inside. How was that even possible?

"Okay," the tequila said. "But I kind of wish you weren't so big right now."

Apparently he was not in the mood to joke, because he froze. "You want me to stop?"

"No, no." I leaned back into him, letting it slip further

inside. "Don't stop."

His hips resumed their deliberate movement. I let my cheek press into the comforter, my eyes falling closed, trying to find the pleasure when he invaded deeper still. Since my eyes where shut, I didn't see him pick the vibrator up or reach it around my body so he could hold it against my clit. It was the low buzzing and the sensation against my slick skin that made my eyes pop open.

Turning up the dial on the vibrator was like turning up the dial on my desire. My stuttering breath increased until I was panting.

"Mmmm . . ." I mumbled into the comforter. It felt good. My attention was on the tingling in between my legs, not so much on the intrusion, but that was starting to feel good too.

"You like that? When I put it here?"

I wasn't sure what he was asking about specifically, but it didn't really matter. At this point it was a definite yes to both the vibrator and his huge dick inside my ass.

"Yes, sir."

He hunched over me, the hand not holding the teasing vibrator was strong on my shoulder, holding on. His lips were on the back of my neck, leaving wet, open-mouthed kisses there between his own labored breaths.

"Are you close?" he whispered.

"Close to coming?" My voice was dubious. "Sorry, no." The buzzing picked up in frequency, and I groaned; he'd just brought it much closer. But I wanted him to enjoy it, and he was still moving so hesitant and timid. "You can go faster if you want to."

Oh my god, he did.

"Holy shit," I gasped. "That feels good."

Saying that only made him go faster and deeper, until

I felt his hips steadily against the skin of my ass. He'd made it all the way inside. I started to writhe, to push back into him. The vibrator stayed firm on me, tormenting me wickedly, hinting that immense pleasure was soon to arrive.

"You like my big cock in your ass?" he asked.

Yes, the filthiest part of me chanted. Yes. I tried to nod, unable to speak.

"Yeah, you like it, dirty girl," the playful tone had returned to his voice, "but I'm about to make you fucking love it."

Abruptly the vibrator was turned all the way up. And then he truly started to fuck me. It wasn't near as fast as I knew he could go, but it was a furious tempo nonetheless, and I cried out at the sensation. Everything from my waist down was in bliss, singing, begging for release. Overload.

"Oh shit, oh shit, oh shit . . . Logan, I'm coming!"

I clasped each hand over his, one on my shoulder and the other between my legs as I fell overboard. I was drowning in the orgasm, shuddering and flailing involuntarily with delight. He dropped the vibrator and it landed buzzing and rattling on the carpet. He shot up and his hands ensnared my waist, holding me as he went faster still.

"Evie . . . fuck, I'm gonna come." Listening to him was so erotic. The deep, sharp breaths. His groan. The final, long sigh after he'd slowed to a stop, where he seemed to pull himself back together. He slid out of me completely and moments later the buzzing was silenced.

I lay there, still face-down and bent on the bed, unable to move.

"Are you okay?" His hands gently clasped my arms, turning me to sit up.

"Yeah." I could see the worry in his deep eyes and wanted it gone. "That was . . . intense. I liked it a lot, but it was intense."

Of course, it was nothing compared to his kiss. Just the gentle caress of his mouth, his tongue tasting me. I let him wrap his arms around me and hold me with his lips still tight against mine. Seconds later I was floating. No, wait. He was carrying me.

"You let me know if the water's too hot this time," he said as he made his way to the bathroom.

I had to brace a hand against the wall when he set me down beside the shower, trying not to sway as he undid the cuffs on my wrists.

"Next time, we both get drunk," I mumbled. It was weird to be buzzed and loopy while he was sober.

His grin was epic. "Already thinking about next time?"

"Not what I meant." I stepped into the shower, and he followed after I heard the lid on his garbage can fall shut.

I cranked the water temperature up since it was lukewarm, and did my best to keep my face out of the water, but he didn't pay attention. I was wrapped in his arms under the stream of water, and I wiped at my eyes, desperate to not end up with oh-so-attractive raccoon eyes.

He gave me a puzzled look.

"I had makeup on, you know. It's probably all under my eyes now."

He stilled my hands and gave me a quick look. "You're fine."

Wow, be still, my beating heart. Logan Stone thinks you look fine. Satisfactory. "Thanks," I muttered.

He bent his head so he could brush his lips on my cheek just beside my ear. "Are you aware that you are the most beautiful woman I've ever seen?"

I laughed. Ridiculous.

"You don't believe me?"

"No, I don't." Did he not remember I'd met his ex, the gorgeous blonde who could be a Victoria's Secret model for all I knew? Did he not remember meeting Payton? Or Tara?

"I told you that I thought you were beautiful the first time we were together, when you still had the blindfold on." He'd told me then, even after he'd paid for me, so there had been no need for him to lie. "When I came in and you were there on that table . . ." He closed his eyes at the memory, and Tara's words returned to me. *You should have seen his face when he came into the room and saw you.*

"Even if you have makeup running down your face," he said, "which you don't, you're still fucking gorgeous to me."

I swayed. Or maybe swooned since I was also drunk. He held me firmly, his eyes confused by my reaction.

"You gave me the tequila, boss." I was going to blame it on that, though it had been his words that made my legs go boneless.

He smiled. "Yeah, and I don't expect to hear you calling in sick with a hangover tomorrow." Another half-joke, half-truth. His fingers followed the trail of water down my back.

"It was three shots, I'll be fine."

"Glad to hear it."

We took our time in the shower. Our bodies were slippery with soap and water, and hands roamed freely, exploring. But it was more about being intimate, rather than trying to arouse each other into another session. After, we dried off, dropped our towels at the edge of the bed, and curled up under the sheets.

"Do you want to stay the night?"

I was tired, and still kind of drunk, but if I slept here, I'd have to go home at the crack of dawn to get ready for work. "I do, but I can't."

"I figured." He sounded disappointed. "I'll drive you home." He hugged me to him. "In a minute or two." I don't think either of us wanted to move.

⌘

On Monday, I didn't see him until the afternoon critique meeting. I followed the herd of designers into the darkened conference room and climbed the aisle of stairs between the tiered tables, filing into a row halfway up. Logan was in the back with his MacBook hooked up to the projector.

Our eyes met for a moment and that was all. His expression didn't change, and I did my best to follow suit. I tried to remember how I'd felt two weeks ago, waiting for him in this room. Indifferent. Annoyed. I had no hope of returning to that mindset.

My feelings for him were strong and disorienting. I kept my eyes fixed on the projection of his desktop and listened to his deep voice behind me. Hearing and not seeing him put non-work related thoughts in my head.

The first slide pulled up – a textured background and angled font with a forced perspective. It was interesting. My eye followed the path down through the brochure just as she'd intended. Critique was anonymous, but we knew each other's work. Kathleen. Her stuff was always strong, and occasionally it was great. She'd been one of the senior designers Logan had beaten out for the promotion.

Kathleen was in her late thirties. She worked hard when she was "on the clock," but when that 5:00 p.m. displayed in the top right corner of her computer screen, it was officially her time. Didn't matter if the client was waiting on a rush proof. She didn't have the drive to go above and beyond.

Logan did. He was like me, anxious to succeed.

Competition was encouraged in the workplace because he wanted to be the manager of the best department in the company.

Was he aware how good he was, outside of the office, in my eyes? It reminded me of the moment I'd complimented his artwork hanging over the couch, the car ad he'd done a while ago. How his expression had softened and he'd come undone. What would be his reaction if I someday told him I was falling for him?

"This is strong work," Logan said. "I'd like to see the same flow mirrored on the back."

Some people didn't attempt to be subtle. Heads turned back to look at Logan, and then on to Kathleen, like they expected her to faint from shock.

A new image filled the screen. An ad for an upcoming wedding expo with the magenta text shaped in the silhouette of a bride, placed on a pale pink background. It was hard to read.

"I appreciate the idea, but this isn't working. It needs an eye-catching photo as the focus to draw us in and make us commit to reading all that text."

I had to remind myself to breathe. This was the exact type of ad Logan would eviscerate. Should have eviscerated. It wasn't good, and not good meant awful to him. Yet, he restrained himself. People's thoughts were loud on their faces. *"Who is this person who looks like Logan, but obviously isn't?"* The next slide was full of drop shadows, and I gripped the edge of the desk tightly. Maybe he'd been saving up his energy to lay into Jamie.

"This is dated and cluttered. Remove the shadows and let the elements breathe. Try an understated take on this."

He moved on, continuing his critique, and it barely

registered when my GoodFoods rebrand package was up for review. I jotted down a note about making it more approachable with less of a hipster feel. The screen went black and there was a soft thump as his laptop shut.

"Any questions?" he asked.

We sat with our butts glued to the seats, stunned.

"If anyone wants to discuss feedback with me, my door is open."

My gaze followed him when he collected his things and moved down the aisle, ending the meeting.

The room erupted in discussion thirty seconds later.

"Did he make an adjustment in his meds?" Gary asked no one in particular.

"This is a joke," Becca said. "We're going to get back to our desks and find out we've all been let go."

Maybe I'd have to tell him to dial it back a little, to ease his way into the constructive critiques. No, wait a minute. This was their problem, not his. His attempt had been perfect.

"Who worked with you on the GoodFoods account?" Kathleen asked me when I came to my feet and pushed in my chair.

"I'm actually handling it on my own right now."

Her jaw set. "Oh, I didn't hear you'd gotten promoted," she said, rather loudly. She knew that I hadn't, and did her best to make sure everyone else knew.

"Not yet." My phone chimed with a text message. From him.

How was that?

I breezed down the hall back toward my cube, barely able to contain my grin.

Perfect.

EIGHTEEN

During the Sunday of Labor Day weekend, Logan drove us out to my parents' house for dinner. It had been four weeks since the night he'd taken off my blindfold and turned my world completely upside-down. The honeymoon phase of our relationship was in full swing, and I was ashamed to admit we'd been neglecting everyone else.

My mother warned that every day she went without meeting Logan would mean more embarrassing marching band and family vacation pictures would surface when that meeting finally happened. It was one of the disadvantages of being an only child; I received one hundred percent of the parental focus. I had to stop her before it escalated to the horrible curling-iron bangs of seventh grade. That was a picture he wouldn't be able to unsee.

"Arlington Heights?" my father repeated, after asking Logan where he was from. "Tell me you're a south-side fan, though."

"I was raised as a right-thinking American, so no." Logan's face was stoic. My father looked at him like I often did. Unsure if that was a joke or not. The corners of Logan's lips twisted upward into a half-smile. Ah, yes. A joke.

My parents still lived in the same two-bedroom house on the outside of Tinley Park, a south suburb of the city. Coming home with Logan was wonderful but odd as my old life collided with my new one. My mother's eyes were glued to the front window when we pulled up in his BMW, and I think she almost fainted when he opened the door for me.

Like with his family, we skirted around the truth of how we began dating. Logan asked me out to dinner, which wasn't a lie— it had happened, but it was after a rather illegal and sordid transaction.

"Oh my goodness, he's crazy about you," my mother whispered in the kitchen while I scooped ice cream on top of the brownies she was plating. "Whatever you're doing, keep doing it."

My hand slipped on the ice cream scooper and went right into the tub, but thankfully went unnoticed by her. I carried the dishes out onto the cement slab patio I'd spent countless hours decorating with colored chalk in my youth, where now my father and boyfriend were discussing politics.

Logan leaned back in his seat and had one arm slung over the back of my empty chair, as if waiting for me. So casual and comfortable, like we'd been together forever.

Yeah, I was so completely in love with him.

When it was time to say goodbye, I was certain my mother was too. She hugged him for an awkwardly long time, but he played it cool. He took my father's offered handshake, the leftover brownies from my mother, and led me down the front steps to his car.

"I like them," he said, sincere, as he pulled out of the subdivision.

"Good. They certainly like you. And I . . ." I said, unable to contain it, "I love you."

His hand tightened on the steering wheel. "You what?"

There was no reaction other than his flat voice. *Oh, no.* What had I done?

When I didn't repeat it, he yanked the steering wheel hard and to the right, so he could turn off the road into the nearest parking lot, and pull in to one of the vacant spots. He threw the gearshift into park and gave me a hard look, his face like stone. I couldn't breathe. My heart stopped beating. I should have kept my stupid mouth shut.

Hands seized my face, gripping it and pulling me in so he could slam his lips on mine. I wanted to melt into the kiss. I wanted the gearshift gone from in between us. There was the sound of his seatbelt unbuckling. The hands trapping my face tightened further, asking for more.

I was more than willing, but . . .

"Logan," I mumbled against his frantic lips, "we can't have sex in the parking lot of a Seven-Eleven."

"I don't remember suggesting that."

"You have to stop."

"Stop what?"

"Kissing me. Touching me, or I'm going to need to have sex with you. Not want, but need."

It was twilight outside, and a mischievous smile flashed across his face, made sexier by the soft light. Like he was thinking about continuing just to see if I'd make good on my threat. But instead he eased up, giving me a gentle, tender kiss.

"All right." His voice was reluctant. "I will stop kissing you now, but I want you to know you started this . . . and I plan on finishing it soon."

It took forever to find a parking space at my place, only increasing the anticipation. He took my keys from me and unlocked my door when I fumbled. I hadn't expected to come back to my place tonight. We were due to meet his friends for drinks, and I assumed after that I'd spend the night at his place. So I hadn't cleaned. He tripped over a pair of heels I'd left in the pathway to the living area.

"Sorry, I didn't think I was going to have company," I

said, taking my keys back from him. There was a pile of clothes on the couch, and he blinked at it. I think it bothered him. I scooped them up and hurried to the closet.

"What are you doing?"

"Cleaning up." I heaved the clothes onto my bed.

"I don't care about that. I don't care about anything right now," he said, his eyes pinning mine, "except hearing you say it again."

All motion ceased and my breath caught, but I was still able to speak. "I love you, Logan."

He was devastatingly beautiful when his eyes filled with love, but they clouded with concern a moment later. "You mean a lot to me, but I'm not sure I'm ready to say that back. Not just yet."

Twelve years echoed in my mind. He was bound to be cautious with his heart. "You'll say it when you're ready. I'm okay with that." I gave him a soft smile, one I hoped conveyed that I understood.

He crossed the room toward me, and I attempted to meet him in the middle, but he lifted me up and carried me backward into the closet, ducking his head under the shelf once we were inside. I hadn't thought through dumping the pile of clothes here on my bed. Now I was on my back on top of them. We both took a moment to push them out of our way and clear space, sending pants and skirts tumbling to the floor. I had a feeling we were going to need every inch of my teenage-sized bed.

Usually I liked being undressed by him, but we both shed our clothes until I was left only in my panties and he was completely naked and on top of me. I wrapped my hands around his warm shoulders, and he pressed the length of himself against me at the same moment he pressed his lips to mine.

We were only a heartbeat away from having sex. He nudged me again, teasing my body through the thin cotton of my panties, and he slipped his tongue into my mouth. I don't think foreplay was on the agenda, and . . . good. I wanted him terribly. I wanted to tell him I loved him while he was moving inside me. My hand drifted down and pulled my panties to the side, guiding him.

God, I loved the sensation when he entered me for the first time, and he fit so perfectly now. It made me mad that he hadn't pursued me sooner. We'd potentially missed out on two years of this. But lord knew I couldn't be mad at him, not when he eased in and out of me, going deep and then pulling almost all the way out, only to plunge back inside.

"I'm never going to get enough of this," he whispered, his head burrowed in the crook of my neck. "Never going to get enough of you."

My eyes fell closed and hot tears stung there, but I held them back. I didn't care that the sides of the bed were scraping against the closet, or that he sent my knee banging into the wall with every thrust. Listening to him, feeling him inside me, connecting with the man I loved. That was what mattered.

I couldn't get enough of kissing him or having my hands on him. I raked one through his hair while his lips skimmed my collarbone. Abruptly he pulled out and stepped back off the bed, and frantic hands yanked my panties down my legs. It was impressive how swiftly he could move. His weight returned to the bed, but he curled beside me, placing my leg over his legs. I was lying on my back and him on his side when he entered me again, his intense eyes watching my expression.

"Oh my god," I whispered. At this angle, he could easily dip his head to lick my breast, which he did. I was right on the edge of an orgasm. The scent of his cologne was all around me, and his hands. . . oh god, his hands. They held me tightly to him.

"I love you." It came from me quiet, but full of emotion.

"Then come for me," he whispered. We'd returned to our games of asking for permission.

"Come with me," I begged.

The weight of our feelings pressed down and hurled us together toward oblivion. For the first time he went before I did, and it triggered my orgasm. His pleasure filled me with pleasure and became mine. Lying beside him was bliss. I didn't want to leave this perfect moment.

He seemed content to stay as he was too. That is, until his phone, still in the pocket of his pants on the floor, chirped with a text message. Lips trailed over my shoulder.

"We should put clothes on or we're going to be late."

"I'm always late," I muttered. The greedy selfishness inside me whined. Couldn't we just have a few more quiet minutes together?

"I noticed. I can help with that, you know."

"Oh, really, boss?"

"Yeah." He propped himself up on an elbow, and his eyes were inky in the shadows of my dimly lit closet. "I can set all your clocks ten minutes fast, or you can start staying at my place more often. This bed isn't good for us long-term."

Long-term. I understood what he was implying. "I like option number two."

⌘

After drinks with his friends, I crashed at his place, but

I woke up alone. Logan had his longest run before the marathon planned for this morning, which meant he'd be gone for a while. The alarm clock had buzzed long ago, and he'd risen, moving silently to the closet to get dressed, and then out the door.

I sat up now, evaluating the room critically. I went into the meticulously organized closet with suits on the left and casual clothes on the right. My haphazard closet must have made him crazy.

After a shower, I cinched the towel tight under my arms, sat with my legs tucked beneath me on the bed, and texted Payton. She called me right back, and we discussed me throwing out the "L" word and Logan's reaction. She was happy for me. She liked Logan.

Once the call was over, I sat on the bed, staring out the window. How were we going to keep pretending we were strangers at the office? And more importantly, why?

The front door opened and shut, followed by his labored breathing and heavy footsteps inside the kitchen. I'd lost all track of time.

My towel was abandoned on the bed when I made my way into the kitchen, stark naked, excited to see sweat rolling down his golden-tan chest. He had the fridge door open when I stepped into the room.

"Are you going to fuck me in the shower, or are you too tired?" I teased.

"Sorry," the smug voice from behind the fridge door replied, "but I'm married now." Then the younger Stone brother rose up into view, and Nick's mouth hit the floor at the sight of my naked flesh.

NINETEEN

Like a fucking idiot, I was paralyzed in shock. Should I dart back into the bedroom? I searched for something to cover up with, thinking that would be faster. There was nothing, because Logan put everything away, everything in its place.

As soon as it registered that I was sans clothes, Nick's eyes went to the ceiling.

"I didn't see anything," he blurted out, although his already flushed face now turned purple. Sweat poured down his forehead and bare chest, and it actually dripped on the floor around him. I scrambled into the bedroom and grabbed my clothes from last night. Logan hadn't mentioned they were training together today.

"I'm sorry," I yelled from the bedroom, "I thought you were Logan." *Oh god, kill me now.* "Where is he?"

"He wanted a longer cool-down. He should be up in a minute."

Now that I was dressed in jeans and a shirt, I wasn't sure what to do. Keep hiding from awkwardness in the bedroom until Logan arrived? I tucked my hair behind an ear and forced myself to go out into the living room.

"How was your honeymoon?" I asked, acting like nothing had happened. "Jamaica, right?"

Nick looked happy to pretend too. "Yeah. It was good. Have you ever been?"

The door swung open and interrupted my normal, clean brain with dirty, impure thoughts. Weren't people supposed to look like crap after they'd just run twenty miles? That did not apply to him.

I watched in fascination as the brothers said nothing to each other and yet moved as an orchestrated pair. Nick handed a Gatorade bottle to Logan while he retrieved a large bag of pretzels out of a cabinet and pulled it open. They drank and ate quickly, stopping only to wipe sweat off with paper towels or open a banana.

When they were finished hydrating and fueling, the iPhones came out of armbands and they critiqued their individual pacing. I felt like I was on Mars. The discussion concluded and Nick grabbed a water bottle from the fridge.

"I'm heading out, I know you've got stuff to do," Nick said. "Evie mentioned she'd like to fuck you in the shower."

Logan's gaze snapped to me and my face burst into flames.

"Great, thanks for that, Nick," I said.

"No problem." He flashed an enormous smile and went out the door.

Logan continued to stare at me with a puzzled expression.

"I thought he was you," I explained. "You failed to mention you weren't running solo and he might pop in."

"You told him you wanted to fuck in the shower?"

"Yeah. And I was naked when I did it."

He scowled and gave a dark, possessive look. "Did you forget what I look like?"

"He was behind the refrigerator door. Like I said, I thought it was you."

He blinked and calmed. A slow smile tweaked across his lips. "I really should recover some more before we get in there."

"It was a joke, I've already showered, boss."

"That's disappointing, Ms. Russell, but you're a dirty girl.

You'll probably need another shower before too long."

The corner of my mouth turned up.

Later, he drove me back to my place, and when he parked, he ran his fingers absentmindedly over my knee.

"Tomorrow I need to be in the office early," he said.

"Oh?" After that dinner, we didn't really talk about work outside of the office. "Why do you need to be in early?"

"I have a meeting with Jon." The VP of sales, his boss's boss. Jon was rarely in the Chicago office, so whatever it was, had to be serious. My face must have shown my concern. "It's no big deal," he said.

Then, why bring it up? He leaned in and kissed me, voiding thought out.

"See you tomorrow," he uttered, a half-smile lurking beneath his lips.

⌘

No big deal. He'd lied to me. At ten-thirty the designers assembled in the conference room for a meeting Logan had scheduled only an hour prior. He didn't sit in the back with his laptop, he stood up front with his boss, Will, the creative director, and Jon. The VP of sales was tall, southern, and always seemed like he'd rather be somewhere else. We only saw him when something had gone wrong, like losing a client. All of the designers went on the defensive when they laid eyes on him, and lowered themselves to sit with straight backs.

Will was in his late fifties. He oversaw all the departments including PR and broadcast, and those departments were far more demanding than ours, so we didn't see him much either. Logan's face was empty. His gaze paused on me, and then went to the room.

"Thank you for being flexible with your schedules," he

said. "By now you might have heard that our company acquired Paradigm Creative, and you're wondering how this will affect our department."

What? Paradigm Creative was a competing agency. They were smaller than we were, but there was sure to be a full design staff there. A spark of panic ignited in my stomach. Was Jon here to break the bad news that our department was being replaced?

"We're bringing on most of PC's design team," Logan continued, "to help with the new workload, and there's going to be a change in structure within our department. A supervisor position will be created from each of the locations, and those new supervisors will report to me."

His eyes flicked my direction for a second. So miniscule no one else probably noticed it.

Holy shit.

A deal this big had been in the works for a while. Logan had known someone in our department was getting promoted, and with that single look, he told me everything. This was why he'd wanted to keep our relationship a secret. Why he'd hesitated when talking about my promotion to senior designer. He had bigger plans for me.

I was the person he'd confessed was the best in the department, but doing something like this was going to make waves. Big fucking ones. If anyone heard we were dating, they would assume I'd slept my way to it, making both Logan and me look bad.

My mind raced with the revelations. Suddenly the meeting was over. Logan was already checking email on his phone and out the door before I shuffled up out of my seat and back to my cube. I had to talk to him. My hands closed around my phone, only to have it chirp with a text message from him.

Lunch @ Spiros, 11:30.

Okay, boss.

Spiro's was eight blocks from the office. It was a hike for mediocre Greek food, and I assumed he'd chosen it exactly for this reason. Our co-workers were unlikely to wander in and see us together. He'd gotten a table in the back, and stood when I came toward him, his suit jacket removed and hanging on the back of his chair. We hadn't set any kind of boundaries for meetings like this, so close to the office and in the middle of the day.

"Hi," he said. "How's your day going?"

I sat in the chair he'd pulled out for me. "It's been interesting. Keeping things quiet about us makes a bit more sense now."

"I'll interview anyone who applies." A coy smile lurked on his face when he sat down beside me. "But, yeah, I already have someone in mind for the position."

"I've only been there a few years, and I'm young."

He looked startled. "You don't want it?"

"You know I do." It would be easier if I didn't, but I was far too driven to pass up the opportunity.

"It's not really about age. It's a confidence and respect thing. They respect you, and we both know you'd be great at it."

I had no idea if I was speaking with my boss or my boyfriend, and it made me dizzy.

"So, are you going to stop by my office later and apply?"

I felt a similar coy smile overtake me. "Yes, sir."

A switch flipped, and I knew exactly whom I was talking to. His gaze filled with so much desire, it left me breathless.

Beneath the table, his hand closed around my knee.

Keeping work and our relationship separate was difficult, but I did my best. We talked about his upcoming marathon. How Payton had seemed kind of down the last time I'd spoken to her. Something was up, and I worried I might have become one of those neglectful friends who drops everything when she has a boyfriend.

The waiter brought the check and jarred me from my thoughts.

"I'm going to have to get back soon," I said, noting the clock on the back wall. Not that I wanted to go. I wanted to stay right where I was. In fact, I wanted his hand to move higher on my thigh. Instead, it tensed.

"Go to the bathroom, now." His voice was urgent enough I didn't question it. I snatched up my purse and went straight back into the restroom, ducking into the first stall.

My thumbs typed furiously on the screen of my phone.

What's going on?

Jamie just came in.

Had she seen us? I waited for him to detail more. But nothing came, so I asked what I should do.

I just left. Stay at least another minute. She might be picking up an order.

I waited in the tiny bathroom, checking my email on my phone and trying not to think about how ridiculous, but necessary, hiding was. Of all people, Jamie was the worst when it came to gossip. She was a magnet for drama.

I waited three minutes for good measure, but it was futile. She'd gotten a table with a guy right up by the front, and I had no choice but to walk past her.

"Evelyn, hey!" she said, forcing me to stop.

"Oh, hey, Jamie."

"This is my boyfriend, Steve."

I smiled at the thin man dressed all in black with a serious face. He nodded back a hello.

"Pretty crazy about that deal with PC, huh?" she asked.

"Yeah. That's good, though. I hear they've got a lot of big accounts. I should probably—"

"You see Logan? He was just in here, too."

Shit. I wasn't a good liar. "Oh? I didn't know this place was so popular."

She shrugged. "The gyros are worth the trip."

"They're just okay," her boyfriend quipped.

"Really?" She shot him a discerning look, like she didn't appreciate him contradicting her.

"I've gotta get back. Nice meeting you," I said. I turned on my heel and raced toward the door, out into the sun.

⌘

I knocked on his office door at four-thirty.

"Are you busy?" I asked, hovering in the doorway.

"Not at the moment. What do you need?" His gaze left his computer screen and glanced my way, then back to the computer. His voice was so . . . direct. He was overcompensating now more than ever.

I strolled up to his desk. With his door open, with him back to pretending he didn't care about me in any capacity other than professional, I viewed him one hundred percent as the boss he was a month ago. The arrogant, all-business jerk who held enormous power over my career. I could do this.

"I'd like to apply for the supervisor position."

His gaze returned to me, like he was evaluating me right then and there, then it drifted back to the computer screen. "Okay. I can set your interview for four tomorrow. Does that work with your schedule?"

"Yes, thank you."

"See you then." The computer dinged with a new email and his focus left me, dismissing me. When I got back to my desk, I pulled up short. Jamie waited in my chair.

"Did you just come from Logan's office?" Suspicion coated her voice.

"Yeah." I tried to hide my frustration. I wasn't pleased she was sitting in my chair, and I was even less thrilled with her question.

"Are you two, like, friends?" She asked it with an even mixture of disdain and accusation.

"No. I applied for the supervisor position."

Her face flooded with surprise. "You did? You're not even a senior."

"Logan didn't say that was a requirement."

She relinquished the chair to me as if just realizing it wasn't hers. "You're right, he didn't. Anyway, I wanted to ask if I could borrow your uncoated swatch deck. Mine's gone missing again."

I dug through my drawer and pulled the fan of color swatches out. She took it and nodded *thanks*, but lingered. "Sorry, I just thought it was weird, seeing Logan and then you at Spiro's, and Debbie said you've been in his office a lot recently."

I shrugged, but inside I cursed nosy Debbie whose cube

was closest to Logan's door. "If I have, it's to go over the GoodFoods account."

A smile broke on her face. "Yeah, of course. You know Debbie," she said, although I really didn't. "Always spreading rumors."

She began her trek back to her cube, but my word stopped her. "Rumors?"

"That you and Logan were friends, maybe more. I told her it wasn't true." She paused. "Unless . . . Are you?"

It wasn't a lie, I told myself. *Be convincing.* "No. Logan Stone and I are not friends."

She flashed me a smile, pulling her hair up into a messy bun as she went. "Yeah, I told her that'd be crazy."

God, it was like being back in high school.

⌘

Logan and I ate frozen pizza at his place, and I debated telling him about my conversation with Jamie. I made it two slices before it spilled out of me.

"There's a rumor going around the office that we're friends."

He blinked. "Wow, juicy."

"Debbie thinks we might be more, just because I've gone into your office a few times. I mean, honestly, she thinks I'm going in there to get it on with you in the middle of the day?"

I could tell from his playful smile he wasn't going to let me off easy. "*Get it on*? Is that what we're doing?"

"Let me revise. Does she think I'm going in there to fuck your brains out?"

The smile widened into a full-out grin. "That does seem to be a more adequate description."

"Stop distracting me from my worrying."

"I'm sure it's fine. They've been running low on drama in the department. When the PC staff comes on board that will give them more to work with."

"Assuming everything . . ." How to phrase it? ". . . works out like you want it to, how long do we have to pretend at the office?"

He considered the statement. "We'll have to play it by ear, but I would think a few months."

It's not like we were in some elaborate scheme, hiding our love. At the same time, I had lied today, and we'd lied to his family about how long we'd been together, lied to my parents about how we'd met . . . The lies were piling up.

"Is that okay?" He seemed to be trying to read my thoughts.

When Kathleen found out she'd been passed over the promotion she thought was in the bag, she was going to be upset. Finding out it went to me, who wasn't even a senior, would leave her beyond pissed. If she had an inkling Logan and I were in a relationship, she'd go screaming to Jon about favoritism in a heartbeat. It would be a disaster, and no matter how Logan defended his position, how could he come through that unscathed?

"Yeah," I said. "I can pretend that we're not . . . getting it on."

"Good. Oh, by the way," he dug a hand in his pocket and set something down on the counter, "this is yours." His palm lifted to reveal metal. A key.

Whoa. It wasn't exactly the same as telling me he loved me, but it was pretty damn close.

"You sure you want to do that? All of your other girlfriends will have to go."

"Yeah," he sighed, mocking me. "And I had so many."

Did he have a clue that being girlfriend number two to

him made me feel like number one?

⌘

I sat at my desk and stared at my uneaten lunch. Knowing Logan had me as the front-runner should have been helpful, but all my nerves whispered back to me was, what would happen if it didn't go well? What if what I said in the interview changed his mind?

The interviews started at one. I saw Gary's mop of black hair turn the corner into Logan's office and shut the door. Gary had even worn a tie. The atmosphere at the agency was relaxed, and a lot of designers wore jeans and flip-flops. Not me. I wanted people to know how seriously I took my work, and looking the part helped.

Gary's interview didn't last too long. Thirty minutes later he was back at his cube and the tie was gone. At two, Maurice was up. He was another senior designer, but honestly, I didn't view him as much competition. He was timid and quiet. I couldn't imagine him managing some of the full-bodied personalities we had here.

My competition went into his office two minutes before three. Kathleen wore a beautifully cut charcoal gray pantsuit with a sunflower yellow necklace. She looked every bit the part of a professional manager when she breezed into Logan's office, and her interview lasted a long time. So long, I began to worry what I was going to do if the interview ran over into my timeslot. Should I knock? Wait outside the door? Thankfully, it swung open before I had to make a decision, and Kathleen exited.

I squashed my nerves for the millionth time and went into his office. They said if you were uncomfortable, you should picture the other person in their underwear. Yeah, well, that wasn't any help. I knew exactly what he looked like in his underwear. Or with absolutely nothing on at all.

I shut the door. When I turned to his desk, he wasn't there, because he was standing before me. I took a confused step toward the pair of chairs facing his desk, but his hands encircled my waist.

"What are you doing?" I whispered in the moment before he set his mouth on mine. His sweet kiss lingered on my lips even after it was gone. "What about my interview?"

"We'll get there. I need a minute to recover. You mind?" His hushed voice was so sexy it made my knees soften.

"Um . . . no, I guess not."

I went to sit and face him while he sat behind his desk. He arched his back and stretched up as if trying to shake loose the tedium of the interviewing process. When it was done, his gaze drifted over my body, upward until his eyes found mine.

"Why do you want the job," he asked, "Evelyn?"

Evelyn, not Evie, because we were at work. Because the interview had now begun. I fed him the talking points I'd drafted from my research. He listened respectfully and said nothing. Then came a sharp look that made me feel about three pixels tall.

"I want to know the real reason you want the position," he said. "Not some bullshit answer you think I want to hear."

His aggressive tone disabled my filter. "Because it's a stepping stone to yours."

"You want my job? What about me?" His eyes glittered with interest.

"You'll be Creative Director."

His mouth went slack with what I guessed was surprise.

"Don't you think that will go to Chase McCutchen in PR

when Will retires?" His voice was . . . unsure. "They're not going to give it to someone in print."

I could see everything behind those gorgeous mahogany irises. Like me, he wanted to reach for a job he might be too inexperienced or too young to land. But I believed no one would work harder or be better at it than he would.

"No, I don't think they'll give it to Chase. Not if he has to go up against you for it."

He blew out a breath and an emotion streaked his face, like I'd just said the most flattering thing he'd ever heard. He hesitated and visibly struggled to pull himself back on topic.

"Tell me about a difficult situation in your work and how you handled it."

I swallowed a breath. This was going to be a gamble. "When I first started, I was paired with a senior designer—"

"Austin."

"He had difficulty working as a team. He fought me on everything, told me that he knew better because he was a senior. He used it as an excuse to steamroll me." I had to still my nervous hands, folding them into my lap. "Austin wouldn't take my suggestions. I tried being nice, I tried to give him time, but when the customer was screaming for a new direction and Austin wouldn't budge, I ran out of options."

"You did it yourself."

"I gave it to our manager and told him Austin and I had collaborated, but Austin hadn't even seen it."

Logan straightened in his chair. "Do you think telling me a story about going behind another designer's back is a good idea?"

"I'm hoping you'll understand I'm willing to do something that makes me unpopular if it's going to get the customer what they want, plus I'm not a pushover. I can stand up to someone who has more experience when I believe they're wrong."

He looked pleased. My opening answer had disappointed him, but this one did not.

"Austin was an asshole and a shit designer. Notice he's not around anymore?" He'd been let go Logan's second week as manager, and the firing had sent a clear message that Logan was going to run a tight ship.

"It didn't make you popular," Logan continued, his voice dropping down low. "But it made people in the department notice you." His expression crept back into a smile. "And, just so you're aware, it put you on my radar."

"Oh." That's all I could get out.

"This position requires you spend less time designing. Will you have a hard time sacrificing that creative outlet so you can manage?" His voice was professional and business-like.

"I've made much bigger sacrifices to get what I want. Was it hard for you to give up the creativity?"

"No."

"Then I'm sure I'll be fine." Because professionally we were so much alike.

"Do you have any questions for me?"

I wanted to ask it in a subtle way, but the interview had gone off the rails the moment he'd kissed me. "Salary?"

"Negotiable, but we'd like it in the upper fifties." Only about ten grand more than I was making now. I fell silent, focusing on that number.

"Any other questions?"

I shook my head.

"Okay, we'll be making a decision sometime in the coming weeks, and I'll let you know. Thanks for your interest, Evelyn."

I climbed out of the chair, and he rose as well. I only made it halfway to the door when a hand curled around my waist.

"Wait." His breath whispered the hair by my ear. "Evie."

He spun me in his hands to face him, and his kiss was untamed. It sank down through my body like liquid love, filling every inch of me. He hadn't said the words, but he had no problem showing them to me. I buried my hands inside his suit jacket, letting fingers dance over his defined chest, covered in the lightly starched dress shirt. Every passing moment he continued to kiss me was more dangerous than the last.

I wanted him. I started to think about locking his office door, or how long we could be in here with the door closed before people would start to wonder why the interview was taking so long. His tongue dipped into my mouth, stroking mine, and desire flamed so hot I knew I was flushed.

My hand had a mind of its own, and inched down until he pushed it away and shot me an annoyed look.

"We can't do that, even if I want to."

I knew he did, because he was sporting a semi. "You want me to throw some cold water on you?" I joked.

"No, I've got my desk to hide behind until that goes away. You, naughty girl, have to go back to your cube now, all flushed."

I bit my lip. "Okay, boss. Just, please tell me you didn't interview Gary this way."

His face got a hard edge. "Wow, look at that. Crisis in my pants solved."

I flashed him a smug smile.

TWENTY

Another two weeks passed before we hit the first bump. I was on my way to Logan's place when Blake called and asked if I was available to grab lunch the next afternoon. Gone was the awkwardness. I firmly loved Logan, and Blake was my friend, so I was happy to get to see him again.

I hadn't seen much of Logan recently. He'd spent the last week evaluating the staff over at PC. Not all of them were going to transition, and he'd been trying to make his own judgments without any office politics in play. As suspected, my only competition for the supervisor position was Kathleen. A follow-up interview had been set with Logan and the creative director for Kathleen and me individually. Ultimately it was Logan's call on who stepped into the role, but Will wanted to help if Logan was on the fence.

I didn't think anything of my lunch appointment until I'd curled up beside Logan right after a mind-draining session, snuggling under his arm. "I was planning on having lunch with Blake tomorrow," I said. "Is that . . . okay?"

He stiffened. "No, not really."

"He's my friend—"

"Evie, he thinks he's in love with you."

"No, not anymore. Besides, that doesn't matter. I love *you*."

He shifted so he was on his side facing me. "I trust you, but him? Don't you remember when he showed up at your place? What if I hadn't been there?"

"What?" What was he talking about?

"He wouldn't take no for an answer until he realized I was there."

I scoffed at this ridiculous accusation. "Blake's not like that."

"I don't know him, and honestly, I don't want to."

I swallowed hard, seeing where this was going. Payton didn't like Blake, but she didn't make me choose between them. But Logan? He didn't want me to be friends with Blake. That drunken moment in my apartment when Blake grabbed me and almost took a swing at Logan had shaped his judgment of Blake.

"So, you want me to cancel?"

"Yeah."

"What do I tell him? That my boyfriend's possessive?"

I wished I could take it back. The bedroom was only lit by his iPad screen, and in the low light Logan's eyes soured. "You can tell him whatever. Tell him your asshole boss needs you to work through lunch."

He wouldn't compromise on this, and he said hardly anything the rest of the night, barely kissing me goodbye when he dropped me off at my place.

⌘

The next afternoon when I called and delivered the fake excuse of work, Blake sighed.

"Well, I was hoping to tell you in person, but . . . Amy's pregnant."

Blake was at that awkward phase in life where you had no idea how to treat this kind of news. Was this a good thing? Was it viewed as a mistake?

"Oh. How are you—?"

"It's good. I'm excited. We're both excited."

I breathed a sigh of relief for him. "Good, that's good." He used to tell me everything, so he was probably desperate to discuss this life-changing event with me.

"You know what?" I said. "Forget work. I'll meet you at Potbelly's in ten minutes."

I was halfway through my sandwich and Blake's story of how they revealed the pregnancy to their parents when my phone buzzed with a text message.

Where are you?

I typed out a response, telling him I'd met Blake for lunch after all, and would explain it later.

"Everything okay?" Blake asked when I set the phone down.

A girl from accounting sat two booths over so I had to choose my words carefully. "My boyfriend's not real happy with me right now. He didn't want me to have lunch with you."

"I get it. I was confused, and I got scared. But, Evie, I'm not anymore. I love Amy. I had to screw everything up to figure it out, and I'm so sorry."

I felt a smile dawn on my face. "I'm happy you got it figured out. Everything works out for a reason."

The phone vibrated on the table.

Where are you specifically?

I made a face. Why did that matter?

I'm at Potbelly's. Be back at my desk in 30.

We chatted about Blake's new plan to propose. Now that he was going to be a father, he couldn't wait to get started on his happily-ever-after with her. That was how he knew Amy was the one.

"Do you know if Logan wants kids?" That forced my eyes to dart around and drew Blake's suspicion. "What is it?"

"We're not public with our relationship. It's complicated right now. But yeah, he wants kids."

"And other than today, things are good between you two?"

"Yes. Yeah." I gave a slight nod. "They're good." And they were. Right?

Blake's amber-colored eyes blinked and his eyebrows lifted. "What is it?"

I'd forgotten how well Blake knew me, and what a terrifically awful liar I was. "I told him I loved him. Like, a while ago. He hasn't said it back."

His eyes widened. "I'm sure he will."

"I know. It's just hard, though. I'm in love with him. Like, head over heels, crazy as hell in love. Birds singing and rainbows and all that shit. He feels it, I think, but I need him to say it."

A half-smile formed on Blake's lips, and the silence made me babble.

"You know," I continued, "I thought he hated me and I couldn't have cared less, because I thought he was an arrogant, self-absorbed jerk. But I was totally wrong, and the whole time I was too blind over you to notice him. I'm pissed at myself for not realizing sooner."

"Realizing?"

Since we were having our first honest conversation with each other in what felt like a lifetime, I pushed through. "That he could be the one I end up with. I know it's too soon, and that's such a ridiculous thing to say. The One. Ridiculous to be feeling, but . . . that's the way it feels."

Blake's gaze left mine and went over my head in alarm.

This restaurant had fast service, was affordable, and close to our office building, which meant it was crawling with coworkers. I'd never thought he'd walk in and risk it, but I'd been wrong.

"Hey, man." Blake's worried focus shifted back to me.

I glanced over my shoulder and couldn't breathe. Logan hesitated behind me, his face unreadable.

"How long have you been there?" It was barely a whisper.

"Since the birds were singing," he replied, his voice unsteady.

Oh shit. Shit! Nothing like confessing you believe he's the one after only two months of dating. He came to the table and stood over us, his wide, hypnotic eyes on mine. At least he hadn't bolted, but I had absolutely no idea what was going on inside his head. I wanted to slide under the table and hide.

The rich brown stare swung away from mine. "I'm Logan Stone." He extended his hand out to Blake, who blinked at the hand, then shook it.

"Blake Haluson."

My brain refused to function. My gaze went to the tabletop and my ears burned in embarrassment. What the hell was I going to do? Just when things couldn't have possibly gotten worse, Debbie materialized from fucking nowhere.

"Hey, guys. You having an impromptu meeting?" she joked, but her eyes clouded with suspicion.

"I was just asking Evelyn and her friend what was good," Logan answered. He was probably looking at me, but all I could do was stare at the dark oak table.

Debbie went on in detail about her favorite sandwich, and he pretended to care with enthusiasm until she flitted past.

"It was nice meeting you," he said to Blake.

"Yeah, you, too."

"I'll see you back at the office, Evelyn."

"Yeah, see you."

I heard his footsteps carry him away. My eyes slid to Blake's. He looked stunned.

"That was interesting." I must have made a face that mirrored the sickening feeling I had inside, because Blake's face filled with concern. "I'm sure it'll be okay."

⌘

I took a deep breath before turning my key in his lock, steeling myself. I'd gotten a text from Logan at twenty to five:

> We need to talk. Dinner at my place.

It wasn't a question.

The train ride to his apartment had been spent mapping out a way to not make me seem like a lovesick, moon-eyed girl who wanted to have ten thousand of his babies.

He wasn't in the kitchen or the living area beyond. I set my purse down on the entry table, then thought better of it and tucked it in the closet where he liked it.

"Logan?"

There wasn't an answer. I checked my phone for text

messages or a missed call. Nothing. Where was he? I sent a text asking when to expect him, and he replied he was stuck in traffic and would be home shortly.

I called Payton, frantic, revealing the whole mess. She tried to calm me, but wasn't much help. Payton was always honest, and given Logan's history, she was worried for me.

Behind me, the front door creaked opened as Logan came in. I turned to face him and almost dropped the phone. "Logan's home, I gotta call you back."

"Hi," he said, setting the plastic bags carrying what I assumed was our dinner on the counter. He set the other item down too – a glass vase bursting with gorgeous red roses. "These are for you."

My shaky hand shoved my phone in my back pocket. "Why?"

He paused. "Why? I can't buy you flowers?"

"It's suspect. Are you breaking up with me for the crazy things you overheard come out of my mouth?"

His smile was mesmerizing. "It didn't sound like you want that." He approached, his arms wrapping around my back and drawing me in. "I was being overly-protective. I came down to that restaurant thinking . . ."

"You were going to challenge Blake to a duel?"

His eyes glinted with amusement, then sobered. "I thought he was going to talk you into leaving me."

"No. He wanted my advice on how to propose to his girlfriend, who's pregnant."

His eyes softened. "So, I bought flowers." He motioned to the vase. "I should have trusted you to have it under control."

"What about what I said? Can you pretend you didn't hear it?"

"Why would I want to?"

He made everything upside-down again. “I don’t know, because it goes against the general rules of dating.”

The devious look he had made my mouth water. “I thought you knew I liked it when you break the rules.”

⌘

I’d forgotten to call Payton back, and the next morning she broke down and called me at work.

“What happened?”

“We’re okay. He was surprisingly cool about it.”

Jamie dropped a birthday card on my desk. It seemed like it was always someone’s birthday in the office, and I signed it before reading who it was addressed to.

“Who’s birthday is it?” I asked her.

She collected the card from me. “Logan’s.” She disappeared, and the gasp on the other end of the phone told me Payton had heard the exchange.

“Did you know it was his birthday today?”

“No.” I was so fucked. I hadn’t the faintest clue what to get him. He had everything he needed. And he’d told me on more than one occasion that having me in his bed was all he wanted. So, what now?

We hung up and Payton immediately started brainstorming ideas, sending me text messages. Stuff for his upcoming marathon? Nope, he had it covered. Some sort of tech item? If he wanted something for himself, he bought it. And what could I afford on my tiny paycheck?

I sent him a text.

Happy birthday, boss. We going out to celebrate?

Thanks, but I've got to cross-train tonite.

We'd agreed no more attempts at lunch after yesterday, so that meant I could go out during my break and get his present, but I had to come up with something first. For as creative as I could be at designing, I was the worst gift-giver on the planet.

Payton texted later.

Lingerie?

Porn?

No, he didn't need porn. He had those cellphone videos of us. Watching us have sex was so much hotter than the fake stuff—

Oh.

Well, that was an idea.

It made my heart race. My throat clamped too tight to talk, and that was fine. I couldn't ask what I was about to out loud, with only a half-wall partition separating me from my coworkers. My nervous fingers tapped out the message to Payton.

Remember what you said about watching us?

TWENTY-ONE

He wouldn't be home until eight. I gave Payton the tour of his place and then pulled down the bottle of tequila.

"You sure you want to do this?" I asked her.

"Hell yeah. Are you?" She motioned to the shot I'd just poured. I downed it and considered her question. When she'd said she wanted to watch us have sex, Logan had said he was flattered. Giving him praise or an ego boost seemed to affect him deeply. He loved it.

So, the plan was to recreate the night Logan and I had truly met, the night we saw each other as we were. Payton would blindfold me, tie me down, and then wait with me until Logan came home. If he wanted to ask her to stay and watch, I was okay with that. I'd have the blindfold on anyway.

I didn't want to get performance anxiety though. Last time I hadn't had any warning that we were going to be exhibitionists. Tonight, I had plenty of time to consider what was going to happen and get worked up over it. My hint of excitement was stifled by nerves. She was my best friend and totally comfortable with anything, but still. What if this made things weird? How could it not? I did a second shot, and she did one, too.

"What level of sloppiness are we shooting for?" she asked when I poured my third.

"Just on the drunk side of drunk."

I didn't eat dinner, so the liquor kicked in fast. Twenty minutes after we'd each done three shots, I swayed into the bedroom, buzzing. I was less anxious about her watching now. Much more eager to hear his reaction when he came home. I giggled to myself when I pulled my top over my head and almost lost my balance in the closet.

"Shit, he's got you hanging up your clothes? You *would* do anything for him." A smile spread across her exotic face. Payton set her purse down beside the chair in the corner. It was the one she'd be watching from if everything played out as I assumed it would.

She pulled a mess of black fabric from her purse and tossed it on the bed. Ribbon to tie me up. I tugged my jeans off and folded them, setting them on the shelf of the closet. At work, I'd snuck away for a late lunch and called Payton from a table in the back of the restaurant so no one could hear the indecent conversation I had with her. She'd agreed right away, even offering to pick up a blindfold and ties, and there was a crinkle of plastic now as she opened the blindfold from its package.

Like all of the other crazy sex decisions I'd made recently, once I'd decided on this I didn't have a lot of regret or hesitation. Only excitement.

Payton bent down and secured one of the ribbons to the bed frame, rising up to view me when it was finished. Her eyes traveled upward over me, and they were hooded when they met mine.

"When do you think he'll come home?"

I bent my arms to unhook my bra. "He's usually back around eight."

The bra was undone, and set on top of my jeans on the shelf. It was odd, the feeling that she was looking at me. She hadn't looked at me like that the night in the club when I'd undressed, or the day I'd stripped in front of Joseph.

Anticipation clung in the air, heavy and thick.

"He might be early," she said, securing the other tie.

And it would look rather awkward if he walked in right now. I hurried, hooked my thumbs under my panties and pulled them off. I thought about leaving them on the floor of his closet, and because I was naked and drunk, I smiled. He disliked clothes on the floor, so I left them there to tease him.

Payton hesitated beside the bed, waiting for me to climb up on it, an expression I didn't understand fixed on her face.

"What's wrong?" I folded the comforter down to the edge of the bed, then again so it was a narrow strip, and climbed onto the sheets.

"I don't want to make things weird between us, but . . ." She paused. "Your tits are amazing."

I laughed at her unexpected compliment. "Okay, thanks. Yours are really nice, too." I mashed the pillow with my hand and lay down on it, spreading my hair out beneath me.

"You've been checking out my rack?" She gave me a pretend judgmental look.

I'd only seen her naked, like, a thousand times. "You hardly ever had clothes on when we lived together."

She handed me the black blindfold and I took it, along with a deep breath. Good things waited for me once I had it on, so I didn't waste time. I positioned it right where I wanted it, slipped into darkness, then surrendered my first wrist to her soft hand.

"Tell me if it's too tight, I'm not so good at tying slipknots."

The ribbon wound around my wrist. A second time, and I felt the tug as she knotted it. It was tight, but not too tight. Her footsteps led her around the bed.

"Scoot over, you're not centered." My heart beat faster at her hushed voice. I slid across the sheets, carrying the pillow with me, and scratched my nose. Of course it had begun to itch. Her grip was light on my free wrist, drawing it up so she could tie it off.

"Now comes the waiting," I said, when it was done.

But the side of the bed dipped down. She'd sat beside me, and with the blindfold on I could focus on her movements by sound. Ends of her hair brushed on my chest when she leaned over me, her breath right beside my face.

My head jolted backward when her lips brushed mine. "What are you doing?" It came out confused and not angry. It wasn't the first time she'd kissed me. We'd been out bar-hopping after graduation, and she'd been hit on relentlessly by this guy who would not take no for an answer. He'd followed us to another bar, and it was the only time I ever saw Payton nervous. So when she told him she wasn't into guys, she turned and kissed me, and I played along.

It hadn't worked. All it did was put me in his sights too, and eventually we hid in the bathroom for twenty minutes and escaped out the back. She'd thanked me, and that had been all. But there was something nice about how she'd kissed me then, tentative and cautious at first, and then greedy and passionate when she knew I was willing to help her sell the lie.

It was sort of the same this time. She didn't answer my question with words. Her satiny lips pressed against mine hesitantly, her breath hurried, and this time I was too stunned to react. A hand slipped behind my neck, and her fingers curled into my hair, and the kiss deepened another shade.

"Whoa, wait," I said, breaking it off, my head spinning. "Payton—"

"I've never been with another woman."

I don't know which was more surprising; the fact that

she hadn't, or that I was technically more experienced than her at something. She tasted like tequila this time, and her sultry kiss was hypnotic. I didn't have use of my hands, so I couldn't stop her, nor could I slide my hands through her hair and hold her into the kiss. And I had absolutely no fucking idea which one I would have done.

The lips abandoned mine and sought out the skin below my ear, and her silky hair fell into my face, pulled into my mouth along with the ragged breaths I was struggling for. "What are you doing?" I asked again, desperate and disoriented.

"Getting you warmed up for him," she purred into my neck. Her palm was flat on my shoulder, inching down, and when I realized where she was heading I jolted again. No idea if it was a recoil or a reaction to the fire her skin on mine created. The hand crept over and down, until . . .

"Your hand is on my boob." Sometimes when I'm drunk I like to say the obvious stuff out loud.

Her mouth returned to mine, muffling any protest I might have made. I couldn't think when she was touching me. Everything scattered hopelessly. What would happen if I asked her to stop? Would things descend into awkwardness? What would happen if I kissed her back? She was a beautiful woman, desired by many, and that she now desired me was powerful.

There was a tiny voice that said this was cheating. I loved Logan. I shouldn't be kissing someone else, and certainly not my best friend. I turned my head again, ending the kiss, but I couldn't do anything about her hand that continued to massage me. Her fingernails scraped lightly over my nipple and I gasped. It felt wrong. And good.

"We can't," I said, breathless. "You're my best friend, and

I'm with Logan."

"You don't want to?"

I struggled to find an answer. One that wouldn't hurt her feelings, wasn't a lie, and wouldn't require me to really consider whether or not I wanted this, because I worried I did. "We shouldn't. It's going to mess things up between us."

She shifted on the bed to where she seemed to be lying beside me. "No, it won't. We could do it as a one-time thing. As long as we communicate and set some rules, I think it could be really fun."

Like I needed more rules. "But Logan—"

"Won't be here for at least a half-hour." Something flat and wet dragged across my nipple, then swirled. Her tongue.

I jerked against the ties. "Oh my god."

She followed it by using her teeth, sucking me into her mouth and nipping at my flesh. I felt a rush of wetness between my thighs at how naughty this was. If Logan walked in right now, what would he do? Would he be angry? Would he want to watch? Encourage?

"Please, Evie?" she whispered against my skin, her lips moving on me. "I'll make you feel so good, and I promise I won't let it get weird."

My conflicted mind, impaired by the tequila, couldn't raise an answer, but my body could. When she kissed me on the lips, I parted mine and gave her tongue entrance into my mouth. I kissed her back, telling myself the liquor had made this decision, like that would absolve me. I moaned against her mouth as her body rose over me and her jean-wrapped legs went on either side of my lap. Her touch was more deliberate now, caressing and exploring my skin, followed by her hot mouth. The weight of her body pressed onto my center, increasing the sensation there.

She lingered over my breasts, following the curve of my body with her delicate hands, all the while her tongue teased mine. I was as interested in her as she was in me. Her kiss was shocking, intense, and so different from his. Foreign and exotic. I sighed into her, and her against me—

She sat up abruptly for the heat of her hands was gone. Had she changed her mind?

"Payton," I gasped, filled with worry. "What's—?"

She moved again, using a knee to guide my legs apart. I hadn't really considered what she'd meant when she said she hadn't been with another woman. It hadn't registered until this moment, when the mattress groaned and her body slipped noisily across the sheets, lower. Until she was, I assumed, kneeling between my legs. Her hair trailed behind her mouth, tickling me as she ventured downward.

"Is this okay with you?" she asked. "If I lick this pussy?"

I couldn't breathe. My hands wrapped around the ties, balling them into fists. If kissing wasn't cheating, this certainly had to be. My traitorous body wanted it, but my mind? That was totally on the fence. Fingertips skimmed over the inside of my thigh when her mouth pressed into the flesh where I had been freshly waxed bare a few days ago. Logan was a fan of the look, and I found it sexy too.

She didn't wait long for my answer, which was good because I pressed my lips together. Her mouth stopped wandering and left my skin, and I heard her settle into the mattress. Warm breath again told me how close she was, only a few inches away.

"Fuck, you're wet," she said. "Is any of that for me, or is it all for him?"

That only made matters worse in that department. I cried out, a mixture of shock and pleasure when her fingertips found me.

"I . . ." That was as far as I got. The fingers touched and explored, steady and even. It was like she was painting bliss with her fingers on me.

"Are you sure this is okay?" she asked again.

But she'd already gone too far for us to turn back. I was panting, and although I probably sounded ridiculous, I couldn't stop myself. I drew a leg up until my knee was bent and let it fall to the side, urging her to do it.

"Oh, holy fuck," I babbled the instant her tongue grazed me. My legs jerked with pleasure, falling farther apart and giving her greater access which she took advantage of. Her hot, wet mouth covered me, and the tongue caressed, back and forth, sizzling. Need built like a volcano and threatened to erupt. "For having never done it before, you're doing a really good job," I uttered on staggered breath.

She let loose a deep, low moan of satisfaction. In fact, she was loud. That wasn't surprising. I'd walked in on her touching herself once and it was quite a production. She'd been so loud, it made me wonder if I wasn't doing it right to myself because I didn't sound like that.

"Does that feel good?" The tongue flicked hard over the tight bundle of nerves. I pushed the thoughts away that Payton was going down on me, and focused on her wicked mouth.

"Yes," I encouraged. "Yes, right there." I trembled under the power of her lips buried against my wet, swollen skin until I was writhing on the bed. I moved beneath her, shifting my hips back and forth, basically fucking her face. I moaned, louder and louder with every pass of her tongue.

"Oh, shit," I blurted out. "You're going to make me come."

"I thought that was the point."

No. And yes, god yes. Her tongue darted all the way

inside. Wet, velvet pleasure. That's what her tongue was. "I'm not allowed without his permission."

She laughed like that was funny, but it was anything but amusing to me. I couldn't disobey his rule with all I was already doing; I was being bad enough.

"Um, what?" she said.

"We have a rule that we can't . . . oh, god . . . not allowed to come without permission."

She paused. "How would he know?"

I don't know how, but I knew it with certainty. "He just would."

Her hands dragged up my thighs until she could use her fingers to spread me back, wider into her sensual kiss. Her mouth focused on my clit, and everything in me focused on that. I fought to steady my breathing.

"Please," I moaned, trying to draw myself away from the edge.

"What do you want to do?"

I could have told her to stop. But no, I was too greedy for the promised orgasm. I hoped it didn't sound as guilty as I felt. "We have to call him."

The mouth stopped and pulled back, and I sighed in frustration. Footsteps carried her away into the kitchen, and she was gone for forever. There was a loud rustling as Payton dug through my purse, and a bang like it fell to the floor, followed by mumbling. She thundered back in, resuming her position on the bed, and a thumb brushed over me seconds before the mouth returned.

"Fuck," I said. In a heartbeat, I was right back at the edge of the orgasm, aching for release. "That feels too good. Did you get my phone?"

She set something cold, heavy and square on my stomach.

"Here you go. Call him."

I couldn't because my arms were tied above my head. Tied well, too. Had she lied and spent the afternoon practicing goddamn knots? "You have to dial and put it on speaker."

"I'm busy." Her tongue lashed at where I was dripping wet.

"Oh my god, Payton, you have to. Please." I bit down on my lip, my face scrunching in concentration on holding it back.

"What do you need to ask him for?"

What? Did eating me out make her forgetful? "I need his permission to come."

"Go ahead," Logan answered.

TWENTY-TWO

A panicked noise tore from my throat, but Payton didn't let it deter her from her task. *Oh shit.* My brain disconnected and shut off, and the tequila told me it had it covered when I tried to find a response. I hadn't seen him at the office once today, although, technically, I wasn't seeing him now either. "Happy birthday."

"Yeah, I'd say so."

His startling announcement that I had permission to come had actually derailed things a bit. My heart raced and my breath came and went is short, gulping gasps, and I was going to die if he didn't say something.

"Logan—"

Two steps, almost silent, thudded on the carpet and his warm hand cupped my face. "Yes, naughty girl?" His deep, quiet voice flooded my ears, filling them with memories of last time I'd had a blindfold on.

"How long have you been there?"

"She was asking me if it was okay to go down on you." His lips touched mine, and the sensation of kissing him, while Payton's tongue dipped between my folds pushed me to the brink. "I'm impressed. Last time you had a blindfold on you were quite the rule-breaker." He kissed me at full intensity and my back arched off the bed. My hands strained to try to wrap around him. I needed him now.

"I want to come with you inside me," I whispered.

"She seems to be doing such a good job, though." He

was quiet, considering. "Can you move up and sit against the headboard?"

I didn't understand, but I did as he asked, sliding up on the bed so I was upright and the wood of the headboard rested flat against my back. Whatever he had planned, she must have understood. Both sets of hands touched my knees, gently pushing them back so I had them spread.

"I like the way she tastes," Payton said. Her tongue swiped again, and I moaned loudly. It felt great, but it wasn't what I wanted.

"Her pussy tastes amazing," he said. The mattress sagged suddenly, like a huge, concentrated amount of weight was on it, and then it shifted again, closer to me. One on either side of my hips. He was standing on the bed, over me. Jeans were unsnapped, a zipper pulled down.

"Open your mouth, naughty girl."

I gasped and parted my lips to draw air in, and the fleshy head of his dick shoved inside. I accepted it, thrilled, but what about what I'd asked for? Fingers trailed up my face, slipping beneath the blindfold to push it up on my forehead. Just enough to give me a peek.

He had one arm bent against the wall, his forehead resting against it and his gorgeous eyes cast down on mine. His other hand was wrapped around his dick, holding himself at the right angle to fuck my mouth. I couldn't see anything else, nor did I want to. I only wanted this man, and told myself the immense pleasure Payton was giving me was from him. He'd allowed this, after all.

"Now you can come while I'm inside you," he said, his eyes gleaming. He slid his dick as far in as I could take it. Then, back and forth, in and out, slowly at first, like he was gauging how I could handle his thrusts with nothing to hold on to. If I'd had any control, I wouldn't have been able to use it anyway. I was reaching a critical stage with my orgasm, and my body seized command.

"I love the way you look while you're sucking my cock," he whispered. I moaned loudly, and the vibration made him issue a sexy moan.

My eyelids fell closed. The crescendo inside me swelled until it was too powerful, and I succumbed to it, surrendering everything with what would have been a scream if my mouth wasn't occupied. The pleasure started at my toes and rolled upward, through my knees and hips and up, up, up. Hands clasped around my head and he drove into my mouth, deep enough that he slammed into the back of my throat.

"Fuck," he cried. "Shit . . . shit, shit!"

His hot, thick liquid filled my mouth and rolled down my throat, and I swallowed it, still quaking around him. My eyes fluttered open to find him staring down at me with that intense expression I so loved from him. He was devastatingly handsome, the most beautiful in this moment.

I'd made it rather clear I'd come, and Payton's mouth had ceased. The bed shifted as she sat back, but right before I got a look, Logan tugged the blindfold down, stealing my vision and my breath in an instant. His zipper rang out once more, but this time it was to do his jeans back up, and I jostled when he stepped off of the bed.

No one spoke, no one moved, leaving me with the impression they were both waiting for me to. But I was still shuddering, and naked, and felt too vulnerable to do anything. Hair swept across my chest and her lips caressed mine.

"Will you share him with me?" she asked.

Blank. That's what my mind went. It felt like ten seconds had passed from the moment I realized Logan was in the room up until now. Nowhere near enough time to consider whether or not I was okay with a full-on threesome.

"I need more tequila," I said, avoiding answering.

"Payton, do you mind? Give us a minute," he said. She made hardly any noise as she departed to the kitchen. I could feel the hesitation in him as he sat on the edge of the bed. The first words out of my mouth had been "Happy birthday," so he had to have assumed I was gifting him a three-way. Was I okay with doing that? She obviously was.

"Do you want to be shared?" I asked him.

His hands cupped my face gently and he feathered a kiss on my lips. "You're more than enough for me, you know that, right? But . . . I'm definitely up for whatever."

I appreciated his skill at sounding indifferent, but he was a man, after all. I knew he wanted it, and he'd said he'd never had one. Men paid thousands of dollars for Payton, and he had paid thousands for me. Both of us at once? How could he not want that?

"What are you thinking?" His mouth danced across my collarbone, working lower.

I had already gone down on another woman in front of him, so the idea of returning the favor on Payton wasn't much of an issue. Honestly, I had already considered that a possibility, depending on how much both of them wanted to recreate that night at the club. She knew it, even without discussing it, because we knew each other so well. And Payton was stunningly beautiful, plus she certainly knew how to have no-strings-attached sex. But sharing him?

"She's a professional," I said.

"You're worried I'll like it better with her?" He licked the side of my breast. "Not fucking possible. You are mine, and I am yours." The mouth on me trailed wet, open kisses from one nipple to the other, teasing me with teeth. "I'm yours to share, or to keep just for yourself."

I loved him so completely, and knew his words were true. "Take off the blindfold," I said, quietly.

He pushed it up onto my forehead and I blinked. The sun had set, but it was still bright enough outside to heat the room with light. Logan sat beside me, leaning close, one hand on the bed on either side of my body, his gaze searing and full of love.

"Okay," I whispered. "But . . . I have rules."

It was like all the air drained from his lungs. Then his mouth crashed into mine with a kiss that dripped with lust and desire and sin, and I knew instantly I wasn't going to regret this choice.

"Payton," he said, his voice raised so she could hear. "Can you join us?"

She sauntered in, clutching the bottle of tequila by the neck, her eyes searching my face for confirmation.

"I have rules," I repeated.

She took a swig off of the bottle, and he held out a hand, requesting she pass it to him. It was so he could take a long pull on it, not me. He set the bottle on his side table, and his deep, intense gaze locked with mine.

"You can't kiss her, not on the lips," I said. That was actually one of Payton's rules anyway. The one thing she didn't check on her willing list.

He gave me a wicked smile, like he was pleased I wanted to save that for myself.

"What else?" he asked. I hesitated, unsure of how to put it into words. His voice fell to a hush when his mouth returned to my breasts. "Tell me, Evie."

"You have to wear a condom with her." I felt like I needed

to explain further. "That connection with nothing between us? It's only with me."

"Yes," he said instantly.

"And you can't come with her," I said. "You have to finish with me."

The wicked smile reappeared. "Absolutely. What else?"

"That's it."

Three simple rules; was there more I was supposed to say?

He straightened with what appeared to be surprise. "So . . . *everything* else is allowed?" His eyes left mine and darted to Payton for a moment, who looked utterly thrilled. When his focus returned to me, it was serious. "I can touch her, anywhere?"

"Yes."

His voice was hypnotic. "I can put my mouth on her, anywhere? Other than her lips?"

"Yes," I answered. Fingertips trailed down my neck, down the flesh of my breasts where my nipples were still hard knots, stopping just above my legs. A mere inch above where the need was beginning again.

"I can put my cock in her, anywhere?" His voice dropped so low it was only a hint of a question.

I swallowed, trying to imagine the concept of watching him fuck her, and unexpected heat poured through me. "Yes."

She didn't need to hear anything else. Her hands yanked her top off, and she dropped it to the floor, exposing her black sheer mesh bra that gave away everything.

"Your tits are amazing," I echoed back to her from before, and Logan startled, as if excited that I would phrase it this way. His hand went behind his back and yanked his t-shirt over his head, discarding it to the floor. Apparently, being tidy wasn't the highest priority right now, but then again, I knew this. He'd left that broken glass of wine on the kitchen floor our first night together.

It was erotic watching them survey each other. He stood and moved deliberately to her, going behind her so both sets of eyes were on me, watching for any signal I'd changed my mind. His fingers crept over her shoulder, gliding down her smooth, tan skin. The fingers slipped under the cup of her bra and touched her while he set his mouth on her opposite shoulder, his unblinking gaze locked with mine.

I wouldn't have thought in a million years I would like watching him put his hands on another woman. I didn't just like it, I fucking loved it. I wanted . . .

"Take off her bra," I commanded.

Oh, he really liked that. I'd never given him much of a command before, but it was obvious I was going to have to do that more often. His hand abandoned her for a moment so he could undo the clasp, and then she pulled the fabric away, arching her back into him when both of his hands encircled her breasts from behind. She made a soft noise of pleasure and her eyes shut, but his continued on mine. Even when he rubbed her full breasts, pushing them together and rolling her dark nipples between his fingers.

It wasn't enough for her. Fingernails lacquered in a dark cherry nail polish flew to the waistband of her jeans and unzipped them.

"Put your hand inside her panties," I said, although I don't know how – I felt like I wasn't breathing. Her moan was filled with aching need when his large hand disappeared inside the undone jeans barely clinging to her hips.

"I think going down on you got her turned on."

His hand stirred inside her pants and she gasped at his touch. I shifted on the bed, closing my legs. I'd never been more turned on. When I'd watched her those years ago on stage, it wasn't anything like this. I'd been turned on, sure, but it was embarrassing with all those other people around. It had filled me with unnecessary shame. Here, this show was only for me.

The hand not inside her pants left her breast to shove her jeans down to the floor, and she stepped out of them, exposing her curvy, long legs. Her matching lace panties let me see exactly what he was doing and how he was touching her.

"You have two hands," I said to him. "One of them is for me."

"You're absolutely right. Payton, sit next to her."

He withdrew from her, and she crawled seductively on her hands and knees across the bed toward me. And just as she leaned in to kiss me, his hands tugged the blindfold back into place. I both wanted it and didn't want it. I heard her shifting on the sheets as she freed herself from her panties, and now she was as naked as I was. Maybe not seeing Logan's eyes on her body was a good thing. Her hip was up against me, and one of her legs went over mine, so we were both spread out before him.

"I'm going to make her come," he said, although I wasn't sure to whom. "Put those in her mouth so she doesn't get too loud."

What—? Wet lace touched my lips, thick with the smell of her. The *taste* of her. The fabric bunched inside my mouth and I moaned against it. Then, hands. Hands everywhere. His fingers pushed inside me, and she moaned loudly in my ear, one of her breasts right up against mine. Her hand was on my clitoris, rubbing furiously, them working together as a team to pleasure me.

The second orgasm stormed onto the scene. Payton's

whimpering was loud, and hurried, too loud to be caused only by what she was doing to me. I couldn't ask because of the panties shoved in my mouth. I couldn't see because of the blindfold, and I couldn't touch because I was bound to the bed. Almost all of my freedoms had been stolen away and I reveled in it. I was sure he was pleasing her the same way he was pleasing me, and I imagined his fingers slipping inside her as his fingers thrust deep inside me. When they curled back, her moans matched mine, identical.

"Are you going to come for me?" he asked.

I nodded my head—

"Yes," she answered on a heavy breath. Hearing that she was so close, just like I was, kicked it up another level so every move of their hands sent waves of bliss dancing through me. Beside me, she tensed and her fingers on my skin drifted to a stop.

"Oh, fuck, I'm gonna come," she cried.

If I had use of my mouth, I would have said the same. I listened to her sharp breaths, heard her cry of ecstasy, and let it pull me right along with her. We both thrashed on the bed in the throes of our orgasms, and he left his fingers inside, giving us something to ride on.

"Good girls." He yanked the panties out of my mouth and filled it with his soft, indecent tongue, like he was fucking me with a kiss. Even though I wasn't cold, I shivered in anticipation. "Can you get on top of her?" He scooped his hands under me and pulled me down so I was flat on my back. When she straddled me, she ground her wet skin against mine, and I gasped at how shockingly pleasurable this action was.

"Fuck." She sounded as surprised as I was. She moved fast, rising off of me and edging her knee inside my thigh to force my leg up and back. She sank back down, positioned over me just so, and our pussies touched.

"Payton, oh my god."

I don't know what Logan was doing, but I could hear his uneven breath, which deepened when she began to slide on me, riding me. Her body ground against mine, bringing us both enjoyment at the same time. Was I supposed to like this? Because I really, really did.

"That's so fucking hot," he said, kissing me again. "You like that pussy on yours?"

"Yes," I whimpered. "Take the blindfold off. Untie me."

He stood and hesitated before answering. "Not yet, naughty girl. You didn't ask permission to come last time."

"You mean when her panties were in my mouth?"

He gave a laugh, edged with wickedness.

There was a rustle and Payton gasped. "Evie, his cock is huge."

His laugh now was soft; startled and pleased. I suppose it's nice to hear that from your girlfriend, but Payton had been with considerably more men than me, so this cemented it as fact. His clothes were off, and the mattress protested as he knelt on it, moving behind her and between my legs. When she lifted up again on her knees and her damp skin drew away, it was replaced with another sensation – her breasts on mine.

She kissed me and I answered back in kind until her mouth traipsed down my neck.

"Fuck, Logan," she sighed against my flesh. "That feels so good."

"What's he doing?"

"He put . . ." she drew in a deep breath, "his tongue in me." The conflict grew in my mind on whether or not I liked this. The possessiveness I'd felt that night Tara had approached us reared its head, and I was thankful he'd left the blindfold on. Yet listening to her fight for breath was audio sex, and the muscles low in my stomach clenched with desire. Maybe I did want to see.

"Yeah? You like eating my pussy?" she asked. "You like fucking me with your mouth?" He didn't answer her, but he must have picked up the pace because a whole bunch of dirty words spilled out, punctuated by her short gasps. Followed by, "I can't wait for you to fuck me with that big, hard cock."

There was a thump as he backed off the bed and padded over toward the headboard. "Come here."

He was talking to both of us. She used her body to guide mine closer to the edge of the mattress. Closer to him. Fingers peeled the mask up and then completely off. At some point, maybe when he'd lost his pants, he'd turned on the lights, and it took me a moment to adjust.

My vision came into focus, up close and personal with Payton's face, her lips wrapped around the head of his dick. My gaze went up to Logan's, and once again, he watched me with an intense expression, gauging my reaction. I . . . didn't mind. It was sexy. Watching the helmet of his massive dick disappear inside her was insane. I couldn't stop watching.

He pulled back from her and set his damp flesh on my lips, asking for entrance. I opened and took him inside.

"Can you . . . untie her?" he asked her. He was so hard in my mouth, and pulsed when I ran my tongue along the length of him. The knot on the far side tugged and jerked, and came free while Logan struggled to undo the one closest to him. I was released a few moments later and, ignoring the ache in my shoulders, I latched a hand on the base of his dick.

I gave myself a few greedy seconds on him, knowing what he wanted. Two mouths on him at once. Because I was beneath her, I pulled off of him and held his dick for her, encouraging her to take over. Meanwhile, I traced a circle lower on his balls, and his whole body shuddered. I let my grip on him fall away, letting Payton do what she wanted so I could focus below.

"Fuck, girls. That's so fucking amazing."

Our tongues met on his skin, and he made a noise of pure, raw satisfaction. We took turns stroking him and sliding him in and out of our mouths, and his face twisted with strangled pleasure, holding himself back. How had this bed not burst into flames? His hand yanked open the drawer and tore a condom off the strip, his shoulders lifting with each deep breath he took.

"Lie down, Payton, on your back." It was a request, not a command, and his voice was uneven. "Evie, come here."

She rolled off of me, and repositioned herself on her back, right at the edge of the bed, touching herself. I rose up onto my knees, a little concerned about his voice.

"What's wrong, boss?" I whispered, and he kissed me passionately, desperate.

"I don't want to fuck things up between us." He dropped the condom packet on the sheet beside me and his hands roamed down my back, pressing me into his hard body and soft skin, and I stretched into his embrace. "Are you sure this is okay?"

I couldn't help that my eyes fell to the condom wrapper he'd yet to tear open. I always regretted the things I didn't do way more than the things I had done. Even though we'd been together for a short time, it felt so much longer. I felt . . . stable. Like nothing could really break us, certainly not something like sex, given how we'd come together in the first place. The dirtiest part of me? She wanted this. Not just the physical act, but the power it gave me.

I lifted the condom wrapper up and tore it open with shaky hands. He pulled it out and proceeded to roll it on, while I grabbed the tequila off the nightstand. I wanted this shockingly twisted act, but a little liquid courage couldn't hurt either. I gagged at the bite of the liquor.

"Don't break my rules," I said, trying to sound playfully stern like he did to me, but it came out anxious.

"I won't." As soon as he was ready, he put his hands on my hips and pressed gently back. And left. He wanted me over her mouth, and she did too.

"Come here," she said, her voice hushed and her hands needy on the skin of my thighs.

I think we were all nervous, all felt like we were right at the edge of something incredibly risky yet thrilling. He put one hand on her knee when he stood in between her legs, and that hand slipped down to touch her quickly, making sure she was ready to take him. His other hand looped behind my neck, his strong arm holding my head, making sure I couldn't look away from him. Like I would want to do that.

Beneath me, her sinful tongue touched my sensitive flesh, and my sharp intake of breath let him know what she'd done. It was hard to focus on it. His dick, glistening from the condom, pressed forward until it was against her. His gaze didn't leave mine. Not even when the head of his dick crept forward, easing inside, and he began to fuck her.

TWENTY-THREE

She groaned, and her hands, wrapped around my spread thighs, tightened their hold. *Oh my god, oh my god.* He pushed deeper, slowly, and his eyes were black holes. Inescapable.

"Yes," she purred, and swiped her tongue over me in response, and I gasped again.

My hands rested on my thighs, but when he advanced further inside her, I trapped his head and yanked it roughly to me. I needed the connection to him right then.

"Fuck," she cried. "Oh god, please fuck me."

I looked down at the body beneath me. Beneath us. Her large, perfect breasts with tight nipples called out to be touched, and since I hadn't done it before, I set the pads of my fingertips on her skin and found it smooth yet firm. Touching her this way was addicting. Then, his first gentle thrust and her breasts shifted and returned to rest.

He had a hand on her hip, bracing himself, and his fingers curled into her flesh, strengthening their hold. His second thrust contained more power and went deeper, and this time her whole body bounced. The moan between my legs was immediately followed by a flurry of activity that had me shaking. Logan thrust again and again, picking up his pace, and with each one I was rewarded by her mouth. Maybe she'd lied about not being with another woman, too, because what she was doing to me was unbelievable.

Or maybe it was the scene before me. His face, full of

concentration, was haunting and erotic as he moved in and out of her. She arched her back and dug her nails into my legs. I was panting when one of his hands grasped my breast and his other hand closed around one of hers.

"Do you like it?" I asked. "Does she feel good?"

The corners of his mouth turned up in a smile, like I'd momentarily broken his concentration. "Yes. Do you like her eating your pussy? Because I could watch her do it all night." His sinful voice wrapped around me. "Would you like that?"

I couldn't render any kind of an answer.

He thrust into her hard, and she let loose an enormous sound of need and desire. "Fuck, Logan, yes. Give it to me."

"Give you what?" he teased, drawing back so he was barely inside.

"Your cock," she whined.

"This is Evie's cock. So you say her name when you come."

I trembled at his words. He drove into her, ruthless and steady, and I could feel her orgasm approaching. Her legs were wrapped tight around his waist. Her toes pointed and her muscles tighten in preparation, and her body arched off the mattress to meet his hips. Her tongue slowed down on teasing me, but watching, hearing . . . feeling her orgasm was fucking sexy. A porn right in front of me, only infinitely hotter.

"Evie, oh fuck, Evie. Shit, I'm coming!"

As it happened, Logan grabbed my shoulder and jerked me into his brutal kiss, like he wanted to devour me. He'd slowed his rhythm as she convulsed and moaned, her cries falling against my skin, but I could feel every thrust he made reverberating up his body, and his lips slammed against mine while his hips beat into her.

As she began to recover, her tongue surged again and my head lolled forward to rest on his shoulder. "Her tongue is inside me," the tequila told him. Like last time, it felt amazing, but I craved more. "Logan—"

He must have sensed what I was about to say. "Not yet. Soon." My gaze fell to between her legs with envy. His dick impaled her over and over again, getting faster and slicker in the aftermath of her orgasm. "I want us to make her come again."

"Yes," she moaned, clearly liking that idea. Her finger worked its way into me, while her mouth continued to suck and stroke, fucking me senseless. Still, no matter how good it felt, it wasn't going to be enough. I needed him, so what I really needed was for her to come again.

"Fuck her harder," I said on a broken breath.

He gazed at me with lust-filled eyes, and rammed into her. She quivered and sighed with delight. "Yes . . . yes . . ."

"Harder," I commanded, this time with a little more weight in my voice. He slipped a hand behind her knee and lifted it, setting her ankle on his shoulder and wrapped his arm around her thigh, pushing deeper with a thrust that knocked her mouth off of me. A sound of enjoyment from him was barely audible over her moans. My thighs were burning with the exertion anyway, so I straightened up on my knees and slid closer. All the way until her leg was sandwiched between Logan and I, and I could flatten my breasts against his damp, bare chest. Hands clamped down on my ass, squeezing. Her hands.

"Yes," she chanted, "yes, yes, yes . . ."

"Harder," I ordered, and a shift went through him. His face was dark, powerful, and streaked with authority. I knew instantly who this was – the man in the shower, the one I hadn't seen since then, even when I'd asked for him. Was there danger unleashing him? I was much too thrilled to care.

He pounded into her, furious and unapologetic, and the hand not holding her leg wrapped around my throat. Fingers squeezed as his grip tightened on me, crossing the threshold into uncomfortable. *Whoa.*

It was gone as quickly as he'd set it on me, moving across my skin to the back of my head, and he jerked a fistful of my hair back, forcing my chin up so his mouth could crash against my neck. I made a noise of deep, raw pleasure.

"Am I fucking her to your satisfaction?" His voice was harsh and rough, and it was like he'd shot me right in my center with heat so acute I couldn't breathe. The ache in my sex was painful, and I was desperate.

"Make her come," I half-ordered, half-pleaded, loud enough to cut through the sound of his skin slapping against hers. He took my hand in his and shoved it down between our bodies, placing my fingers on her swollen nub.

The bed shook with his powerful thrusts, and I rubbed her flesh, not caring that his thrusts were crushing my fingers against her.

"Shit, oh shit," she babbled. Her hand slapped my ass and kneaded the flesh. "Don't stop. Don't fucking stop."

I was wildly out of control, and yet in control when she came again, seizing and screaming on the mattress. Before me, the look of aggression began to wane from Logan's face when his pace slowed to a stop. Breathing sounded like a struggle for Payton, a struggle she was just starting to win when he abruptly pulled out of her. His hand hooked around the back of my neck and he shoved me down roughly, so my head was right in between her legs.

The tight, pink skin was before me and I closed my eyes, inching forward. I ran my tongue down through her crevice, and she jolted, mumbling something I couldn't understand but that sounded like encouragement.

I focused on my job, anxious to return the pleasure and see if I could do as well as she'd done. My tongue gathered up her wetness as I fluttered it, and I shifted into a position more comfortable for pleasing her—

"I want to fuck you while you do that."

Yes. I climbed off of her and put my feet on the carpet, rising to stand before him. I didn't have to ask how he wanted me. He turned me toward her as she slid backward, her whole body now on the bed, and she bent her knees, opening her legs. Payton drew up onto her elbows, her tousled hair hanging to brush over her breasts, and she curled a finger at me in a seductive *"Come hither."* The desire and sex filled every goddamn inch of the room and I was powerless to disobey.

My legs shook as I placed my hands on her knees, letting them glide down the curve of her long legs toward her center as I lowered into her. There was the subtle noise of Logan pulling the condom off and tossing it in the trash can.

I brushed my thumb over her, rolling a circle where I liked it best, figuring that's where she would like it too. Oh, yeah, she did. Her enormous sigh made the muscles of my sex clench. Hands grasped my waist, and his hard dick, the one I'd been without forever, nudged me. I set my mouth on her, and he dipped the head of his dick . . . the head of *my* cock . . . inside me.

"More, Logan," I begged. "I want all of you."

He inched forward. "Fuck, Evie."

I stopped thinking about what I was doing with my mouth and let my body take over when he was filling me, completing me. Her moans intensified as I pressed my tongue hard and flat against her and licked like she was an ice cream cone, but had to stop when he began fucking me, pushing deep.

"I need permission," I cried.

He hesitated. "No. I'm too close already."

I groaned. It felt so good. How could I not come? He'd backed off and the tiny, slow thrusts teased and tormented, and from this angle, all of him was touching me inside and out. The pressure inside me multiplied as he grew deeper. Harder. Faster. I was in big, fucking trouble.

"Yellow," I said. I returned my attention to her, sucking her into my mouth. Her hand was on the back of my head, running her fingers through my hair. I had to think about this tender action, her soft mewing and not the dick that rammed into me. *Shit* –

"Red!"

He didn't just stop at my warning, he pulled out all together. I turned over my shoulder, stunned at his action.

"You weren't the only one at red." He was breathing rapidly, standing with one hand clenched around his dick, strangling back his orgasm.

I sighed back into her pussy, letting her taste coat my lips and slide into my mouth. She was sweet and salty and interesting. Behind me, his breathing slowed and a hand caressed my ass.

"Green?" His voice was like velvet.

"Green."

He pressed back inside, filling me in one swift move, and I was right back in the big, fucking trouble from before. The connection with him was too great, too powerful to hold back much longer. Things began to blur as pleasure spilled over. Pleasure from listening to his groans of satisfaction and his quiet comment about how unbelievable it felt. Pleasure from the woman in front of me who I was giving this intimate kiss to, going where no other woman had. She'd chosen me for this.

His hard dick hit exactly where I wanted it to each and every time, and my whole body trembled. It screamed for release.

"God, Logan, please . . ." I said with every thrust he made. "Please . . . Please . . ."

"I want us all to do it together."

I pulled my mouth away so I could look at her stunning eyes. Was that even possible? She nodded. "Put your fingers in me while you're fucking me with that mouth."

I slipped my middle finger into her wet heat that was unbelievably soft, and my tongue wandered in the area above, coaxing the orgasm closer. It brought my orgasm closer, too. Every plunge of my finger into her was mirrored between my legs. Building, and building . . . threatening an avalanche of bliss.

My index finger joined in so I filled her with two fingers now, shoving them deep inside and curled them back, searching for the spot guaranteed to send me into a frenzy, hoping it was the same for her.

"I'm going to come," she exclaimed, shocked. "I'm coming!"

"Evie," Logan cried. Before he'd finished my name, I reached the apex of my orgasm. The explosion inside me, as our mutual orgasm tore through my body, rocked my foundation. He clamped his hands down as he came, clenching my hips tight against him so my insides milked him dry. The orgasm was so intense it forced tears in my eyes, but I blinked them back.

His sweat-coated arms were tight as a vise around me, holding me to him as his lips trailed a line across my back, up to the edge of my shoulder. Payton sat up, leaned forward, and cradled my face in her hands. Her kiss was gentle and tender, like the desire in her had finally been sated.

I couldn't stand any more and a half-second before my legs gave out, he released me and urged me forward to collapse on the bed. I shifted and rolled onto my back, my head landing on his pillow. Did we snuggle as a threesome afterward? He moved to curl up beside me, and we both looked at her, sitting on the edge of the bed, unsure.

She flashed a sexy, half-smile. *Oh, right.* Payton didn't snuggle. She'd kick guys out of her bed if they tried. She loved sex, but feared intimacy with men. She climbed to her feet and began snatching her clothes off the floor, dropping them in a clump at our feet on the bed while she pulled her panties on.

"I hate to fuck and run," she said, hooking the bra closed, "but that's what I'm gonna do."

"Payton," I started.

"I hope you liked it as much as I did." She stepped one foot and then the other into her jeans and shimmied them on.

"I did." My voice was quiet, but only from exhaustion and not embarrassment.

Her top was put in place and she came to us, leaning over him to kiss me goodbye. It was quick, light, friendly and not sexual. She straightened and cast her gaze on Logan. "Happy birthday."

He took a deep breath. "Thank you."

When she was gone, he turned onto his side and kissed me, one that tasted like love and not sex. It was quiet for a moment, and I began to pull at the thread of worry about what kind of impact this was going to have on . . . well, everything.

"I can't wait to see what you get me next year." He dragged me into his arms and squeezed me, and I put the worry away for later.

⌘

We went to a movie with Logan's friends on Sunday afternoon, and Payton tagged along. Because we were in a group, the initial awkwardness for me was easy to disguise. Logan, ever the actor, seemed unfazed. When the movie was over and the group migrated several blocks down to a restaurant, she pulled me aside.

"Hey," she said, "what we did was amazing. I don't regret it. Do you?"

"No."

"Good. Don't read anything into it, but that was a one-time thing for me. What you and Logan have . . ." Her eyes glanced at him and then returned to me. "It's great."

"It is great."

We'd had a long talk and reached that same conclusion. We'd done it once— an experience we shared together, but I didn't want to share him again. And Logan had admitted he'd felt pressure to perform, and constant fear I would change my mind and he'd hurt me.

I'd been right. Nothing could come between Logan and me in the bedroom. There, we were rock solid. I didn't consider another aspect of our relationship could be a problem, but I was naïve.

⌘

In the Monday afternoon critique, I ended up in the front row, far from Logan. We'd fallen perfectly into the rhythm of compartmentalizing the office from personal. Here, I was Evelyn, a designer on his team in the running to be named the design department branch manager. At his place, I was Evie, his naughty girl who occasionally left her dirty dishes in the sink.

One more day. Jon would be in the office tomorrow, and it would be announced I had landed the position I desperately wanted. Then I'd be the one leading these meetings. He'd come a long way with his criticisms, but Logan asked my advice the night before. He was grateful to be passing the torch.

"There's one more thing," Logan said, when the final critique was over. "Hess Sports is planning another direct mail campaign. Who wants the project?"

I think if we could have put our fingers on our noses to signal *"Not It,"* we would have, to determine the poor soul who was saddled with this client. Hess was picky, ignored deadlines, and had no concept of how design worked. Earlier this year one of the designers had spent weeks on a tri-fold brochure, proof after endless proof, only to have Hess tell us they wanted to change to a postcard, and all of the text on the double-sided brochure needed to fit on a tiny, one-sided card. Oh, and not look like garbage.

"Someone needs to jump on this grenade," Logan said.

People were suddenly fascinated with the tabletop in front of them. I chewed back a groan and swiveled in my seat. "I'll take it."

He nodded. "Thanks, Evie."

For a moment, no one moved. Then the collective mouth of the design team fell open upon hearing my nickname, the one none of them had heard before, come out of Logan's mouth.

"Evelyn," he corrected, but it was far too late.

My face heated red despite my every effort to stop it, and each pair of eyes in the room turned to me. I turned as well, facing front and swallowing hard, feeling their gazes boring into my back. I took a deep breath and prayed it wasn't as bad as it seemed.

"All right, thanks everyone," he mumbled, snapping shut his MacBook, and fled from the room.

It took Jamie two seconds to make it over to me. "What was that about?"

"Hmm?" I pretended to be clueless. Debbie lingered nearby.

"Logan just called you Evie. Like you two are friends or something."

I shrugged and pulled myself to my feet, but Jamie stood in my way. The expression on her face widened with surprise when my denial wasn't immediate.

"Oh my god, are you two—?"

"No," I said. It came out too quickly. "I heard he has a girlfriend." Not a lie, since I was so terrible at telling them.

"Yeah? I hadn't heard that. What department does she work in?" Jamie asked and Debbie slid closer, giggling.

I blinked. "What's that mean?"

"You know, how he gets around." The confused expression on my face prompted Jamie to clarify. "He's slept with half the accounting department, Chloe in PR . . . I think someone else too—"

"That administrative assistant who was here last year," Debbie chimed in. "She had that southern name?"

"Oh!" It was like a light bulb went off in Jamie. "Scarlet."

My stomach churned. I didn't want to hear any of this. "No, I hadn't heard." Definitely not a lie. I did my best not to look upset when I pushed past them and went to my desk.

SHIT.

That's what the text message he sent me said. I responded

instantly:

Yeah, shit is right.

At four, Logan dropped the project folder for Hess Sports on my desk, hardly uttering a word, and I didn't acknowledge his presence, but it didn't matter. The rumor mill was in full force.

Jamie flitted over to my desk. "There is so something going on with you two," she said, smug. "Don't worry, your secret's safe with me."

I wouldn't have believed her no matter what, but watching her head straight for Debbie's desk? That girl had no shame.

TWENTY-FOUR

He'd beaten me to his place, and when I came in, he rose up from the couch. He hadn't changed out of his suit. It looked like he'd gone straight to the fridge, grabbed a beer and waited for me.

I gave him a plain look. "Smooth."

"Yeah, it sure was," he responded. "Did anyone say anything about it to you?"

"Jamie's convinced there's something going on between us. Anyone say anything to you?"

He put the bottle down and trapped my waist in his hands, tipping his head down so he could set his forehead against mine. "No, but I don't think anyone would. Is it going to be a problem?"

I shrugged. "Maybe, but I don't know what we can do about it."

"I can't believe I did that."

"It was a simple mistake."

He probably expected me to slide my arms across his shoulders and press into him, but instead I remained, neither softening into him nor pushing him away.

"What's going on?" His voice was concerned. "Have I done something else?"

"I don't know." No, wait, I did know what he'd done. "Chloe. Scarlet. Half of the accounting department."

"What?"

"Is it true? That that's the list of women you've slept with at the office?"

He tore his gaze away, guilty. The tension in his hands faded and released me. He slammed a huge sip of his beer. "I'd say that list is inaccurate."

All of the breath left my lungs. "Inaccurate how?" *Oh, god.* "There are more?"

"No. I haven't slept with half of the accounting department. Only Rachel."

"But Scarlet and Chloe?"

He sighed. "Yes. Rachel was right after April, during my post-breakup phase."

"Phase?"

"I lost my virginity to April, and I didn't cheat on her. So, after we broke up . . ."

He went and fucked a lot of other women, making up for lost time. I followed him into the bedroom and his fingers worked to unbutton his dress shirt.

"Scarlet asked me out," he continued, "the day after she gave her two weeks' notice, and I hooked up with Chloe at Jemma's New Year's Eve party."

Jemma, the accounts manager, was Jon's second-in-command and the most outgoing person on the face of the earth. Sweet as could be, that girl could do anything, including inviting the entire office to her NYE bash. I'd already made plans with Blake, otherwise I would have gone too. Maybe I would have ended up kissing Logan that night instead of Blake.

"Are you upset I slept with a few women you happen to know, long before we got together?"

"No," I said. "But you should've told me."

He hung up his shirt, giving me a view of his hard abs and muscular arms, and it was so unfair that I was annoyed and yet turned on at the sight of him.

"You're right. Okay, then, full disclosure. There's one more person at the office I've slept with."

My annoyance grew ten-fold. "Who?"

"You, naughty girl." He undid his pants and stepped out, his eyes on me. "You forgive me, or do you want to stay like that and have angry sex?"

Had he actually said he was sorry? "I'm not angry, Logan." Because, as usual, he was right. It seemed stupid to be mad at him for what he'd done before.

"Is that a no to the sex?"

I took my shirt off and made a production of dropping it on the floor. I saw the fire begin in his eyes and the excitement when he understood the game I wanted to play.

"Hang it up."

His commanding tone sent a delicious shiver through me. I yanked my black dress slacks off and held them in outstretched arms. Then I dropped them right on top of my shirt, my lips pulling back in an evil smile.

"As a rule, I don't like clothes on the floor."

"Too bad," I said. "Besides, I thought you liked it when I broke your rules."

He whirled me into his arms, rough and then tender. "Not as much as you like breaking them."

⌘

The next morning I had a perma-smile on my face. Logan had a lunch appointment, but after that he'd make the announcement. I'd dressed in the most professional outfit I had – a black tailored business suit that might have been too wintery, but I didn't care. I'd pulled my hair back to make myself look older, although it was probably a lost cause.

Kathleen was going to be upset. She might even make a comment about my age, and even with my hair up, I still looked impossibly young.

I was at my desk and on my second can of Diet Coke when Jamie made her gossip rounds and hovered.

"Why are you all dressed up?" she asked.

"I don't know, I felt like it."

"I hear Logan's dressed up today too." She gave me a suspicious look.

"He's not dressed up today any more than he usually is."

Her eyes lit up with a '*gotcha.*' "When did you see him? Debbie said he's been in the conference room with Jon and Will all morning."

My mind scrambled for an excuse, but it was too slow. She leaned in. "Did he stay at your place last night, or did you stay at his? I always make Steve stay at mine. His place is gross and I'm not lugging my stuff over there, you know?"

I had to keep my stupid mouth shut to prevent things from getting any worse. Thankfully, my desk phone rang and it forced Jamie on her way.

"Hey, Evelyn, this is Rachel from Accounting." My breath caught. "Were you the one handling Player's account? There's a billing issue, and I can't reach Logan."

Now my breathing stopped all together. "What kind of billing issue?"

"Well, did they order an extra run or something, and pay through us? I've got a line item from the printer that's been paid, but I don't have a PO for it."

My hands were so sweaty I almost dropped the phone. "Uh . . . I know a second run was ordered. I think they paid for it, I know it wasn't us." Thank god she couldn't see my terrible liar face.

"Oh, okay. It's been paid, so it's not really an issue, but it was strange to see a charge for four thousand dollars and not have any paperwork, so I thought I'd check."

"Did you say four thousand?"

"Yeah, I know, weird. You want me to email you a copy so you can take a look?"

It came through into my inbox, and I stared at it in disbelief. Ninety-six hundred was what he'd told me. So why the fuck did the printer show the second run only cost $3,975? It became difficult to focus on anything other than his closed office door.

The clock was a goddamn liar. It said only twenty minutes had passed since the email appeared in my inbox, but it was a freaking lifetime before Logan finally pushed open his door and flipped the light on. I snatched up the print copy I'd made and marched to his office. We were already under the microscope, but I couldn't help it.

When I shut the door, he scowled and moved to re-open it, probably thinking that this was a bad idea. "Whatever it is, it has to wait until later."

"No, it really can't." I thrust the paper in his face.

He scanned it and looked angry. "I don't know how many times I told that billing department not to put it on the summary. How'd you get this?"

"Rachel called, wanting to know if Player's had ordered an additional run because she didn't have a PO."

"Is that what you told her?"

"Basically."

Relief washed over his face. "Okay, then, we're fine. I'll call her and confirm that's what happened." When I continued to stare at him, he looked confused. How could he be so clueless?

"The amount, Logan."

The relief vanished in a heartbeat. "Oh."

"Oh?" I repeated. "Can you please explain?"

He wadded up the printout and tossed it in the trash. But he couldn't stall forever. "I was able to get the printer to do the job at-cost."

"But you—" Rising anger closed my throat.

"I lied to you. I thought when you heard how much money you were going to have to come up with, you'd back down. But you didn't. So I was going to let you sweat it for a couple days and then tell you the truth." The color faded from him like a gradient washing from pale to completely white. "But when I learned how you were planning to get the money . . . then I couldn't tell you the truth. I didn't *want* you to back down."

He didn't want me to have any other option. He'd forced me into that club and onto that table. If I had known it was less than four thousand, I probably could have scraped that money up in between my parents and Payton. I couldn't look at his lying face another second.

"Evie, stop," he said, hushed. "Please. I should have told you, and I tried, but I was so worried I was going to lose you, and then too much time went by . . ."

Surely he was trying to get me to look at him, but I refused. It wasn't so much the initial lie that hurt, but the time he continued to let it exist that had me so upset.

"People in love don't keep secrets from each other."

"I didn't want to hurt you—"

"Bullshit. You weren't protecting me, you were protecting yourself." I set my gaze on him, finally meeting his eyes. He stood a few feet from me with his hands on his hips, like he wasn't sure where else to put them, worry streaking his face.

"Yes," he admitted. "I'm sorry."

An *actual* apology.

My brain went to war with itself. If he hadn't lied, I wouldn't have gone to that club, and who knows if we'd have ever gotten together. The night he'd met Payton and confessed his guilt about what he'd done showed even then he was filled with regret about the lie.

I believed you didn't get to pick and choose the parts of a person you loved. You loved the good and the bad. All of it. So, he'd been bad and he'd hurt me, and while I wasn't happy with him right now, I still loved him.

"You lied to me. Don't do it again."

He seemed to swallow hard, and nodded in agreement. As I reached for the doorknob –

"Wait." His hollow voice lined my stomach with lead. "My lunch appointment, it's with April."

Everything went cold.

"Why are you having lunch with your ex?" I bit the words out. If I hadn't caught him in that previous lie, was the plan to get away with this one, too?

"Her father passed away on Sunday night. It was very sudden, and she's having a hard time. She's falling apart." His words got me to stop and focus on what he was saying. In spite of my anger, it was difficult not to feel heartache for her. "I told you that I cut her out completely." His gorgeous brown eyes never left mine, but there was guilt behind them. "I think her father's death made her realize she needs closure. A conversation for us both to reflect on why it went wrong, and to say goodbye."

I took a deep breath to remain rational. "All right, you need to see her, fine. If you'd explained that, I would've understood. But you were going to –"

"I went crazy when you went out with Blake, and you two were only friends. I thought you were going to say no, and I owed her, so I'd planned to tell you . . . after."

"God, Logan. I trust you completely, I mean . . . " My voice fell to almost nothing. "The stuff we did with Payton. How can you not trust me?"

I chose to ignore the pained look in his eyes. "I was going to tell you, you have to believe me."

"Why should I? You've been lying to me for months." My voice sounded as cold as I felt. "Go. Have your lunch with April and give her the closure she needs. You and I can discuss this later. After I've cooled off."

I fixed a hand on the doorknob and pulled air into my lungs, desperate to find a blank expression to hide the hurt and anger, and yanked the door open.

I was determined not to let this crush the day. Just a few more hours. Then, it will be negotiations on salary and discussion of which office would be mine, and I could sort the personal stuff out at home tonight.

Lunch was left in the fridge. I was too full of churning emotion to want to eat. I broke down and purchased a third can of Diet Coke from the vending machine while Logan disappeared from his office and went to have lunch with her. My silver can of crack and work weren't enough of a distraction, and my mind worried about what he was doing. There was so much history between them, I couldn't even fathom it. I tortured myself relentlessly. What if she didn't want closure, but wanted him back? I imagined her begging him for another chance, telling him she was willing to compromise for him.

"Can I see you in my office, Evelyn?" His deep voice caused me to jolt in my seat. By the time I'd turned to face Logan, he was already halfway down the aisle.

As soon as he shut the door, his arms encircled me.

"No." I pushed away from his hold, but it was futile. He blew out a breath and I could smell the faint hint of alcohol. "You had drinks at lunch?"

"Yeah. It was difficult, and I'm glad it's over."

His clear eyes rendered me motionless. It was over between him and her, at least I could tell that wasn't a lie.

"I'm also not looking forward to the conversation about the management position," he added.

"No, I can't imagine Kathleen will take it well."

He left me standing by the door and paced to his desk, running a worried hand through his hair. "I'm sorry if I hurt you. I don't ever want to do that." The expression on his face was heartbreaking, and I fought the urge to soften. I believed he didn't want to hurt me, but he'd done a piss-poor job of it.

"Like I said, I'm pissed, but we're at work and we've both got things we need to do. We can talk about it later."

He sank down into his seat and worry grew on his face. Was he really that torn up about Kathleen? I sat down in the opposing chair.

"We both know you don't have a problem being direct," I said, "but be honest with Kathleen. Do it fast, and then try to listen when she responds."

"That's how you'd want it done?"

Something was off. He'd fired Austin with his cold professionalism intact, or so I'd heard, and that had to be much harder than letting someone know they'd lost out on a promotion.

"I'm not saying you shouldn't soften the landing. Make sure you tell her she's a great designer. She'll be upset, but she's an adult and can handle it."

"I hope so, Evie." His expression changed, like he was

done fighting whatever had filled him with reluctance. "I need to speak with Evelyn now."

The air around me shifted, and I should have seen it coming.

"While we appreciate you expressing interest in the position," he said, "we've chosen to offer it to a different candidate. You've got a great career ahead of you here, and—"

"No, Logan."

"—think you're an excellent designer, the best I've—"

I shot to my feet so fast I got dizzy. "Why?"

God, his face. He looked like his own words were destroying him. "This morning Will asked if we'd slept together. I could've lied and said no, but it didn't matter. He'd already made up his mind."

"You wanted me for that position before we started dating." I couldn't organize my thoughts. "Over time, they'll see I earned it and you didn't hand it to me because I was your girlfriend."

"It's too damaging to both of our careers. You're young. You'll have plenty more opportunities to advance."

It was all slipping away, my dream job vanishing before my eyes. Taken from me because of the simple mistake of uttering my name. His mistake.

"Don't do this."

He took an enormous breath as if steeling himself. "It's already done. Kathleen accepted the position twenty minutes ago."

I stumbled backward, away from his eyes that frantically searched mine. With all of his lies this morning, the roller coaster of emotions, and now this, it was too much. I couldn't take any more, and it broke me.

"Take a minute," he urged. "Don't go out there like that."

"Like what?" I hissed.

"Looking like I just broke your heart."

A cruel, bitter laugh bubbled up from inside. "What difference does it make what they think of me now?"

The door banged against the doorstop when I yanked it open. Jamie's head popped up over the cubicle wall to spy me heading back to my desk. I leaned over the keyboard and began shutting down my system.

I couldn't stay here. An emotional meltdown was imminent and I wasn't interested in trying to cry quietly in a bathroom stall for the next thirty minutes. I certainly didn't want to be here when the announcement was made about Kathleen's promotion. This was quickly becoming the worst day ever, and I just wanted it over already.

I put my phone in my purse, tossed my soda can in the recycling bin, and cursed the Mac to hurry up.

"Where are you going?" he asked softly, lingering just to the side of my cube.

"I don't feel well, Logan. I'm going home." Maybe it was unprofessional, but I didn't give a rat's ass just then. After everything that had happened, I did feel sick to my stomach, so it wasn't a lie.

"You're not feeling well, how?"

The tension in my body was building to a level I couldn't manage. The words came out too loud and angry for the surrounding designers to ignore. "Why do you care?"

I knew he could feel the eyes on us as much as I could from his sudden, hurried breath. His eyes set. "I care because I'm in love with you, Evie."

He'd said it as loudly as I had, straight up declaring it for the whole office to hear. Debbie gasped, but that and a phone ringing somewhere off in HR were the only sounds in the aftermath. Perhaps he'd thought this would make me feel better, but, no. I couldn't feel anything but crushing disappointment in him and my situation. I put my purse on my shoulder and straightened to leave.

"My name," I said through clenched teeth, "is Evelyn."

TWENTY-FIVE

I went home, curled up on the bed that now seemed so tiny, and unleashed my emotions with my face pressed into the mattress. Afterward, I sat up, filled my lungs with air, and blew it out, feeling empty. I'd started the day happy and in love, only hours away from landing my dream job. Now it was early afternoon and I wasn't at work. I was here, and alone.

I'd called Payton on the train ride and filled her in on the details, arranged to go to her place for dinner, and then turned my phone off. I didn't want to talk to him right now.

The joke was on me, though. I changed into a tank-top and yoga pants that absolutely did not flatter my large thighs, and I started to clean. In the few months since we'd gotten together, I'd learned to enjoy the empty countertops and clean floors. I polished the sink, and when that was done, I moved on to wiping down the insides of cabinets. After that, I took a wet rag and started to scrub the corners of the floor where the baseboards looked like they'd never been cleaned.

A sharp knock on my front door snapped reality back on me. Holy shit, what time was it? I knew who it would be, so I didn't rush to get to my feet or hurry to the door.

"Jesus, would you please turn your phone back on?" Logan's face was streaked with concern as he came in. "I've been so worried about you."

He was still in his suit, and I glanced at the clock on the microwave. "It's not even five."

"Yeah, I left right after the meeting." The one where he

had made the announcement, no doubt.

"It's Tuesday, what about your cross training?"

He gave me a look like I was being ridiculous. "Fuck that, we need to talk."

I went back to sitting on the carpet, crossing my legs beneath me and scrubbing the rag over the dingy ivory-colored trim. "Go ahead, boss, talk."

He went into a whole long apology, but honestly, I didn't need to hear it. He knew he'd screwed up. I heard him take off his jacket and set it down somewhere, probably folded neatly. At least there were plenty of clean surfaces for him to do so now.

"Say something," he asked, hushed. "Tell me you're okay."

"I'm okay." My voice was flat, emotionless.

"Please look at me. Tell me we're okay."

I turned to see him standing with his tie loosened and his sleeves pushed up, devastatingly handsome. My body wanted him regardless of what my mind told it, but thankfully my mind was stronger. "I'm not going to tell you we're okay. I'm not going to lie to you."

His approach was too rapid to react to, and hands scooped under my arms, lifting me to my feet. "Then tell me what I can do."

"I love you, but I'm not happy. You have to let me be unhappy about this. I lost that promotion because of what you said."

Logan loved compliments, but he didn't like anyone to point out his faults. "It was a simple mistake. We both know you've made one before."

I could only imagine the shocked look that splashed on my face, and I shoved his hands off. I didn't need a reminder of my disaster with the legal disclaimer, and not today of all days.

"Fuck. I didn't mean that, I'm sorry." He tried to pull me into his arms, but I would have none of it. I backed up a few steps, but then the wall was flat against my back, and it left me with nowhere to go. His hands trapped me there beneath his intense gaze. "I'm so sorry. I love you. Please tell me how I can help."

His mouth lowered to mine, but I shifted away. His lips were the most persuasive when they weren't talking. My head tilted back and thudded against the wall while he mouthed aggressive kisses down my neck.

"Logan, no." My eyes fell closed. I was still too upset, too conflicted. "You can't fix it that way."

It was like I'd just punched him, he was that stunned. "I wasn't trying to. I love you and I can't help it," he said, his eyes pleading. "I can't stand that I did this to you, that I hurt you."

Once those three words passed his lips in the office, he didn't have any trouble saying them, but part of me worried this was manipulative.

"I need space," I said. "You have to let me work through this on my own."

"Space," he repeated with horror. "How much space?"

"I don't know. A few days."

His chest lifted in a breath. He didn't want space, but I wasn't going to back down on this, either. The struggle in his eyes as he faced his first ever compromise from me was fierce.

But it was blinked away and the hesitant words from him were whisper quiet. "All right. I can do that."

He brushed a hand over the back of my head, pressing my forehead to his lips in a chaste kiss, lingering. "Are you sure?"

I nodded, but said nothing as he left, his shoulders sagging.

Logan had only had one girlfriend in his life before me, and he'd been the one to walk away, which meant he'd never had it end on someone else's terms. Not that it ended between us. At least, I didn't think.

I had intended to maintain radio silence for one day, but one night became two after I watched Kathleen gloat around the office. No one spoke to me. I was literally sleeping with the enemy as far as they were concerned. After his declaration of love, he retreated into his cold, professional version like someone had deactivated the other part of him. On Thursday night he asked hesitantly if we could get dinner.

But I still needed more space. I couldn't get past the failure. For once, Payton and Blake saw eye to eye, and they both told me I needed to forgive Logan and stop blaming him for a decision I probably would have made if the roles were reversed. I wanted to forgive him. I missed him, but as more time went by, it became harder and harder to find a way back to what we had.

When I rounded the corner into my cube on Friday morning, he was there, leaning against my desk. That same steel-colored button down and gun-metal gray tie he'd worn the day we'd gone into his office . . . and later that night he'd become my boyfriend. Outwardly, no one would notice the drastic difference in him, but not me. He hadn't shaved. The faint lines around his eyes and the way his shoulders hung told me something was wrong.

"The train was late," I said. If it hadn't been, I might actually have been on time this morning.

"Can we talk in my office?" He asked it softly, and it filled me with unease. He didn't move until I nodded.

I sat down and heard the dull thud of his door shutting behind me.

"Evie, I promised I wasn't going to keep things from you, so there's something you should know." He came to stand in front of me and leaned back against the desk, his face serious. "I'm giving Will my notice today."

What the hell was he talking about? "You're leaving?" He'd been in talks with another company and hadn't told me? I jumped right into anger. "Where are you going?"

He sighed. "I haven't figured that out yet."

"What?"

"If I'm gone, Kathleen will step into my role and you'll get the position you deserve."

I launched to my feet and came eye to eye with him. "Don't be ridiculous. You're not going to quit; you're like me. Your job is everything to you."

The mocha-colored eyes blinked slowly. "No, it's not. I can find another job, but I can't find another you."

This was impossible. Here he was, willing to fall on his sword for me and give me exactly what I wanted. But how could I let him do that? How would he not resent me if I allowed this?

"No," I said. "Just wait a minute."

"I can't do another day of this. I tried not to fall in love with you, but you made that impossible. I can't rein this back in. And I don't want to."

He was only inches from my face, gazing at me, and he hadn't moved. I'd been the one to close the distance between us. Logan had lost control over his carefully maintained self, because of me.

"We'll figure it out," I said. "We're both too determined not to, so don't go quitting in the meantime. I just need a few more days to accept what happened."

"You don't have to. Let me make it right."

"Wait," I said, frantic. "Logan, just wait." And I think my panicked voice echoed that night when I'd been strapped to the table and unable to follow him. His hand slipped behind my neck, cradling my head into his kiss that was exactly like our first, magnified a thousand percent. Slow. Seductive. Filled with so much love and intensity I was powerless to stop my surrender.

"I'd wait forever for you," he uttered and returned to his task of shutting my brain down with the simple touch of his lips.

My hands came to rest on his jaw, gritting against the stubble there when I eased it back. I held his face in my hands, his eyes on mine. And in this moment, I knew we would be all right. He was willing to give everything up for me, and I knew I'd give everything up for him, if I had to.

"Give me the weekend," I said. "Don't do anything until Monday."

Disappointment ringed his eyes. "The weekend? You're not coming Sunday?" Because Sunday was the marathon.

"I don't know," I lied, and hoped it was convincing, since a plan was rapidly taking shape in my mind. He'd caught me completely off balance when he'd taken off my blindfold, and a little part of me hungered to do the same to him.

He let me slip from his hold, confirming again he wouldn't do anything foolish before we spoke again on Monday. I hurried to my cube, ignoring the dirty looks. They could go fuck themselves. I didn't need that supervisor position. This company had already given me more than enough.

It gave me him.

I ducked out of the building at lunch to call Nick,

thankful I had the number saved in my phone from the time he'd texted me their progress on a run. His voice was so much like Logan's it was unnerving. "I was hoping you could help me," I said.

"I'm still married, so if this is another shower request, my answer is no."

"You're hilarious." I was glad he couldn't see me blush. "I wanted to surprise Logan . . ." I just realized he might not know that Logan and I were taking space. "Have you talked to him recently?"

"Yeah, I had to call him on Wednesday to tell him about the awesome stress fracture in my foot."

"In your foot? What about your race?"

"I guess I'll have to try to beat Logan next year."

Months of training, gone. "God, that's awful."

He made a noise, sort of an *oh well.* "It happens. What did you want to talk about? Logan said he'd screwed something up at the office and you weren't too thrilled with him right now."

"I've gotten over it," I announced to myself. "But Logan doesn't know that yet, and I was kind of hoping to show him on Sunday. If you're not running, are you still planning on going?"

"Oh yeah. Hilary had made up some signs for me, and I thought I could use them on Logan. Some of them will be epic."

"Do you mind if I still tag along?"

"Of course not."

"Great, thanks. Can we keep it on the down-low? "

His half-laugh was similar to Logan's. "I'll try my best."

⌘

I dressed in skinny jeans, a gray long-sleeved shirt and

knee-high boots, looping a scarf around my neck. It was warm for October in Chicago, but not all that warm. Sunny with a slight breeze, and perfect marathon weather. Hilary said Nick had bitched about missing out the whole time as they walked with Logan to the starting corral. I'd met them just past mile four with coffees I'd grabbed for them at a Starbucks.

"How is he?" I asked.

"He's fine," Nick said. "He was disappointed you weren't with us."

Hilary smiled. "He's just nervous."

I couldn't meet Logan as he made his way to the starting gate. I wanted that moment when he was running along and spotted me in the crowd cheering for him. I hadn't been allowed to ask questions when he'd taken off the blindfold, and now he wouldn't be able to either. Not when he was trying to break his personal record.

The streets were thick with people, but Nick knew where the best spots were for spectators, and his phone chimed with an automated text when Logan's bib crossed the start so we had a rough idea of when to expect him.

"If he's keeping pace, we've only got another minute," Nick said. He looked through the signs Hilary had in her enormous purse, and selected one.

"Really?" she asked. The sign read: "I'm so proud of you, Snuggles."

"Snuggles?" A grin widened on my face.

Nick shrugged it off. "I like to hold my woman close, what's the big deal?"

We moved deeper into the crowd of people, edging our way up to the road. Runners flew past, and I watched in disbelief. They were going fast, much faster than I could ever run. They'd just done four miles, with another twenty-two to go. Insane.

"What's he wearing?" I asked.

"White shirt, black shorts and hat."

A whole herd of runners went by with women who looked like there wasn't an ounce of fat on their bodies. The crowd was thick.

"Did we miss him?"

"There he is!" Nick pointed out in the distance to the wave of runners barreling toward us. He extended the sign out toward his brother. "Logan! You got this, man."

Logan looked relaxed and focused. His eyes glanced at the sign in Nick's hands and a faint smile curled on his face. I was vaguely aware Hilary was clapping and saying something like, "Go, Logan!" I thought I was clapping. Thought was difficult when our eyes met.

He didn't slow down, nor did his eyes widen in surprise. An enormous grin burst on his face, and he was so handsome I thought my heart exploded. How could I ever stay away from him? Then he went past, his feet slapping the pavement in quick bursts, carrying him down the road alongside dozens of other runners.

We had to hurry to the next stop and almost missed him.

"He's ahead of his pace," Nick said with a scowl.

"Isn't that a good thing?"

"He doesn't want to peak too soon and then not have enough to finish strong."

Nick told him as much at the stop, and Logan nodded, his warm eyes locked on mine. He was sweaty, and gorgeous, and I wanted to yell at him to take his shirt off.

It was frantic going from stop to stop because Logan was moving so fast and the crowd was dense no matter where we went. He'd dialed it back too much at the third stop and had fallen behind the pace he wanted to maintain, which made Nick pull out the "You're so sexy when you're sweaty" sign. I gave Hilary a smile, letting her know I thoroughly agreed.

"Mile twenty-five's going to be slammed," Nick said. "You two go ahead and get a spot, and I'll text you when I see him at twenty-one."

The finish line was closed to spectators, so this was the closest we could get to see him finishing. We watched as a guy, younger than Logan, pulled off to the side and was eventually helped away by EMTs. How was Logan fairing? This wasn't his first marathon, but still. He'd looked less relaxed last time we'd seen him, but Nick was also shouting out that he'd fallen off pace.

I was nervous for him, and once Hilary got the text, my nerves kicked up.

"It won't be long now, he's going to do these last miles quick," she said. "I hope Nick can make it in time, but he fucking better not run."

"Is it killing him not to be out there?"

"No, he's okay. I think he's getting a kick out of helping Logan."

Twenty minutes later, Nick pushed his way through the people and found us. "He's fading, but I think he'll do it."

Logan wanted to finish under four hours. He'd told me his last marathon he'd finished in four hours and two minutes. So close to hitting a sub-four hour race. Every time Nick glanced down to check his phone, I glanced with him. Three hours and forty-one minutes.

Time kept ticking by, and no Logan. The playful banter between the newlyweds ceased, and I thought we were all chanting in our heads for Logan to be the next racer to turn the corner.

"Yeah, man!" Nick suddenly cried. "Holy shit, he's gonna get it."

Logan's shirt was pasted to his body in sweat, or possibly water he'd tossed on himself, and there was a focused expression I'd never seen before. Utterly competitive and driven. It turned my insides into liquid, flooding me with desire.

He swung his arms, one hand clutching a black pouch of energy gel, and seeing us gave him the final burst I think he needed. Every second brought him closer, and closer, and closer to me. And then, he was gone, streaming toward the finish.

We hurried toward the runner reunion area in Grant Park, and a few minutes later Nick's phone buzzed with notification of Logan's unofficial time. He'd done it.

His younger brother was all smiles. "He'll have to go through gear check, but it shouldn't be much longer."

We waited outside the tall green fence as runners meandered out the exit, finisher medals and shiny Mylar blankets draped over their fatigued bodies, but smiles on their faces.

Then, he appeared through the line of runners.

"Hell, yeah," Nick said. "Three hours, fifty-seven minutes, forty-two seconds."

It's like Logan wasn't even listening. His focused look was on me.

"Hi," he said loudly over the fans around us as he approached.

"Hi, boss," I yelled back. "I'm so proud of—"

"I have to tell you something." It was hard to hear, and I worked through the crowd, Hilary and Nick following me.

"What is it?" I was concerned when I reached him. He looked . . . weird. Exhausted from the race, but also nervous.

Nick passed a black pouch of energy gel to him and took the gear bag from Logan's hands. To my side, Hilary had her phone out. Was she taking pictures?

"I don't want to keep anything from you," he said. "So you should know I bought an engagement ring."

I couldn't hear the people around us anymore. "What? When?"

"That day you had lunch with Blake."

Right after he'd heard me confess I thought he could be the one. *Oh. My. God.* I wasn't sure how to respond to this stunning information. And that black pouch wasn't energy gel. It wasn't plastic, but fabric. My body tingled with anticipation and nerves.

"I have rules." His fingers disappeared into the pouch. "Just one, actually. You have to answer my questions honestly."

It was a platinum band with a large emerald-cut diamond surrounded by smaller diamonds, and the moment it came out he sank to one knee. I pressed my fingers to my lips, my gaze going from his, to the ring he held up, and then back to him. My body froze into a statue.

There was a red observation tower nearby that elevated the race spotters a few feet above the crowd and, when Logan knelt down, the spotter went on high alert.

"Runner down," he yelled into a megaphone. "Runner down."

Logan's gaze went to the man in the tower and turned to his brother. "Is he talking about me?"

Nick yelled to the spotter that Logan was fine. That he was proposing. It wouldn't sink in, even after hearing that. Logan Stone was down on one knee, proposing. To me. His focus returned to mine when it was clear the spotter got what was happening.

"Do you love me?" he asked.

I nodded, my eyes wet with tears. "Yes."

"Do you know how much I love you?"

"Yes."

He was breathing rapidly, but I had no idea if it was from what he was saying, or the twenty-six miles he'd just run. "Do you want to spend the rest of your life with me?"

My idiot brain tried to come back online, and I shot an accusatory look at his brother. Nick had been carrying that ring all morning and had passed it to Logan without a word. "You told him I was coming."

"Yeah," Nick said, sheepish. "I was worried it would mess with his head too much if you weren't there, and then showed up."

"You're breaking my rule, Evie," Logan said. My overwhelmed mind struggled to figure out if he'd meant it playfully or seriously. Emotional tears blurred my vision.

"Will you marry me?"

He'd been with April twelve years and never done this. In less than three months with me, he was sure. And I was sure too. I wouldn't fail at loving him. Wasn't even possible.

"Yes," I said.

It was barely a word, but it registered all the same. He took my shaky hand and slipped the band onto my finger, where it felt like it belonged. Strangers around us cheered and congratulated us. All I wanted was to be in his arms, and it looked like he had the same desire.

Then Logan made the mistake of trying to stand, and his face filled with alarm. "I'm not sure I can move."

Nick hooked a hand under an arm and hauled Logan's stiff body upright, ignoring the groan of discomfort this action caused his older brother. I ignored it too. I threw my arms around Logan's neck, his sweat-soaked shirt beneath my hands. I loved it. I loved everything about him.

His mouth was hot and tasted like cherries from his energy gels, and he answered my urgent kiss by matching my intensity. A hand snaked behind my back to hold me against him, pressing me into his damp body and heaving chest.

"Did that really just happen?" I said in between his breathy kisses.

"I asked Hilary to get it on video because there are some people who are going to need visual proof."

"Like Mom," Nick chimed in.

I stared at the ring on my left hand which was still trembling when lips found mine and stole my focus. Holy shit, my fiancé knew how to kiss.

"Okay," Nick interrupted, "congrats and all, but can you maybe hydrate so I don't have to carry you when your muscles cramp up?"

I don't think Logan wanted to. When I tried to release him so he could head to the table with water bottles, his arm remained locked around me.

"Are you okay?" I whispered.

He grinned. "Oh, yeah."

He was sweaty, and gorgeous, and . . . happy.

And he was mine.

TWENTY-SIX

The Saturday after Thanksgiving, my phone rang at five forty-five in the morning, bathing our bedroom in pale blue light. My hand fumbled and yanked it off the charger, and my bleary eyes looked at the screen. It was a number I didn't recognize.

"Hello?"

"Hey, it's Payton."

"Who's dead?" I whispered into the phone, terrified. She knew better than to call this early.

"I am." Payton's voice was frantic. "Sorry I woke you."

I sat up, concern flooding my body. "What's wrong?"

"I need to talk to you, I'm kind of freaking out. And I'm coming over."

"Okay, but what's happened? Are you all right?"

She paused, which only made my worry grow. "I'm okay. Well, no, not really. I'm gonna grab some coffee and then I'm headed your way."

Logan was out cold, deep in a NyQuil coma. My fiancé had been fighting a cold for at least two days, refusing to admit defeat until last night. As we were getting ready to go out for drinks with our friends, he'd curled up under the covers, shivering. We ended up canceling, and I spent the night in bed, reading his iPad while he snored and coughed beside me. He looked better this morning. Also, he looked like he might sleep another four hours, which was good. Whatever was going on with Payton sounded serious.

The entire time I was in the shower I was worrying about her, and then a knot formed in my stomach. Oh, god, was she pregnant? She was careful in her personal life, and it was required at the club, but accidents did happen.

My shower was brief. I'd learned pretty soon after moving in with Logan that showering in the big glass enclosure by myself was a great way to end up cold. No wonder he always had the water so hot. I pulled my bin of cosmetics and hair stuff out from beneath the sink and dug out a ponytail holder, wrapped my wet hair back into a bun, and stored the bin away. I'd only moved in a week ago and was determined to keep my sloppiness to a minimum. I padded out into the kitchen and sat at the breakfast bar, staring out at the gorgeous view I'd never get used to.

I'd never get used to him, either, and didn't want to. I couldn't get enough of him. Ironically, I saw less of Logan at the office, but now that the cat was out of the bag and I was reporting to Kathleen, things improved everywhere else. Logan and I got ready in the mornings together, commuted together. We ate lunch out in the open when his schedule allowed it, and at the end of the day we came home together.

Jamie was instantly my new best friend when she saw me sporting the rock on my hand. Custom designed by Logan, of course. I think she wanted to swing an invite to the wedding, or possibly help me plan it. She'd been dropping some not-so-subtle hints like talking about how she'd planned her sister's wedding. Even when Kathleen promoted me to Senior Designer over her, Jamie took it in stride.

At six-fifteen there was a sharp, single knock on the door, jarring me from my thoughts.

Payton came in like a blur, dropping a tray of coffee cups on the counter. Was all that coffee for her? Or had she been so freaked out she'd forgotten I didn't drink the stuff? When I pull an all-nighter I look like death warmed over, but of course, not her. Her hair looked perfectly messy and tousled, and her makeup smudged to give her sexy, smoky eyes like a magazine ad. I could tell she hadn't slept, though.

"Are you pregnant?" That was the greeting I gave her.

"What? No." She yanked her coffee out of the tray with too much force and sent coffee slinging everywhere. She was vibrating with nervous, chaotic energy, and witnessing her like that was scary.

"What's wrong?"

"I got let go from the club." Her face was white. "I mean, I got fired."

I froze with the paper towel in my hand, ready to clean up the coffee. "What?"

Her face fell into her hands. "What am I going to do?"

"Again, what? What happened?"

"This is all his fault, you know. He shouldn't have said a damn thing." She paced a circle in the living room. "Fuck, it was so much money."

"Could you be more cryptic? Who are we talking about?"

She pulled to a stop and glared at me like I should know. "We're talking about the guy who got me fired; the one who fucked up my life."

"Your life?" I said, dubious. "You like what you do there, but, come on. That place is not your life." Did she think that was rich coming from me, given what I'd done to keep my job?

"Ugh, no, I'm not talking about the club." She set her coffee down that had been nothing more than a prop to occupy her busy hands. "Look at me, I'm a fucking mess. He owes me at least an apology. He should have warned me."

"Jesus, Payton, who?"

Her gaze hardened. "Logan."

What? "Logan got you fired? How?"

"Because of what he did last night."

She was making absolutely no sense. "Last night–? He was sick, and he was here with me."

"Yeah," she snapped. "I'm aware."

She resumed her random pacing without explaining. It was like she was coming apart, and I couldn't do a thing to stop it. Worse, I couldn't help her without understanding what had happened, and she wasn't making sense, so I stormed into the bedroom and latched a hand on Logan's bare shoulder.

"Hey," I said softly, nudging him awake.

"Hey," he mumbled back.

"So, uh, Payton's in the living room."

Logan rolled slowly onto his back, blinking his sleepy eyes at me, still not really awake.

"She got fired from the club last night."

His eyes went clear and he launched upright, fully awake. "Payton was working at the club?"

"Apparently, and she thinks you're the reason she got fired. Why's that?"

"She must have gone in," he said on a whisper, "when we canceled last night." It was like he was thinking out loud.

His phone rang on the nightstand, the screen flashing an impossibly long number, and Logan's alarm grew when he glanced at it. I could barely hear him over the ringtone.

"Oh, shit, Evie," he said. "I think I did something I shouldn't have."

THANK YOU

To my awesome husband. You are the fucking best.

To my beta reader Robin Bateman for your amazing notes and fantastic support.

To my editor Lori Whitwam for your hard work, putting up with my overuse of the word "that," and your enthusiasm for the book.

To my best friend Amanda (don't you dare call her Mandy) for showing me that my ending needed tweaking when you ran a kick-ass Chicago Marathon.

To my former boss Adam for blowing off the meeting I spent months preparing for, so you could go get a massage the Friday before your race weekend. When I needed to introduce Logan's character in an asshole way, I instantly thought of you.

OTHER BOOKS BY NIKKI SLOANE

THE BLINDFOLD CLUB SERIES

Three Simple Rules

Three Hard Lessons

Three Little Mistakes

Three Dirty Secrets

Three Sweet Nothings

Three Guilty Pleasures

THE SORDID SERIES

Sordid

Torrid

SPORTS ROMANCE

The Rivalry

THE NASHVILLE NEIGHBORHOOD

The Doctor

The Pool Boy

The Architect

The Frat Boy

The Good Girl

FILTHY RICH AMERICANS

The Initiation

The Obsession

The Deception

The Redemption

The Temptation

ABOUT THE AUTHOR

USA Today bestselling author Nikki Sloane landed in graphic design after her careers as a waitress, a screenwriter, and a ballroom dance instructor fell through. Now she writes full-time and lives in Kentucky with her husband, two sons, and a pair of super destructive cats.

She is a four-time Romance Writers of America RITA® & Vivian® Finalist, a Passionate Plume & HOLT Medallion winner, a Goodreads Choice Awards semifinalist, and couldn't be any happier that people enjoy reading her sexy words.

Made in United States
Troutdale, OR
05/22/2024

20032026R00192